STITCHES

AMANDA MEUWISSEN

DREAMSPINNER PRESS

Published by
DREAMSPINNER PRESS

5032 Capital Circle SW, Suite 2, PMB# 279, Tallahassee, FL 32305-7886 USA
www.dreamspinnerpress.com

This is a work of fiction. Names, characters, places, and incidents either are the product of author imagination or are used fictitiously, and any resemblance to actual persons, living or dead, business establishments, events, or locales is entirely coincidental.

Trade Paperback ISBN: 978-1-64108-364-5
Digital ISBN: 978-1-64108-363-8
Trade Paperback published April 2022
v. 1.0

Printed in the United States of America

This paper meets the requirements of
ANSI/NISO Z39.48-1992 (Permanence of Paper).

Readers Love AMANDA MEUWISSEN

A Model Escort

"The aspect of "Beauty and the Geek" is subtle but effective here.... This would be an attractive story for readers looking for more STEAM/STEM in their romances."

—*Library Journal*

Their Dark Reflections

"I thoroughly devoured this book. Amanda Meuwissen has a gift for creating multi-dimensional characters, full of moral ambiguity, and making you fall in love with them. This book is no exception."

—Paranormal Romance Guild

"The concept of the story was simple, the execution – delightful – one that kept me turning the page."

—Love Bytes

After Vertigo

"With its endearing main characters and a story that held my attention, *After Vertigo* was a fun read and perfect to unwind with at the end of long day."

—Joyfully Jay

Coming Up for Air

"*Coming Up For Air* by Amanda Meuwissen is the first book that I've read by this author, but it won't be the last..."

—OptimuMM

By Amanda Meuwissen

By the Red Moonlight
Coming Up for Air
Their Dark Reflections

DREAMSPUN DESIRES
A Model Escort
Interpretive Hearts

TALES FROM THE GEMSTONE KINGDOM
The Prince and the Ice King
Stitches

Published by DSP Publications
After Vertigo

Published by Dreamspinner Press

CHAPTER 1

THE SOUND of a nail striking the metal plate of Ashmedai's candle clock alerted him that it was morning. He closed his book, careful as always with his sharp clawlike nails around the delicate pages. He had been reading by the light of the bright white crystal in his study. Candles were far too dim and better used to tell time than as light sources, especially in a kingdom where the sky was always dark.

Every morning was the same for Ashmedai, ruler of the Shadow Lands—a lonely rousing from a familiar book and a solitary walk through an empty castle. Once, a thousand years ago, the Amethyst palace would have been filled with attendants, even when the only member of the royal bloodline was a prince not yet married to call himself king.

Ashmedai was not that prince, but even without a consort, they still called him king.

He had read everything within the shelves of the large black bookcase beside his chair by the window. They were his favorite tales, though had also read every book on every other shelf in the castle countless times. Even after centuries, well-written stories never grew stale.

Ashmedai rose and crossed to the candle clock. The metal mount holding it to the wall was almost reflective enough to be a mirror, marking down the hours as each inch of wax melted away. Within its surface, Ashmedai could only faintly make out his white skin, long black hair, and pointed ears. The image was distorted. Fitting, since he preferred to not see himself except when dressing to look presentable.

He ran his tongue across his sharp teeth while staring at his indistinct eyes glowing within the metal—white-on-black. This was the largest candle clock in the castle, meant to monitor an entire day and night. Ashmedai placed a nail at the base each morning, and now, he plucked it from the plate, blew the candle out, and swept with his hand from the base upward to rebuild the candle anew, using its own discarded wax collected beneath the plate in a basin.

Like before, Ashmedai secured the nail into the lowest portion of the wax. Then he snapped his fingers for the wick to relight. He paused a while to watch the flickering flame. Leaving his study was always the hardest part of each morning, but eventually he had to.

The castle no longer looked as it once had. Polished stone and marble in brighter hues had all been turned black. The red and gold accents Ashmedai had added over the years only solidified the macabre atmosphere, though frankly, that was his preference while living alone.

"Prrp!" A chirp from his pet, Aurora, preceded her appearance as a reminder that he was not entirely alone, but the floating, translucent feline wasn't quite enough to fill the void of lost companionship.

Ashmedai stroked the shimmer of her lustrous not-quite-fur regardless, pleased to have her with him and enjoying the way she purred and rolled in midair at his attentions.

Many of Ashmedai's subjects had volunteered to retain positions in the palace to help with upkeep, but their labor was better served farming, hunting, preserving the city, or pursuing their own passions. Besides, their offers were from the belief that they owed him, when in truth, Ashmedai's solitude was the punishment he had bestowed upon himself for failing them.

For failing *him*.

A toll of the bell that someone was outside was not uncommon each morning, usually marking the arrival of the same citizen—Ashmedai's advisor Dreya. His customary walk was almost always a precursor to a meeting with her as the start to his day. Some days she was his only interaction.

He supposed he hadn't always secluded himself. Once, in *the* beginning, people other than Dreya frequented these halls quite often, and Ashmedai would venture out to visit friends, especially his dearest friend, the alchemist, Braxton. But as the years passed, Ashmedai had shuttered himself away more and more, rarely admitting guests and only leaving the castle when he had responsibilities to attend to.

He loved his people, whether those from the beginning of their endless curse or those newly born into it. Ashmedai's penance was to rule them and to ensure they never learned the truth of what had caused humans, elves, and dwarves alike to become incomprehensible monsters, turning what once had been Amethyst into the Dark Kingdom.

Forever.

"Good morning, Dreya," Ashmedai greeted as he opened the doors.

"Good morning, Ash!" She breezed past him, full of energy and on a new mission each day. "Ready to work?"

Dreya was a mayor of sorts, a representative of the people in charge of morale and day-to-day management. She was also the youngest of Ashmedai's advisors, as she had only been born thirty years prior, not an original inhabitant when the curse struck.

Her parents resembled a dryad and a satyr, and she was a perfect mix of both. She had bark and moss along her arms and legs, with a furred lower half from her knees up. Her ears were long and drooping like a satyr's, but she had leaves for hair that changed from green to red in autumn and were nearly black now in winter, with two medium-sized horns protruding from the top of her head.

She also wore a miniature top hat, which rested somewhat lopsided in front of her horns. As someone who had never been outside the Shadow Lands, Dreya was fascinated with what the rest of the world was like. Hats had gone out of fashion here centuries ago, since most of the citizens couldn't properly wear one anymore, but although that was also true for Dreya, she didn't let it stop her.

Covering her horns with a larger hat, she'd told Ashmedai once, would look ridiculous.

"But first!" Dreya turned about as Ashmedai shut the doors. She clicked her tongue to capture Aurora's attention and conjured a small squishy red ball between her thumb and pointer finger.

Dreya's innate magic to conjure something out of nothing— especially something solid, even if only nonliving, nonmagical items— was invaluable but could only be exploited so much. Everything she conjured had an equal cost of energy, but she always spared a little each day for Aurora.

"Who's a good kitty?" she cooed and tossed the ball across the foyer, where it rolled into an adjoining room, and Aurora took off through the air after it.

Dreya paused, craning her ears as she waited, and Ashmedai waited patiently with her. Every day, Dreya hoped Aurora would bring the ball back, playing a true game of fetch. Ashmedai was certain he'd open a closet someday and become buried in balls Aurora had been hoarding over the years.

"Anyway—" Dreya shrugged, disappointed but undaunted that once again Aurora hadn't returned. "—shall we discuss the hunt? Or start right on Festival Day?" She conjured a thin slab of wood, a piece of parchment, and a quill. "Only a few weeks to go!"

Mention of the yearly celebration almost made Ashmedai wince, but he managed to suppress it. He knew it was better that his people looked back with fondness on the day of the curse, but their good nature to make the most of an unfixable situation didn't change the tragedy of it.

Or the tragic loss of Prince Cullen.

Ashmedai cleared his throat to cover the sting of memory and gestured Dreya toward his sitting room. "Whatever you'd prefer."

LEVI HID his face with the hood of his cloak before entering the market. He didn't think himself ugly, but compared to everyone else in the Shadow Lands, surely he was almost….

Ordinary.

He crept down the stone steps into the market square. Behind him was the entrance archway, covered in a glittering black awning with two glowing crystals in silver sconces on either side. These crystals were warm orangey-red, though light sources throughout the Dark Kingdom could be many colors. Crystals in lampposts along the market path were green, blue, even violet, like the Source Crystal in the town square at the center of the market.

Instead of heading down the market steps, farther behind where Levi had come from, one could have turned right toward the residential area, with its long road eventually leading to the Shadow King's castle, or left, toward Braxton's tower at the edge of the wood, where Levi lived.

Braxton Leviathan was Levi's master. His creator. It was difficult sometimes being only a few weeks old, but Braxton insisted that Levi's shyness would fade. That's why Braxton had tasked Levi with doing the shopping, and because using steps was difficult for the enigmatic inventor.

As Levi descended the long stone staircase, the voices of the people below were welcoming, as if it were a midday bazar. But there was no day in the Shadow Lands. Eternal night shone above, with ever-present stars and a never-waning full moon.

Levi didn't know what day looked like. Many people who lived in the Dark Kingdom had never seen it, and those who existed before the curse barely remembered what the warmth of the sun felt like. Levi only knew "sun" and "day" existed because he had been told.

"Newest silks from Emerald!" a man at one of the first stalls shouted as soon as Levi reached the bottom. The merchant had the appearance of a fish, with bulging eyes, though his fins were still shaped into something like webbed fingers, and he had legs, as well as gills on his neck to prove he could leap right into the Black Lake and not resurface until he wished it. "Who knows if the next caravan will contain more! Get it while you can!"

Levi pulled his hood lower and scurried away. He was meant to engage the sellers, for how else could he conquer his shyness, but did they have to be so loud?

"Careful!" a woman with a forked tongue hissed at Levi when he nearly ran into her. Unlike the fish-man, she had no legs but moved like an upright snake, a naga with slitted eyes and hair plaited as though made of scales like the rest of her.

"S-sorry!" Levi hurried onward, trying to keep his face hidden while taking more care with where he was going. He liked the people, the swarm of them here, all so different, never two exactly alike, but it was also overwhelming when any of them paid attention to him.

He'd start with Daedlys's shop like usual to calm himself. Daedlys spoke in a naturally pleasant whisper—as long as he wasn't screaming, but he didn't scream often since it could be painful to others, being a banshee. Plus, Daedlys was friendly and had doted on Levi ever since he first ventured out of the tower.

"If it isn't our sweet Stitches," Daedlys said like an echo on the wind when Levi entered the shop. As a general store with various wares, it was one of the few businesses inside a building rather than a stall.

Levi threw his hood back when he saw that no one else was inside, revealing his red hair, wavy and messy, curling around his slightly pointed ears.

Daedlys could see through things anyway, with his pitlike black eyes. The banshee had long white hair, his face gaunt and body thin, fading where feet should have been to a wisp almost like the tail of the naga woman outside, though Daedlys floated, transparent like a phantom, wearing an equally diaphanous black robe. Daedlys could wear anything, but whatever he put on his body became as see-through as he was.

"Hello, Sir Daedlys. I have a list today," Levi said, carefully pulling it from his cloak. Usually he kept his hands hidden too, while trekking through the market, afraid that someone might find his blue skin or the stitches holding his parts together off-putting, but Daedlys had called him "Stitches" with a smile ever since they met. It made Levi less self-conscious of his appearance while in this shop.

"Lyssy, my love?" Daedlys's husband, Klarent, called before entering from the back.

Klarent almost seemed to float too, though that was because his tentacles carried him across the floor. His skin was orange, and his arms were also made of tentacles, three each that worked in tandem like large fingers. Tentacles made up what might have been hair as well, and covered his face like a beard. Levi distinctly heard a voice, however, and not one in his mind, so he knew a mouth had to exist beneath the tendrils somewhere.

"Levi!" Klarent exclaimed when he saw him, loud, perhaps, but cordial, and not so loud that Levi shrank back or regretted removing his hood.

Levi remembered how surprised he'd been to discover the two were married, given their vast differences in species, but then, everyone in the Dark Kingdom was a different species.

"Perhaps you can offer your opinion as one untainted by too much life experience." Klarent approached Levi, holding out a beautifully bound tome edged in gold with a depiction of the Source Crystal on the front.

"Tainted, he calls me," Daedlys scoffed.

Klarent waved at him in dismissal, focusing on Levi. "What do you think?" He coiled a tentacle toward the cover, and the painted picture of the crystal glowed with violet light like the real thing. "Too ostentatious?"

Not everyone in the Dark Kingdom could cast magic. Klarent could only minimally, with small tricks like the light, and Levi's magic wasn't much stronger, since he was a construct. Even fewer people understood alchemy the way Braxton did, but enough were attuned to magic to keep the crystals glowing so that, even without torches, it was never dark in the land of night.

Levi might have guessed that the Source Crystal itself gave illumination to the other crystals, but the Amethyst gemstone was the source of the kingdom's curse, not its magic or light.

That was another reason why Levi kept his face hidden—because his eyes glowed violet like the Amethyst.

"It's lovely, Sir Klarent," Levi said. "What does this one chronicle?"

"Why, the story of the Source Crystal and the curse that afflicts our lands, of course, and how King Ashmedai rallied the people when we might have descended into chaos. I think this shall be a gift for him come Festival Day."

"Suck-up," Daedlys muttered fondly.

Klarent turned on him with a huff that upset his mouth tendrils. "I am the official chronicler of our history!"

"Which you appointed *yourself* a few hundred years ago. And we have endless accounts of the night of the curse, my love—most by you."

"Am I not allowed to make improvements over the years? After all, some things get better with age."

It was only playful banter, Levi knew, for he had experienced the pair many times now and was not surprised when Klarent coiled his arm tentacles toward his husband, slithering them up and around his ghostly form so that Daedlys seemed to emanate bits of mist wherever he was touched.

"Darling! Not when we have a customer."

Klarent laughed. "What are your thoughts then, Lyssy? Too much?"

Daedlys shivered with a ripple of his form that almost made him disappear. "I think the glow is a nice touch."

"Thank you."

They were like one being for a moment, not kissing or embracing exactly, but something unique to them and equally as intimate, before Klarent released Daedlys.

That sort of closeness seemed such a precious thing to Levi, and he wondered if he'd ever get to experience it.

"Gather whatever you need, sweet Stitches." Daedlys returned his attention to Levi. "I know Braxton is good for any trades. What's he have for me today?"

Levi removed the item from his bag and set it before Daedlys and Klarent on a nearby table. It was a black crystal that Braxton had crafted with alchemy.

"Brace yourselves a moment," Levi warned. He touched the crystal, and all the other crystals inside the shop went dark, plunging them into shadow. Levi touched the crystal again and the light returned.

"Fascinating!" Klarent declared.

"Master Braxton said he can make more for you to trade at the shop if you like it," Levi said.

"A master switch to dim every crystal in a room?" Daedlys carefully studied the black crystal, which was no larger than a goblet.

"Within the walls of any *building*, more than just a room."

Daedlys stared until the black of his eyes mirrored the black brilliance of the crystal. "Every home will want one," he said breathlessly. "You bet I'll take more. Pick out something for yourself while you're at it. This is the best invention yet!" He snatched the crystal up, though touching it this time did not sink them into darkness.

"You must will the lights to darken, so there's no risk of setting it off accidentally," Levi explained, refilling his pack with the supplies on Braxton's list and then hoisting it over his shoulder again as he began to look around the room with more scrutiny.

There were always wondrous things in this shop, but food and supplies were plentiful elsewhere. What caught Levi's eye were fabrics and jewelry and all the ways he might make himself look more like a denizen of the Shadow Lands instead of a newborn creation.

"I should chronicle this," Klarent said, watching Daedlys inspect the crystal and then setting his tome aside to gather paper and a quill and sit at the desk where he did the shop's bookkeeping. "Braxton invents so much, I can hardly keep track."

Only half paying them as much mind, Levi tentatively touched a violet tunic on display. "Is this silk from Emerald?"

"Indeed it is. Don't listen to Gordoc at the steps," Daedlys said. "There's plenty of silk yet and more likely to come with the next caravan. You go right ahead and claim that, darling. It would look lovely on you."

The tunic was far more ostentatious than anything Levi had worn before, with long sleeves edged in silver thread. It was slightly longer on the left and right sides, where it would drape near his knees, almost like a skirt, bound together at the collar with deep purple cord, and bearing a hood with similar silver embroidery as the sleeves.

"Claim a belt as well," Daedlys added.

"Oh!" Levi snapped back from touching the tunic. "I can't actually take this. Master Braxton—"

"Can let you indulge if I'm offering. He treats you too much like a servant. Honestly, just because he made you in his workshop."

But Levi *was* a servant. It was his place. He owed his life to his maker.

He wasn't planning on taking the tunic or a belt, but at the last second, he shoved both into his bag, just as the shop door opened to admit someone new.

Levi drew up his hood. Everyone knew about him, he just… didn't like the way most people stared.

"Ash!" Klarent proclaimed. "We were just talking about you."

Levi's eyes snapped to the man who had entered.

Ashmedai.

The Shadow King.

Every time Levi saw him, it was as if his stitched-together limbs were about to unravel, and he felt both unable to move and as if he might collapse to the ground in pieces at any moment.

The king was just so beautiful. Levi didn't even know if he understood beauty, but to him, Ashmedai was it.

His skin was white as bone, his hair long, straight, and ebony black, with black in place of the whites of his eyes, white irises, long nails, almost like claws, all his teeth razor-sharp, and pointier ears than Levi's subtle tips, like Levi had read about elves.

Like Daedlys, Ashmedai wore all black, but with stitching and accents in red and gold. He looked so royal, with a brocade tunic and long cloak. He wore no crown, but when he moved, the shadows moved with him, as if drawn to his regal presence.

Levi could relate.

"Daedlys, my friend, Dreya pointed out that my sword belt is in need of mending, possibly replacement, before next week's hunt. What do you recommend? And what's this about talking about me?" He turned with a mildly amused smile toward Klarent.

Ashmedai's voice was deep and penetrating, so much so that Levi could feel it rumble through his chest. Ashmedai was king and not often seen around town, yet he acted toward his people as if they were all the same station, allowing anyone who wished it to call him "Ash" and consider him friend. From what Levi had been told, Ashmedai had always been that way, since the start of the curse, when the once Amethyst Kingdom's prince brought calamity upon the people and Ashmedai became king in his stead to save them.

Levi watched Klarent try to inconspicuously hide the book he meant to give Ashmedai later, rising in the same motion to draw attention elsewhere. Daedlys waved a hand to assist, finishing hiding the book beneath the desk. Telekinesis wasn't his main magic. If anyone asked, he'd say that flawless visualization to create clothing without using patterns, as well as other items, was his true gift.

"Why, we were saying how long it's been since we last saw you and how much you'd enjoy learning of Brax's newest invention. Show him, my love."

Daedlys did so, touching the black crystal with intent this time and briefly shrouding them in darkness. When the lights returned, he said, "Can you imagine how convenient it will be to turn out all one's lights at once before going to bed? Tell you what, my king, I'll give you a deal on the first one, so long as I can keep it on display until Brax sends me more."

Ashmedai approached the crystal, eyeing it with the same subtle smile and a curious tilt of his head. He didn't float like the others but carried such a commanding presence in his steps, Levi's breath was lost again and again while looking at him.

The white-on-black eyes Levi was staring at suddenly turned toward him, likely having felt the weight of his gaze, and all at once, Levi could move again—because he had to.

"Th-thank you, Sir Daedlys," Levi stuttered, half muffled by the fabric of his hood. His feet reacted before he'd consciously considered running, because the panic of being perceived by the king made him desperate to get out from under those eyes.

"Hang on, Stitches, have you met—"

"Another time!" Levi all but shrieked, ducking his head to scurry from the shop, and then just as quickly fled from the market.

ONCE UP the market steps, it wasn't far to Braxton's tower, but Levi was still out of breath when he reached it. He hadn't needed to keep such a fast pace after he'd turned toward the wood—almost no one visited

Braxton other than the king, and he had only stopped by once since Levi was created.

Levi had stayed hidden in his room the entire time.

"Levi? Back so soon?"

The immediate call of Braxton's voice as Levi fell against the front door made his shoulders hunch up to his ears. "Y-yes, Master."

"That was hardly enough time to complete your errands." Braxton's head appeared at an almost ninety-degree angle, peeking at Levi from the workshop entrance across the main level. Besides appearing older, like a human man closer to forty than twenty, Braxton looked very much like Levi since Levi had been made from copies of Braxton's own parts. Braxton's hair was the same red color, though more meticulously styled, and the rest of his coloring was what Levi's would have been if he were alive instead of animated through alchemy—pale peach skin and blue eyes.

"I completed the trade, I simply—"

"Rushed on back like a scared child," Braxton huffed, head disappearing. His disappointed tone was enough to make Levi sag heavier against the door.

There was a faint purple glow coming from the workshop, pulsing every so often with brighter and brighter light. Braxton's specialty with alchemy was to always use the Source Crystal to power his creations. That was why some of the smaller crystals near the Amethyst gemstone were also violet, as conduits to transfer its magic, in essence, combining magic with science. As Braxton once explained to Levi, magic is innate, alchemy requires materials, and both have a cost.

The only time outside of Braxton's work when violet became the primary color for crystals or decoration was during Festival Day. No one in the Shadow Lands would have dared channel that power any other day, afraid the demon that caused them to become monsters and trapped them within the barrier of the wood would snatch them up if they tried.

They didn't mind if Braxton took that risk, however, so long as they could reap the benefits.

The door to the workshop was rarely open while Braxton was working. Levi was only allowed inside after the fact, and only to clean the space like he cleaned the rest of the tower. That purple glow like the Source Crystal, like the image on Klarent's book cover, and like Levi's eyes, intrigued him, coaxing him from the comfort of the door.

"May I offer my assistance, Master?" Levi asked.

"Blasted thing," Braxton muttered.

The pulses were growing faster.

Levi crept closer. Perhaps Braxton hadn't heard him. He should call again and wait for instructions, but his feet continued their momentum.

Faster and faster the light became, such a rich violet color, like Levi imagined might be contained in a sunset, if he had ever seen one outside of paintings and books. The frequency became so intense, it was almost too fast to discern the intervals, though not yet static light, making Levi's eyes sting and his head feel dizzy to stare at it.

He reached for the doorframe.

Blackness.

Leaping backward, Levi managed to get several feet away before Braxton exited with a swift slam of the workshop door. It never ceased to amaze Levi how quickly Braxton could move in his wheeled chair.

From what Levi had learned of the original races that lived in the Amethyst Kingdom, Braxton was human and still looked like one now. He had been in the wood, one of the farthest people from the Source Crystal, when the demon cursed the lands, and for that he had been both one of the most and least affected by it. He looked as he once did, but he could not leave his chair.

Braxton chose to wear simple robes that reached to his ankles, with long sleeves and high collars, keeping him fully covered but making it easier to dress on his own. Bathing and dressing him were some of the few chores Braxton never asked of Levi.

"What were you doing?" Braxton asked with a stern wrinkle of his brow.

"N-nothing. I asked if you required assistance." Levi straightened his stance, hands at his sides and head pointing forward.

"And what is the rule when I am working?"

"To leave you to it," Levi said, keeping his shoulders back but feeling a dip in his stomach.

"Exactly." Braxton wheeled closer, ceasing his approach a short pace in front of Levi.

The tower didn't appear large overall, mostly just tall, but the workshop expanded farther than seemed possible to someone who had only ever seen the tower's exterior, expanding beneath the large hill it was built against. The main room was completely open, with a small kitchen and space to sit. The only part sectioned off was the washroom. Stairs ascended to the second floor where supplies were stored, then farther up was Levi's room at the top of the tower. The building was stone and quite cold in both temperature and décor, though since there was always a fire in the hearth, Levi assumed he felt the cold more acutely because of what he was.

He was glad that, although it was winter, the Shadow Lands kept a constant temperature year-round. He didn't like feeling cold. Although he did wonder what it might be like to experience snow. The stars and full moon were only ever covered for an occasional thunderstorm.

"Now, you delivered the dousing crystal and acquired everything on my list?"

"Y-yes, Master. I'll unpack it all for you immediately." Levi offered Braxton a small bow, but before he could step away, Braxton stopped him with a grasp of his wrist.

"Are you flush?"

Levi felt added heat fill his cheeks at the mere mention, enjoying the warmth, but not if it was visible. "I-I… is that possible when I am not truly alive?"

"You still eat and drink, and blood still flows in your veins." Braxton tugged Levi down to his level, locking eyes with him and reaching up to feel Levi's cheek.

That warmth might have been welcome too, if Levi didn't worry Braxton would be angry to learn of his infatuation with the king. The two were close friends, after all, and what could a construct ever be to royalty?

"Did you run back? Are you still so frightened of being outside these walls? You'll never get used to Amethyst if you don't interact with its people." Braxton's touch and expression seemed less scrutinizing, almost sympathetic, as he stroked Levi's cheek before releasing him.

Braxton was cold too, in disposition, but Levi believed he meant well.

"I'm managing, Master. Truly. Daedlys and Klarent are always kind to me."

"Those two are kind to everyone," Braxton said with a wry smile. "Not all people are as cordial, Levi, and you need to learn to handle others. Would you rather I kept you locked in the tower?"

"*No.*" Levi's eyes snapped wide.

"Then allow yourself to unwind instead of staying taut like a spring trap. No one will hurt you. Perhaps with words, but no one harms another in the Shadow Lands. I've told you."

"I know." But words, however temporary, still carried the weight of actions.

"Did you take your draught this morning?"

Levi couldn't help the scrunch of his nose. "I… forgot."

"Levi, the purpose of that draught is to help ease your mind and acclimate you to life here."

"I know. I'm sorry, Master, it just… tastes awful."

Another wry smile touched Braxton's lips. "Things that are good for you often do." He wheeled around Levi toward the kitchen, where the kettle was on simmer, keeping the brewed draught warm where Levi was intended to take it with breakfast. There was an inherent bitterness to it, but Levi could admit that after drinking it, he always felt a sense of contentment far stronger than if it was merely herbal tea.

Braxton poured some of the brew into a ready teacup and handed it to Levi. Trying not to scrunch his nose quite so obviously this time, Levi swallowed a large, acrid gulp.

"There you are. Honestly, sometimes I regret you have a soul. So much more effort than my other constructs."

Levi's stomach dipped far deeper than could be caused by Braxton's anger or a nauseating drink. Braxton was all he had; he wanted to please him. "I'm sorry, Master."

"You can make it up to me by going to the city council meeting later." Braxton wheeled away without waiting for Levi's response. "I'm far too busy."

"T-truly?" Levi nearly dropped his cup. "B-b-but I—"

"You can handle that, can't you?" Braxton interrupted without looking back. "I'll need a full account in case Ash needs anything of me. Ah, and I have some previous requests you can deliver to him afterward." Braxton tapped a waiting list on the kitchen table as he passed it.

Requests for the *king*?

"B-b-but—"

"But what?" Braxton finally pivoted to fix Levi with a steady stare.

Levi clutched his teacup in both hands and lowered his eyes at the quiet reprimand. "N-nothing, Master."

Braxton sighed. "When I have time, I'll have to do something about that stutter. Go on now. Put the supplies away, and then you can do as you please until the meeting."

Levi had almost forgotten the pack slung over his body, filled with supplies for Braxton—and a tunic and belt for Levi.

Any concern over Braxton discovering there were extra items in the bag washed away as Braxton returned to his workshop, closing the door behind him. Even so, Levi gulped down his remaining draught with a grimace and set to work unloading the pack and putting everything in its place.

Then he grabbed the list from the table, all basic enough requests, such as additional warding crystals. Those were likely for the upcoming hunt, since they could warn people should they venture too close to the barrier's edge. A perimeter of the crystals lined the barrier, but they could be disturbed by animals and didn't stay lit forever, often needing to be replaced. The barrier was invisible otherwise and very difficult to detect.

Anyone who unwittingly crossed it disintegrated, like being erased from existence.

Levi left the task of gathering items for the king until later, bypassing the first upstairs level upon his ascent and continuing for his room. Braxton slept in his workroom and was a man of simple needs, so the top floor was all Levi's. He didn't have much—a bed, a wardrobe, an extra washbasin. The rest of the room was lined with bookshelves and filled with nearly every tome Braxton owned. He'd gifted Levi with much natural knowledge upon his creation but told him that expansion of it was up to him, and that every new thing learned made him more useful, which was Levi's only goal in life.

That and to perhaps manage a conversation with the king without stammering.

Levi's wardrobe was meager, but then, he didn't require much. He still managed to hide the new tunic between a few other sets of garments and hung the belt with it.

He couldn't truly say why he felt the need to hide new clothing. He hadn't stolen it. He hadn't paid for it with goods he wasn't allowed to trade. It was a bonus, a gift. Yet still, it felt like something precious that he needed to keep for himself.

Braxton gave Levi everything he needed—*more* than he needed— but Levi's favorite was the room itself, with a window that looked out of the tower upon the entirety of the Shadow Lands, all the way from the tower's great hill to the hill of the Shadow King's castle, and every expanse within the valley between.

The Black Lake was to the west, the wood to the east, and the castle straight ahead, as if Levi could look directly into the king's own bedchambers if their hills were closer.

The thought made Levi's cheeks grow warm again.

He had a chair pulled up beside the window where he often read. He sat there now, leaning his arms upon the windowsill and his head on his hands, thinking of the king. He'd run from him today without so much as a bow. Later, he had to talk to him. There would be no hiding or running then.

With a furtive glance aside, Levi flicked a finger at the corner of his room, and where he indicated, a figure blossomed—Ashmedai, just as he'd looked in Daedlys's shop, standing there with a soft smile.

Illusion magic was the extent of Levi's power. He could create images as real as flesh, but only in appearance. While it looked as though the true Ashmedai stood before him, when Levi lifted from his seat to reach out and touch Ashmedai's face, his fingers fell right through him. The illusion was still beautiful, though.

Levi waved his hand to banish the mirage. He would have to face the real thing soon, and though nervous energy coursed through him as he turned to begin gathering the requested items for the king, most of that energy was becoming excitement.

"WHAT SAY you, Ash?"

"Hm?" Ashmedai looked up, chastising himself for drifting.

Much as he kept to himself most days, he enjoyed city council meetings, a chance for his people to directly tell him and his advisors how their lives might improve. Talk of Festival Day, however, continued to make him think on the lost prince, even after all these centuries.

"Apologies, Dreya," Ashmedai said to her at his right.

City council meetings were held in the grand hall in the middle of what was otherwise the residential area, with rows of seating for anyone who wished to attend, and a head table for Ashmedai and his advisors.

Ashmedai turned from Dreya's patient, smiling face to address the subject standing before them. "Apologies to you also, Grillo. Were you requesting clearance for additional lumber for festival structures?"

"That's right," Grillo answered.

He was a minotaur and one of the kingdom's more towering subjects at over eight feet tall—though part of that height was from his impressive horns that curled up and then down like a ram's. His face still retained an almost humanness, more than that of a bull, but he had hooves and a tail and massive muscles covered in fur.

He was an excellent carpenter due to his strength, often able to cut down trees with a single swing of his axe. One would likewise think that would make him an excellent hunter, but his wife surpassed him in that regard.

"Have you discussed with Yentriss your planned section of the wood?" Ashmedai nodded to Yentriss at his right.

Ashmedai might be king, but he took to heart his advisors' counsel, and Grillo's wife, Yentriss, was watchman in charge of the kingdom's safety, which included its streets and settling disputes, as well as protection from outside threats.

"Grillo has proposed his route, yes," Yentriss said, stern and without favoritism.

She was like a dragon without wings, average in stature, especially compared to Grillo, but whereas he had fur, Yentriss was covered in scales. Her face was even more human than her husband's, despite green and gold plating, but her head elongated back to three hornlike points in place of hair.

"It is borderline," Yentriss continued, "but there are too few mature trees within safer zones."

"Is it necessary then to build such structures purely for the festival?" Ashmedai asked.

"If I may, Ash," Grillo spoke up, "I'm not planning to build for building's sake. The primary focus will be to rebuild dilapidated stalls, both in the market and those currently stored away. Many have gone without mending for far too many years, and I fear not making such changes could be a threat to public safety."

"Much as I may be wary, he's right," Yentriss agreed.

The people here no longer aged. Their children did, but only to adulthood. No one died. A few people had gone missing over the centuries, believed by the masses to have been erased by the demon for venturing too near the barrier, but that was rare.

The problem was when people did want children, there wasn't much room left where they could expand. They had already taken too much from the wood without time for the trees to grow again. Risks were becoming necessary.

"For the upcoming hunt, I have requested more warding crystals from Brax," Ashmedai began, only to pause as he caught sight of shuffling at the back of the hall. Many people were here tonight, so several were standing, but at the very back in the far-right corner was a cloaked figure.

The one advisor missing from the head table, who should have been beside Yentriss, was Braxton, in charge of development and technology. Ashmedai realized he knew the cloak that had moved upon the mention of Braxton's name. He'd seen it scurry away from him earlier that day.

Levi.

Maybe it wasn't merely festival talk that had distracted Ashmedai, but his not quite close encounter with Braxton's creation. He couldn't help it, but the one time he'd caught sight of the young man's eyes, it cut him to the quick.

Violet—just like Cullen's.

Ashmedai cleared his throat to cover that he had drifted once more and began again. "Grillo, we will equip you with some of the excess warding crystals to ensure your safety. If possible, I would also like to insist that you not enter the wood alone. Agreed?" he asked of Yentriss.

She nodded, and Grillo looked relieved.

"What if crystals aren't enough?" someone asked.

It was a new mother, Ashmedai recalled, someone who had, in turn, been born here within the curse, never having known something different. She resembled a Gorgon with blank white eyes and a head of snakes, though her bottom half was that of a spider.

Ashmedai gestured her forward to take Grillo's place in front of him.

"What happens after these trees are taken?" she continued. "What of the next time we need to build or expand? What of the rumors that we have not only reached our limit, but that the barrier is shrinking in on us?"

A murmur tittered through the crowd.

"Hold on now!" Dreya stomped one of her hooves to regain the room. "Are we a people of discussion or hearsay? A rumor is merely a rumor, Shevah. The barrier is not shrinking. You'll recall Braxton disproved that months ago."

That was true—the barrier wasn't shrinking—but the rumors weren't wrong that they were running out of resources, and Ashmedai had tasked Braxton with solving that quandary above all else. He didn't want his people to panic until he knew for sure what might be done.

"Calm yourselves," added Luccite, their healer and the final advisor, seated beside Dreya. "If Brax's crystals ever fail or do not warn someone in time, I have perfected many ways to adapt after disintegration."

Luccite was like a panther on two legs, with a very humanoid body but a feline head, and a cat's sly smile to match. She was shorter than most, however, and quite stout, often wearing robes that hung off her body, like today's, in deep emerald. Her fur was a rich gray but with brown at its roots, giving her shimmering dimension, and her eyes were slitted gold. She lounged like a cat too, practically leaning on Dreya, who didn't seem to mind.

"There is nothing to adapt if someone disintegrates entirely," Shevah hissed back.

It wounded Ashmedai to hear such things, but he understood his people's fear. He had kept them mostly safe for nearly a thousand years. The limited space was bound to catch up to them eventually.

"Your words are heard, Shevah," Yentriss said, "and rest assured that concerns over the barrier are our top priority. Do you doubt the resolve of your king to keep you as safe as he is capable?"

Shevah's stony expression wavered, her white eyes turning to Ashmedai, which caused her to look immediately cowed. "No. Never. Surely the demon would have killed us all by now without your guidance." She bowed.

That wounded Ashmedai more, because his people loved him without question. No one knew what really happened that night.

Other than Ashmedai and Braxton.

"Shall we move on to the Emerald shipment and call it an evening?" Dreya broke in with a chipper tone, ever vigilant to the shifting mood of the room.

Shevah returned to her seat, and Ashmedai listened with only half an ear as various other citizens came forward to make requests of items that would likely be on the monthly caravan from the Emerald Kingdom or made suggestions for new things to send. The other half of Ashmedai's attention was on the hooded figure of Levi.

He wished he could see Levi's face.

"Another note? It's a waste of time!" a louder voice brought Ashmedai back again. It was Lauffy, a naga woman in the crowd, whereas Gordoc stood before the table.

"There's no harm in trying," Gordoc argued. "I'll pen the note myself. If they ignore it again, so be it. One day, they might finally take to heart specific trade requests."

Ashmedai remembered soon after the curse befell them when he had penned the first note. He'd explained what had happened and warned the people of Emerald to stay away for fear that they might be taken by the curse too should they cross into Amethyst. There was never a response, but occasionally people would venture close, and Ashmedai's fears were realized.

If anyone crossed into the barrier, they couldn't leave. They would morph into monsters, and if they tried to escape afterward, they'd disintegrate as soon as they were out again.

For a while Ashmedai had set up sentries to warn people away, but when they saw the monsters the citizens of Amethyst had become, they'd run in fear as if they had gone mad. It was from the shrieks of those escaping, and from the few outsiders claimed by the curse in its early years, that they learned of the kingdom's new name.

The Shadow Lands, they were called now, forever cloaked in darkness.

People who had crossed over and stayed never recalled being told of notes with the caravan. It was assumed that someone, either royalty or a guard, must have been snatching them up and tossing them aside. These days, only a small few still called the lands Amethyst, like it had been when Ashmedai fell in love with it—and its people.

And….

"Perhaps not this time, Gordoc," Ashmedai said. "While I appreciate your willingness to try, with the festival soon upon us and so much else on everyone's minds, I ask that you wait until at least the shipment afterward. Is that all?" He looked to his advisors for anything forgotten, then to the crowd for other voices, but all was quiet. "Good evening, then, and thank you."

There was a bustle as the crowd began to disperse. Yentriss and Luccite left with little more than brief good nights, but after watching them leave, Dreya turned to Ashmedai, immediately starting in on something or another to keep his attention.

She meant well and could rarely contain her excitement about this or that to keep things running and the people happy. Ashmedai had added her as an advisor for that very reason—because she'd done the same even before she had the position—but as he noticed that a sole figure lingered at the back while everyone else continued to leave, he spoke over Dreya.

"It seems someone else needs my ear tonight. May we reconvene tomorrow morning?"

Dreya's drooping ears sank lower to her shoulders, but then perked back up as she smiled, never one to be glum for long. "Of course! Have a pleasant evening, Ash. I'll come by the castle nice and early."

She always did.

After Dreya left, Ashmedai moved around the table toward the robed figure, who had set a basket against the wall and stood to wait until everyone else had gone.

Then Levi dropped his hood.

"G-good evening, sire. M-m-may I... um.... F-forgive me." He paused to collect himself and took a heavy breath. "I have some things for you from Master Braxton," he said more slowly.

Ashmedai had only ever seen Levi lurking or in passing on the street, never full-on before, but he saw now that it wasn't only Levi's eyes that made him look like Cullen. Levi resembled the lost prince nearly as much as he resembled Braxton. Besides the almost mix of Braxton and Cullen's faces, all that kept Levi from being Cullen's twin was that his hair was red, not brown, and his skin blue instead of cream.

Ashmedai had also noticed the lines across Levi's face, assuming they might be scars, or maybe markings he was created with, but each line was actually very fine stitches. They were on his hands too, and around his neck. He must be like that everywhere, not a singularly created homunculus but pieces stitched together.

"M-Master Braxton made me," Levi stuttered again, gaze drifting downward. "You knew that, didn't you?"

"Yes. Apologies for staring, I... I never noticed *how* he made you before."

"H-he's… tried to create a construct many times, but they were all failures, s-so he stitched the best parts of each together and got me. Sometimes, when I disappoint him, he says I'm a failure too, that he'll cut my stitches so I fall apart."

A crack of possession raged through Ashmedai, which must have been very visible in his expression, because when Levi glanced up, he was quick to correct himself.

"He doesn't mean it! He just gets angry when I'm not good enough or don't listen."

The instinct in Ashmedai to protect this young man didn't dwindle, but even as ruler of their small kingdom, he couldn't overstep, especially with a friend as dear to him as Braxton.

There were no laws around a creature like Levi.

"You don't quite look like him," Ashmedai said. "Younger, certainly, and you look as though you could be related, but not identical like his other constructs."

"Th-that's because of being made from pieces." Levi kept looking away, only glancing at Ashmedai briefly as he spoke, like he wasn't used to eye contact with anyone outside of Braxton. "He says being reanimated that way is why I have a soul. Why I'm… wrong sometimes and not as obedient as I should be."

"He doesn't want you to have independence?"

"He does." Levi frowned. "But… he gave me life. I am his. I attend to everything he wants of me, as I should."

"*Everything* he wants of you?"

"Not like that!" A flush filled Levi's face, like deep purple in his azure cheeks.

At least Brax isn't a complete narcissist, Ashmedai thought, filled with relief as strong as his possessive anger. "You could look even more your own man without those." He gestured at the stitches. "I could fix them for you."

"What?" Levi gaped at him.

Ashmedai took Levi's hand, which made Levi flinch at first, but he soon relaxed and looked on with rapt attention as Ashmedai delicately moved his thumb and middle finger around Levi's wrist in slow strokes, careful not to catch the skin with his claws. The visible stitches started to pulse with an inversion of light like the deepest of shadows.

When the shadows faded, there was just smooth, connected skin.

"See?"

Levi stared with something between awe and horror.

"It's all right. I can fix the others too. I'm surprised Brax never—"

"I need to go." Levi jerked away before Ashmedai could take his other wrist.

"Levi—"

"Please accept our offering." Levi shuffled back faster, leaving the basket by the wall. "It was nice to finally meet you, Master Ashmedai."

"Just—" Ashmedai tried to correct him, but before he could finish, Levi was already out the door. "—Ash."

He hadn't meant to upset Levi. Selfishly, however, he had wanted an excuse to touch him.

It seemed it was Ashmedai's true curse to be left to emptiness like the now vacant hall, with only the shadows that flocked to him and the faintest light from the crystals to keep him company.

He was cursed to keep watching that same face leave him....

Tomorrow, Ashmedai would see Braxton.

CHAPTER 2

"IF I'D known you were going to visit today, I wouldn't have had Levi bring your shipment to the meeting last night. Though more important was having him there as proxy, I suppose. Seems things went well?"

Ashmedai sat with Braxton in the tower's lower level. The kitchen table sat only two, but like the last time Ashmedai had come for a visit, Levi was nowhere to be seen.

"I wish you'd attend those meetings yourself more often," Ashmedai said, sipping from his tea. It was black and strongly caffeinated, the way Ashmedai liked, and it had been waiting for him when he arrived, despite Braxton coming out of his workroom at Ashmedai's knock, surprised to see him. "You are one of my advisors, are you not?"

Braxton sipped from his tea with a wrinkle of his nose. "Do you want me attending meetings or solving our kingdom's problems?"

"What of that new black crystal you gave Daedlys?" Ashmedai volleyed back. "While useful, how does convenience of turning off lights solve lacking resources?"

"My friend—" Braxton smirked at Ashmedai's jab. "—do you trust me?"

Ashmedai responded, as he always did to that question, "With my very soul."

"Then *trust me*. It's all part of the same solution. If useful trinkets come out of grander experiments, so be it." Braxton pushed his tea away and regarded Ashmedai across the table. He looked so human, like he always had, making him unique among the Dark Kingdom's subjects. "Why are you here, Ash? Really?"

Ashmedai set his tea down too. He listened for a moment with his keen, elf-like ears. All was quiet around the tower, but he kept his voice low regardless. "Levi is different from your other constructs."

"Yes," Braxton said evenly. "A cloned body was getting me nowhere, but a combination finally gave me someone who could think. Can you blame me for wanting additional hands around this place? Or *feet*, rather."

The comment wasn't meant as a barb, yet it pricked like one. "You could ask any number of people to help you here," Ashmedai said. "Take someone on as an apprentice—"

"I need someone to live here—to have their *life* here. I wasn't going to get that from the average citizen. But you don't have a statement for me, old friend. You have a question."

Ashmedai never could hide anything from Braxton. "Why not ask me to smooth Levi's stitches? Surely you could as well, but it would be no trouble for me."

"Why? For vanity's sake? He hardly needs it."

"Have you asked if he wants it?"

"Are you interested in my little puppet?" Braxton's smile turned crooked.

"I'm interested in all my people. And he's hardly a puppet."

"True. He is the only one of my constructs that has ever been truly alive."

"Exactly. He's alive. You won't discard him like you did the others."

"Oh?" Braxton leveled Ashmedai with an intensity in his pale eyes like moonlight on a still pond. "That didn't sound like a suggestion."

"I'd prefer it didn't have to be," Ashmedai said. He didn't often feel passion, angry or pleasant, but he couldn't deny the emotions that stirred in him now.

Their gazes remained locked for several beats, and then Braxton chuckled. "I have no intention of discarding him. He isn't used parts to me, Ash. He's… Levi."

The tension drained from Ashmedai at his friend's break in stoicism. "You like him too."

"What can I say? It's hard to find good conversation these days."

That *was* a barb, however playful, since Ashmedai used to visit Braxton daily, but lately, he might not venture to the edge of the wood but once a month. That wouldn't be a problem if Brax left the tower more, but it brought them to a crossroads.

Ashmedai reclaimed his tea and finished it in a gulp.

"You *are* interested in him," Braxton said.

"Curious, that's all."

Braxton's smile lingered cryptically. Then he headed to the sink, taking their cups, and dumped the remainders from his own.

It was the loss of Braxton's gaze that bolstered Ashmedai to ask his real question. "Brax... why does he look like Cullen?"

Braxton's head lifted without turning to look at Ashmedai. "I can't help that the power that gave Levi life comes from the Source Crystal."

"It's not only his eyes. His face, he...."

"He looks like me."

"Yes, but... maybe it's the stitches, or...."

Braxton turned to stare with such incredulity that Ashmedai had to wonder if he was imagining the resemblance—or if he simply wanted it to be so.

"Never mind. I'm sorry, it's just...."

"Festival Day."

"Yes."

The sorrow that filled Braxton's expression mirrored Ashmedai's own. "It's been a thousand years, Ash."

"I know. And it can be a thousand more. I'll still wonder what might have happened differently."

The commiseration on Braxton's face was a connection that Ashmedai could achieve with no one else in all the Shadow Lands.

Especially when Braxton said, "So will I."

THE FRONT door opened—Levi heard it distinctly and flattened himself to the wall of the tower. He'd been gardening. He would swear to Braxton if questioned later that that's all he'd been doing since he hurriedly made tea and then dashed out the back door after seeing Ashmedai approaching.

It wasn't Levi's fault if he'd left the kitchen window open a crack and stuck close to that window while Braxton and Ashmedai spoke.

He wondered what Prince Cullen must have looked like if Ashmedai saw a resemblance in Levi. There were few surviving paintings or tapestries from that time. The people of the Dark Kingdom preferred to think of the now and their history after the curse, rather than who they'd been before.

While Levi could only vaguely imagine how the Amethyst Kingdom and its people might have appeared before the curse, he did sometimes think on it. The trees, many near him where the wood began, wouldn't have been black or shimmered as though covered in diamond dust, but brown with bright green foliage. Well, in autumn they might have been any number of colors, and in winter, they would have been barren like now, but they had variation throughout the seasons, like Dreya's hair. In the Shadow Lands, trees were always the same.

So too the luminescent plant life they cultivated and oftentimes ate would have been more greens and browns instead of colors like iridescent blue.

What had Ashmedai looked like before, Levi wondered? An elf, still with pointed ears? Still pale? Still commanding? Still beautiful?

Oh, he must have still been beautiful.

Levi readied himself to turn and risk a peek around the tower to see how far the king had gotten. Perhaps he would follow for a little while—

"Are you a doll?"

The unexpected voice nearly caused Levi to yelp, and he threw his hands up to cover his mouth and prevent it. The voice had come from behind him, but it wasn't Ashmedai, for the voice was small and higher pitched.

Slowly Levi lowered his hands and turned to take in the boy who had snuck up on him. Levi hadn't heard the tiny feet creeping closer from the very direction he'd been about to look.

The boy had a human face, but most of him was covered in a fine layer of light brown fur. Conversely, the edges of his body, such as his cheekbones, elbows, and knees, were lined with shimmering green scales. He had small ram horns protruding from the sides of his head, as well as faint claws on his hands and bare feet—like a lizard combined with a bull.

Grillo and Yentriss's son, Kenner.

"Are you?" Kenner came closer, with a tilt of his head. "You're stitched like a doll."

"I-I, um...." Normally Levi would have put up his hood. He was wearing his cloak, but it seemed silly to hide himself when the boy was already staring. "N-not exactly. Master Braxton made me."

"The other ones he made were dolls, even without stitches. They didn't talk."

"I suppose they didn't." Levi relaxed from the wall. "I'm different. Is... that okay? Are my stitches strange to you?"

Kenner giggled like that was a silly question. "Who isn't different here? I'm Kenner." He thrust out his hand. The top of it had scales too.

"It's nice to meet you, Kenner." Levi accepted the gesture, grasping Kenner at the wrist and giving a gentle squeeze before letting go. "I'm Levi."

"Like Leviathan, right? Brax's surname? You're a junior?"

The assessment caused Levi to giggle too. "Maybe so. What are you doing here? Did you pass the king on the road?"

"Uh-huh. I ran ahead of my parents. There's always new stuff by the tower, but you're the newest, so I wanted to come see. Can you do anything neat?"

"Neat? I don't know. Like what?"

"You know, alchemy, like Brax. Or magic! I haven't come into any magic of my own yet, but since Father doesn't have any, I might not either."

Levi smiled. There were so few children in the Shadow Lands. Children who had been turned at the start of the curse had long since become adults, and back then, people hadn't realized they could no longer have children until years passed with no new babes. They thought it a blessing initially, hoping for decades that there was a way to break the curse. Once the allure of that faded, effort was put into magical workarounds for couples to have children again, regardless of species or gender. It was still rare that a couple chose to.

Kenner was about ten years old, and there hadn't been another babe after him until Shevah's a few months ago. Although this was Levi's first encounter with a child, he thought Kenner much easier to be around than adults.

"Magic like this?" Levi flared his fingers toward the garden, and among the plants—some phosphorescent perennials, some vegetables they grew to eat—lights in the shape of tiny dancing fairies began to weave the way a bee might carry pollen.

Bees in the Shadow Lands were very much like fairies, Levi supposed, since they glowed like pricks of light. He was certain bees elsewhere didn't do that. Kenner seemed entranced regardless, giggling once more and bounding toward the garden to give chase.

Levi was careful to direct the fairies away from where playful feet might trample the plant life, and soon the fairies were dancing around Kenner in synchronizing patterns and causing him to twirl in delight.

"I've always said that the best magic is pure of intention."

Levi did yelp this time—because that *was* Ashmedai.

"M-M-Master—" Levi faltered upon spinning and discovering the king leaning casually against the tower wall not two paces from him.

"Ash," he interrupted. "And before you try, not Master Ash, or sire, or Ashmedai. Just Ash."

Like before, Levi's knee-jerk reaction was to pull up his hood, but he refrained. "Kenner said he passed you!" he blurted.

"He did. I turned around."

Levi could hear voices now. Kenner had said he'd run ahead of his parents, so of course they were on their way here. With Levi's attention distracted, the fairy illusions snuffed out, and Kenner groaned in disappointment.

Then Yentriss's voice came more clearly. "Kenner! What are you up to?"

The boy perked up, sprinting the way he had come from. "Hey, Ash! Bye, Levi!" he called as he went, leaving the two alone.

Levi had no idea what to say.

"Festival business, I'd imagine." Ashmedai saved him the trouble. He was so enchanting, stately and exquisite, even with his arms crossed and one foot propped back on the wall. "They're here for Brax, and likely me too. Before they steal me away… may I apologize for startling you in the hall?"

Levi's hand went to the wrist Ashmedai had rid of stitches. "I-I'm the one who should apologize. It was wrong of me to run. It just felt so tingly and warm and… I-I mean… I feared Master Braxton might be angry. He didn't even notice. May I ask…."

"Yes?" Ashmedai pushed from the wall, bringing them as close as they had been last night.

"How did you do it? I didn't know you were a healer."

"It's not healing really, just revealing what's already there, like… something hiding in the shadows." Ashmedai's smile stretched to show his sharp teeth. Levi really liked those teeth. "If I could heal, we wouldn't need Luccite."

"R-right. Then…." Levi looked at his wrist, his other hand still holding the smooth skin. "This is the real me?"

"Isn't it?" Ashmedai asked softly.

When Levi looked up, it seemed the king had stepped closer. His white-on-black eyes could have held Levi captive forever.

"There you are! Ah, and Levi too. Just who we were looking for."

A sharp intake of breath made it easy for Levi to step back without looking too much like he was retreating.

Dreya had spoken, accompanying Yentriss and Grillo with Kenner at their heels.

Levi had never been around so many people before without being hidden in his cloak.

"Did I pronounce that right?" Dreya asked, coming toward Levi boldly, without so much as a stray of her eyes at Levi's stitches. She wore a tiny hat askew on her head and a dress that looked like it was made of the same leaves as her hair. "Or is it more like *levy*?"

"Um… the first way was right," Levi said meekly. "You were looking for me?"

"And Brax," Grillo said, "but this will be your first Festival Day, won't it? We thought you might want to help. Daedlys recommended we ask. I hope the little one wasn't bothering you." He lightly gripped one of Kenner's horns and gave it a tug that toppled the boy against his side, where he hugged him closer. He'd seemed so serious at the council meeting, but he appeared warm and personable now, the complete opposite of his wife.

"Levi made fairies in the flowers!" Kenner exclaimed.

"He was curious," Levi offered, "not a bother."

"Can't deny we're all curious." Dreya was suddenly close enough that Levi had to tip backward or risk their noses bumping. It wasn't his stitches she was getting a better look at, but his violet eyes. "You've kept to yourself all these weeks, but what a wonder you are. Some people can be funny about that color, but I think it's one of the prettiest there is. And new life is always a wonder, as most parents would agree, I'm sure." She glanced at Grillo and Yentriss, who shared a tender look.

"Levi's a child like me?" Kenner asked.

"More a newly minted adult," Ashmedai said.

Levi was glad the king didn't think of him as a child.

"Are you really only here for Brax and Levi," Ashmedai continued, focusing on Dreya, "or did you stalk me from the castle?"

She bristled in a way that ruffled her leaves. "It's hardly stalking when you left a note on the castle doors so I'd know where you'd gone!"

Grillo failed to suppress a snort, while Yentriss's mouth merely gave a slight twitch.

"I shudder to think what terror you might have wrought if I hadn't," Ashmedai said.

It was likely due to his pleasant tone that Dreya knew he was teasing, and she pursed her lips with a budding smile.

"Well then." Ashmedai turned to Levi. "You'll help, won't you? I'm sure Brax will have no objections."

"Oh, I…." Levi was trapped, both by Ashmedai's stare and the request of him—more like *command*, for how could Levi possibly say no to the king?

He didn't want to say no. Not really. And having everyone's attention on him wasn't nearly as overwhelming as he'd feared. "I can help," Levi said finally, looking back at the others with nervous enthusiasm. "What would you have me do?"

"I was hoping you'd assist me," Grillo said. "As a guide using Brax's crystals. It can be seen as dangerous to venture too near the barrier, but I hoped you wouldn't be as afraid as others I've asked, since you live so near it. What say you?"

Levi had never feared the wood or the barrier. The view of trees was part of his first memories from when Braxton brought him to life. "I can do that."

"Wonderful!" Grillo said. The others all looked pleased, save maybe Yentriss, who had a scrutinizing skepticism about her, as though she thought Levi somewhat unimpressive.

"Wonderful indeed," Ashmedai echoed, catching Levi's eye again. "I suppose we all have work to do."

BRAXTON HAD no objections to Levi being stolen away. He wanted Levi to acclimate, and being sequestered did nothing to foster that.

Levi had hoped, however, that Ashmedai might join him and Grillo, only for the king to get monopolized by Dreya the moment they reached the edge of the city. Levi stayed with Grillo alone as they gathered some of the crystals spared for the upcoming hunt, as well as Grillo's axe and other tools for bundling and bringing back lumber, and then off they went.

They headed almost all the way back to the tower, but then cut into the trees along a narrow path before the final bend in the road.

"We'll need to gather wood for several days to have enough for all I have planned. That work for you?" Grillo asked.

"Yes, Master Grillo. As long as I can attend to my other chores."

"*Grillo*." Grillo glanced at Levi with a wide smile and a snort from his long snout. "There are no masters among our people, not even Ash. Does Brax really make you call him that?"

Levi clung unconsciously to the bag filled with warding crystals draped across his body. He also pulled the wagon that would carry the lumber they collected. It was large but light enough, with an easy grip. Levi had offered to pull it initially since Grillo would have to do the heavy lifting once it was full.

An even larger wagon pulled by Braxton's mechanical horses would have been better, but that would never have fit along this path or between the closely rooted trees. Besides, the horses that existed traveled almost constantly, rarely used for anything other than bringing the trading carriages back and forth from Emerald.

"He doesn't *make* me call him that," Levi said, "but when I first woke to this world, he said he was my maker, my master, and so I have called him that ever since."

He'd never told Levi to stop calling him that either.

A rustle in the trees made Levi's head snap up. He hadn't thought he'd be afraid, but then, he'd never ventured very far into the wood. The shadows here seemed thicker, or maybe the glow from the plant life was dimmer. Whereas the shadows that followed Ashmedai were swirling and inviting, here the added darkness made the hair on Levi's arms and neck extend like during a lightning storm.

"Glider monkey."

"Hm?" Levi returned his attention to Grillo.

Grillo pointed ahead at a tree that was slightly swaying. In its branches, peering at them from the dark, was a small animal covered in fur. Its ears were longer than the length of its head, its body compact given its lanky arms and legs. Its thumbs looked apposable around the branches it clung to, and connecting from its wrists to its body was an extension of furred skin almost like wings or a cloak.

Levi had only ever seen the ones people kept as pets, but because of that, he knew the monkey was both friendly and not for eating.

It leapt to another tree with a graceful glide and disappeared.

Grillo was getting ahead of Levi, so he hurried to catch up.

"Is it much farther?" Levi asked.

"Not so much now. Best take out one of those crystals," Grillo said.

Levi fumbled to do just that. Warding crystals were smaller than most but still filled the entirety of Levi's hand. They were clear, and if the person holding it ventured too close to the barrier, it would begin to glow with white light.

For now, it was dormant.

"There are many buildings in the city," Levi said as he matched pace with Grillo. "Some from stone, but most from wood. After a thousand years, it's impressive so many mature trees still thrive."

"Not enough," Grillo said. "And the ones around us aren't quite mature enough yet, which is why we're heading deeper. Our trees grow faster than those outside the Shadow Lands, but we must still be vigilant and adhere to careful coppicing. How the trees are cut ensures for better, faster regrowth."

Levi nodded. He'd devoured every book and subject Braxton could supply to him. His swiftness in reading and learning was something Braxton often praised him for, however much he might chide him for other things. Levi had not learned much of woodcutting, however.

"What of the stone?" Levi asked. "We have no quarries, do we?"

"Some stone can be found in the hills and near the Black Lake. Thankfully, a good stone structure can last for centuries, so we've rarely needed to repair or replace them. New structures, however, are often wood, since that is what we have in abundance. But the more our people grow and spread, the less we have to work with." Grillo sounded sad, Levi thought—resigned.

"Master Braxton is working on a solution. He'll find the answer."

The comment caused a curl of Grillo's lips. "If anyone can, it's Brax."

Another rustle of the trees made Levi look up in search of the glider monkey, wondering if it had decided to follow them, but the trees ahead were still. He paused, peering cautiously behind them. No higher branches were wavering there either.

"G-Grillo—"

"Boo!" A small figure lunged at Levi from out of the shadows, and Levi dropped the handle of the cart, skittering backward.

"*Kenner*," Grillo scolded in a low, parental tone, wiping the smile from the boy's face. "You know better than to traipse into the wood alone!"

Kenner's arms, which had been up like a playful mimic of a monster with claws, sagged to his sides. Well, like a monster with sharper claws than the boy.

"I wasn't alone!" Kenner defended. "I followed *you*."

"And we will purposely be getting near the barrier. Do you understand? I will be safe thanks to Levi and the warding crystals, but you—"

"I can keep an eye on Kenner," Levi said, causing father and son to stare at him in equal surprise. Perhaps it was the rapport Levi and Kenner had already formed, or simply that it eased Levi to know that even a boy could make it through the wood unharmed. "Would that not be safer than him heading back alone?"

Grillo's brow furrowed at the suggestion. "I suppose that's true. But do not think for a second this is a prize for disobedience." He centered on his son. "You will have no sweets after dinner for being so reckless. Understood?"

Kenner nodded emphatically, clearly happier to have his way now, even at the cost of something later.

"You stick to Levi like planks nailed to a wall and watch the crystal just as vigilantly."

Kenner nodded again.

"Come on then." Grillo faced forward, and a smile lit up Kenner's face as he scurried to Levi's side.

With Levi pulling the cart once more, the three walked in close formation, the crystal held outward in Levi's free hand.

"Did you think me the demon?" Kenner asked, his voice a whisper, though they were far too close to Grillo for anything to be kept secret.

"Or a dangerous animal," Levi admitted, keeping his voice low too. "You believe in the demon? That it lives in the wood?"

"Of course!"

"Yet you boldly entered it?"

"After you and Father. I know I'm safe," Kenner said without falter.

A quiet snort came from Grillo, but he said nothing.

"Then you are braver than me." Levi glanced around at the glittering trees and the all too silent dark. "I always thought the wood comforting—from afar. Being amidst the trees, I feel less certain."

"I'll protect you," Kenner declared more loudly. "I'm really strong. I'm gonna be strong like Father, and with, um… procession like Mother!"

Levi stared at the boy in thought. "Precision?"

"Yes, that! She's the best hunter in all the Dark Kingdom, you know."

"So I have heard. What does the demon look like, do you think? I haven't read many stories about it, other than basic accounts of the curse."

"You don't know the whole story? There are tons of them! Mostly the same though."

And mostly by Klarent, apparently. "I know a demon cursed the old prince, who was lost," Levi said, "and King Ashmedai, who wasn't king at the time, defeated it and took over after everyone turned into monsters."

"But did you know the prince *summoned* the demon?"

"He did? Why?"

"Some think for more magic, but others say the old prince would never have done that, that he didn't care about power. Some think it was so he could pass the kingdom to someone else, since he didn't want to be king and no one else did either. He thought a demon was his only choice."

"What happened?" Levi asked.

"The demon tricked him, what else? He killed the prince for his, um… humorous?"

"Hubris," Grillo supplied.

"What's that mean?"

"It means the prince was prideful," Grillo explained, "overconfident, and because of it, he caused tragedy. Like a little boy wandering into the wood when he knows he shouldn't."

Kenner ducked his head, otherwise ignoring the comment. "Anyway, the demon cursed everyone using the Source Crystal, which used to be a symbol for the Amethyst Kingdom. Nothing can destroy it, and people have tried. Or used to try. It's what keeps the barrier up. And if anyone crosses it, the demon waits in the wood to eat them."

"Eat them?" Levi said as his stomach dropped. "I thought people disappeared if they crossed the barrier?"

"Well, yeah, coz he eats them. Oh! He's big with bat wings, claws, horns, a tail, and tons of scary teeth. His skin is so dark you can't see him in the shadows until he smiles and shows all his fangs, or when his eyes glow. And when he wants to eat someone, his mouth gets so big, he can swallow them whole."

In many ways, that description shouldn't be scary. It wasn't exactly like one person in the Dark Kingdom, but its pieces were definitely present in various people.

Yet still, the image filled Levi with dread, and he couldn't shake the sensation of being watched from the shadows. When the people first saw the demon, none of them had been monsters yet, none of them had ever seen a monster, so it must have been terrifying.

Wait….

"Have other people seen the demon?" Levi asked. "I thought only Braxton and the king were present."

"Others were there after the prince died. Then Ash and Brax chased the demon into the wood. Almost everyone saw it then. Right, Father?"

Grillo was about to answer when a flicker from the warding crystal lit up the expanse around them. In the distance, they could see the perimeter of crystals faintly glowing too, though a few were clearly missing or had gone out. "Time to head left," Grillo said, taking his son's shoulder to steer him. "Levi?"

Levi shivered as he stared at the flickering crystal in his palm. The thought that some unknown beast waited just beyond the barrier made a lump form in his throat, but he had a job to do. Slowly, he approached the barrier and replaced the missing or unlit crystals with ones from his bag, and then chose a new crystal to carry in his hand.

Across the barrier was seemingly more darkness, but with a shimmer in the air almost impossible to notice. The shadows *were* watching them—animals, like the glider monkey. Levi hoped that's all it was, and not foolish highwaymen willing to press their luck by crossing over. Or something worse.

He hurried back to keep pace with Grillo and Kenner, and after a few strides heading left, the new crystal he held went dormant.

The next time they hit a spot where the crystal flickered, Levi did the same, and that was where they stopped. Grillo would be taking the trees from just before the line of the perimeter, as many as could fit on the cart after they were felled and trimmed.

"Kenner, you don't get even close to that line of crystals. Understood?"

"Yes, Father. I don't want to get eaten."

Much as Levi felt differently about the wood now, so deep in its ominous embrace, that feeling of being watched never became more than that—a feeling. Grillo chopped trees, Levi and Kenner helped stack the lumber, and when there was hardly any room left in the cart and Grillo announced one more tree should do it, Kenner darted farther into the safe zone, beckoning Levi to give chase.

The line of crystals was behind them, with Grillo still in sight without any shout of reprimand, so Levi complied. He even conjured a few more fairies to chase after Kenner as they ran between the trees, this way and that. Kenner always stayed one step ahead of Levi. Most of the trees were skinny and difficult to hide behind unless there was a cluster, but there was one just wide enough that when Kenner dashed behind it, he disappeared.

A different boy emerged from the other side.

"Slowpoke!" he called.

Levi froze. The boy was an elf. A half-elf maybe?

With pale skin and red hair.

"Levi?"

Levi blinked and Kenner was in front of him—*right* in front of him, peering up at Levi with concern in his eyes.

"Why are you crying? Did you stub a toe?"

Levi's hands went to his cheeks. They were wet. "I... I must have. I'm fine now."

"Time to head back!" Grillo called, hefting the final tree into the cart.

Levi scrubbed away his tears, smiling at Kenner and then beginning to chase him once more back toward Grillo.

He'd lied, though. He had no idea why he'd been crying.

"*ASH*." DREYA'S tone was both reprimanding and playful, pulling Ashmedai's attention back from the path leading to the wood.

While his people all knew to forego formalities with him, only his advisors were comfortable admonishing him—Dreya most often, despite being the youngest.

Perhaps because of that.

"You are a million miles away," she continued. "Someone needs to choose who gets to run the archery booth, and that someone needs to be you. Otherwise, Sarek and Nonn will hem and haw until my ears wilt." Her ears sagged as she said that, hanging low along the sides of her head.

There were always plenty of volunteers for the festival, and usually an appointed organizer, though Dreya had taken over that task ever since ascending to her role as advisor. The entirety of the market would be transformed for the event, but some of the activity would be in the area just outside the start of the residential sector, by the market steps, where Ashmedai and Dreya stood now amongst the bustle of initial stalls being planned and built.

Festival Day was the biggest event of the year, like the liveliest of city fairs. Since many of the booths, such as archery, were an excuse for advertising a person's profession or wares, sometimes a lottery needed to be waged. Other times, Ashmedai had to pick someone, for he was the only person the people believed to be impartial.

He was often more mediator than ruler, really, which was fine by him.

"Sarek," Ashmedai said. "Nonn has supplied bows for the hunt all year."

"Very fair," Dreya agreed.

Ashmedai meant to stay focused after that, but when his gaze drifted once more to the road, this time, he caught sight of Levi returning with Grillo, Kenner, and a full lumber cart. The delight that fluttered through him dwarfed putting attention on anything else.

He'd hoped that having Levi assist with the festival would mean more time to get to know him, that maybe he could have snuck away to watch over Levi. He'd had any number of excuses for Dreya, but she'd shot down every attempt he made to escape.

"He is rather fascinating, isn't he?"

Ashmedai startled. There was no denying where his attention had shifted. "Yes, he is."

"I can barely remember being a child, and for me, it wasn't that long ago." Dreya laughed lightly. "Can you imagine what it must be like to experience the world for the first time as an adult? I suppose I might get to find out if the barrier is ever gone. My parents have told me stories of the world before the curse, but they're farmers. They never traveled. Not like Luccite, who came from Ruby and had seen the world before settling here. Levi is lucky in a way."

"Yes, I suppose he is. My dear Dreya," Ashmedai said before she could jump into whatever topic she planned on next, "can we resume tomorrow? We have made much progress due to your diligence, but we do have weeks yet before the festival."

She seemed about to protest, but like last night after the council meeting, a kind request was often enough for her to acquiesce. "It has been a long day. Will you be at the castle tomorrow morning or somewhere I need to track down?"

Ashmedai smiled at the gentle tease. "I will be there."

Levi and the others were nearly back when Ashmedai left Dreya to intercept—

"Ash!"

—only for Klarent to intercept *him*.

The tentacled scholar blocked Levi from Ashmedai's sight. He held a load of books and was clearly excited, given the way his beard tentacles quivered.

"Yes, Klarent, how may I help you?" Ashmedai hoped to settle this quickly.

"The festival could use more culture, I thought—more stories and performances, rather than just games and feats of physical skill. So, this year—"

"You're planning a booth to allow the people to show off more artistic talents?"

"Exactly so! I myself hope to do a few dramatic readings, but it would serve the booth schedule well if your voice joined mine in recruiting. We haven't filled the open slots nearly enough, and I want the booth to be a resounding success!"

"Certainly, Klarent. I can even mention it at the next city council meeting. Now—"

"And I would like for you to promise to be present for my opening act. Without spoiling the surprise, I have a gift for you."

"For me?"

"I'm hoping it will be quite the spectacle, so I ask that you not get whisked away to other activities until after I've had the opportunity to present it to you at the opening."

Surprised and warmed in equal measure, Ashmedai smiled fondly at his friend but was still eager to escape. "I will keep a keen eye on the time and be at the very front, I swear to you. Now—" he tried once more, meaning to sidestep Klarent, only for Klarent to turn on his own with a bright declaration.

"Levi! Lyssy will be so pleased to know you accepted Grillo's request. He hoped you wouldn't be too upset that he recommended you."

The focus of Ashmedai's drifting thoughts had come to him, with Grillo and Kenner continuing past with the loaded cart. Levi's eyes were on Ashmedai at first, but they shifted shyly to Klarent.

"Oh, not at all. It was… enjoyable."

Ashmedai could tell Levi meant that, yet there was something off about him, a twitch and hidden sorrow behind his eyes.

"Lyssy is watching the shop," Klarent said, "but I'll let him know. Now, Ash, remember, you promised to be at the opening of my booth."

Ashmedai offered a small bow. "And a promise is something I never break."

"I, um… I should head home," Levi said once they were alone.

"May I accompany you?"

"Y-y-y-you…." Levi trailed off when he couldn't contain his stuttering, collecting himself and finally answering with a short, "Yes."

They walked a pace or two in silence, leaving the hubbub behind them, but eventually, Levi spoke again, as Ashmedai had hoped. He wanted Levi to feel comfortable speaking openly with him.

"So…. Ash, did you enjoy your festival work today?"

"Well enough." Ashmedai smiled, pleased he hadn't needed to correct Levi this time. "Some of Dreya's tasks for me revolved around next week's hunt. We tend to need more food come Festival Day, given people are more likely to indulge."

Many things were edible in the Shadow Lands, but there weren't many animals, and even fewer that were hunted for meat. The people dried most of what they caught to last longer, hunting only monthly and keeping a close eye on the various herds.

"Master Braxton can replicate some foods with alchemy, can't he?"

"He can, and he does, but while nutritious, something replicated isn't quite like the real thing. As I have heard from far too many citizens—it doesn't taste the same." Ashmedai chuckled, enjoying the soft smile Levi echoed back at him. "If I may ask, why did you wait so long to be among the people more?"

"I-I was nervous," Levi said with a drop of his head. "I thought they might think me strange."

Ashmedai stared at him in disbelief.

"I wasn't born here!" Levi hurried to explain. "I was made. I didn't know what others might think strange, especially with my stitches and… my eyes."

"Let me reassure you," Ashmedai said, "you are wonderfully unique, Levi, like everyone in the Dark Kingdom, but unique in a way all your own."

"Isn't that strange?"

"I suppose it is." Ashmedai chuckled again. "You simply need to stop thinking that strange is a bad thing."

"Even if my eyes match the Source Crystal?" Levi asked more dejectedly.

Something thick stuck in Ashmedai's throat, but he managed to say, "It is hardly an unsightly color. The people trust in Brax. They'll trust you. Has anyone proven otherwise?"

"No. Everyone's been wonderful." Levi smiled.

The distance from the market steps to Braxton's tower wasn't far, so Ashmedai slowed for their walk to last longer.

"What about you?" Levi asked, keeping pace with him. "You live in the castle all alone. Even Master Braxton made me so he wouldn't be alone."

Besides Levi's adult figure, it was his shrewdness that made Ashmedai think of him as a man and not a creation of only a few weeks. "Maybe I have trouble sometimes thinking my strangeness is a good thing too."

That caused another smile to brighten Levi's face, and their stroll almost came to a stop as they enjoyed the quiet moment that passed between them.

Then Levi looked down, continuing onward, and Ashmedai was reminded of the shadows behind those violet eyes.

"Are you all right?" Ashmedai asked. "You seemed off when you returned with Grillo, as if something had upset you."

Levi often seemed hunched, like he wished he could hide within himself the way he used to hide in his cloak. "I had a... a daydream, I think?"

"A daydream?"

"It was odd. Kenner and I were playing. One minute he was dashing behind a tree, the next, someone else stepped from behind it. Still a boy but... a half-elf with red hair."

"Like you?"

"I don't think so. I don't know. He had no stitches. And I've never been a boy."

"Perhaps you longed that you might have been, watching Kenner."

"Perhaps." Levi gazed timidly at Ashmedai, letting some of his smile return. "Silly, isn't it?"

"No. We all long for things we can never have."

Another quiet moment passed, the slow progression of their feet coming to a full stop.

"Were you... going to come in?" Levi asked.

"Oh." Ashmedai hadn't realized they were at the tower door until he looked up. No wonder Levi had stopped. Ashmedai had simply followed his lead. "Brax might not want to be interrupted unannounced but please let him know that I would like tea again sometime soon. And in general, more often. You and I can be a positive influence on each other, I think. I don't need to be such a hermit, especially with my dearest friend."

"You and Master Braxton are very close," Levi said. "I guess I thought you were close with everyone."

"I try to be. Admittedly, I could be better. Brax and I just understand each other more than most."

Levi seemed hesitant to say more. What he did say was a simple, "Tomorrow?"

"We'll see each other when you return to assist Grillo. I look forward to it. And Levi," he called when Levi reached for the door. Ashmedai had his hesitancies too, but he couldn't deny that he hadn't found a reason to be less of a hermit in a long time.

He took Levi's hand and slid his fingers up Levi's wrist that still bore a line of stitches.

"These are not something you need to hide or be ashamed of, but if you ever wish for me to take more of them away, all you need to do is ask."

The soft thrum of Levi's pulse could be felt beneath Ashmedai's fingers, and he thought he felt its steady beat speed up. "Maybe I will. Good evening, Ash." Levi slid his hand from Ashmedai's grasp slowly and offered one last smile.

After Levi entered the tower, Ashmedai couldn't bring himself to leave right away. He was certain he wasn't imagining that Levi looked like Cullen, no matter what Braxton said, but it wasn't only his appearance that was familiar. Levi was gentle and curious like Cullen too.

"Aren't there better options for the king than a lowly construct?"

Ashmedai jumped. He needed to stop getting so lost in his thoughts.

Braxton had opened the door and was peering at him with a faint scowl. Levi must have gone upstairs, for even a crane of Ashmedai's neck to see farther inside showed no sign of him.

"You said it yourself," Ashmedai answered. "He's different."

"Is it that, or because he reminds you of another man with violet eyes?"

"You admit it?"

"I admit he's different, Ash. He isn't Cullen."

Hearing or saying the name was always so different from thinking it. "I know. I'll visit again soon. Good evening, Brax."

Ashmedai turned to take his leave, and the road back into the city felt lonelier than ever, even with the lights and sounds of the people becoming more vibrant the closer he got to the market steps.

A daydream, Levi had said.

Ashmedai wondered if that's all it was.

CHAPTER 3

LEVI WHIRLED around the tower, hurrying to finish his chores so he could meet up with Grillo sooner—and hopefully see Ashmedai again.

He was almost through putting away the dishes and cleaning the kitchen, with tea for Braxton and Levi's draught both heating up on the stove. The draught was easy enough to prepare, a powder Braxton had created that dissolved in hot water. Levi didn't even mind the idea of drinking it this morning; he was too excited to go out, to be something—anything—other than only Braxton's.

Ashmedai had admitted he was closer to Braxton than to anyone else in the entire kingdom, yet Levi was the one he'd walked home and touched with gentle fingers. If Levi wanted, Ashmedai could take away all his stitches, and he'd be whole someday, his own man. The thought both terrified and excited him. He wasn't sure when or how he would get up the nerve to ask for that, but the memory of Ashmedai's touch was potent encouragement.

Maybe someday Ashmedai would be as close or closer to Levi than he was to Braxton, which was a terribly jealous, selfish thought, but Levi couldn't shake it.

"Is there a storm passing through?"

"Hm?" Levi barely paused in his closing of cupboards to answer Braxton.

"You are making quite the ruckus out here. In such a hurry?"

"I'm sorry, Master. I do not want to make Grillo wait on me. I finished all my chores." Levi spun around, with the final tidying complete. "May I leave now? Do you need anything else of me?"

Studying Levi as he wheeled toward him, Braxton answered slowly, "I suppose not. But are thoughts of Grillo the only reason you're spinning like a top?"

Levi fought to keep his cheeks from flushing or from averting his eyes too obviously. "I… enjoy being around others too. Like you wanted! As long as it's not too many."

Braxton said nothing but continued surveying Levi with an unreadable air.

Levi felt a twinge of guilt for longing to have a closeness with the king that surpassed his master's. After all, Braxton had only the two of them. "Master? Are you very busy?"

"I am always busy," Braxton said, despite having left his workshop and making no move to return yet.

"You take breaks, though, like now."

"When someone is being especially noisy, yes."

Levi dropped his head. "I will be quieter next time. But, if I may say, Master, as important as your work is, you need rest and distraction too. I was talking with Ash about how he hopes to get out more, see others more, have tea with you more."

"With *Ash*, were you?"

"Y-yes." Levi chose not to comment on the stress of the name. "I wondered… why don't you go out more and make friends, as you've encouraged me?"

Braxton patted the armrests of his chair. "You know it is difficult for me to get around."

"I could help with that. I could carry you down the market steps. You still can get out more if you want to."

"*You* can. I have no interest in friends."

"You're friends with the king."

"He is the exception." Very little space separated them, but Braxton wheeled closer anyway, close enough that one of his wheels brushed Levi's shin. "He is exceptional. You seem to agree."

"I-I-I…." Levi tensed, eyes widening.

"You handle the friend-making, Levi. I'll continue my experiments. Don't neglect your draught now."

"Y-yes, Master." Levi bowed and then went to retrieve the draught. "I made tea for you as well. Would you like some?"

"Is it the bitter stuff you made for Ash?"

"No, Master. Your herbal tea."

"Then yes, thank you."

Levi poured the draught, then poured some tea for Braxton, drinking his even as he moved to hand Braxton his cup.

Braxton turned away without further comment, but the last few words between them echoed in Levi's mind.

Yes, Master.

No, Master.

"Must I call you Master?"

"Excuse me?" Braxton turned before exiting into his workshop.

Levi hadn't meant to say it, but now that he had, he didn't want to lose his momentum. "May I call you Braxton as others do? I'm more than a servant, aren't I?"

It was clear that Braxton hadn't expected the request. He looked unreadable again but didn't seem angry. "I suppose you can call me what you like so long as you do as you're told."

"Yes, Ma—" Levi stopped himself, taking a breath before correcting. "Braxton." He smiled in gratitude.

Braxton nodded and went on his way.

Levi downed the rest of his draught, eager to be on his way as well. His desire to see Ashmedai only grew stronger.

And see Ashmedai he did—for a few moments with barely a good morning passing between them. Levi was all too quickly ushered into the wood to accompany Grillo again. Kenner didn't join them this time, but he did stop by to say hello to Levi before they left.

In some ways, the day went much as the one before. The shadows still seemed to be watching Levi, but he chose to ignore the feeling and enjoyed working in a way that wasn't focused on the tower.

The best repeat of the day before was when Ashmedai offered to walk Levi home.

"Would you have any interest in joining the hunt next week?" Ashmedai asked.

"Would I be of use?"

"Your illusion magic—do you have limitations, or can you make anything appear?"

Levi didn't mean to blush, but he felt heat fill his cheeks, thinking of the many times he had conjured a vision of Ashmedai. "I-I can make anything."

"Then you may be more useful than you'd think. And I'd have an excuse to spend more time with you outside a brief stroll."

Ashmedai took Levi's hand, also echoing the day before, only this time, it was the hand he had healed, and he ran his thumb across Levi's smooth wrist.

"I-I'd like that," Levi said with a shudder. He wanted to ask for more stitches to be cleansed, to feel more of Ashmedai's skin on his, and the pleasant scratch of his clawlike nails, but it felt too intimate to do so outside the tower. "Tomorrow?"

Ashmedai smiled, gently squeezing Levi's wrist. "Tomorrow."

THE HUNT was days away, but the first thing Levi did when tomorrow came was leave even earlier than the day before to stop by Daedlys's shop.

"Stitches! I hear you're the talk of the town," Daedlys said as he floated over upon Levi's entrance. "Well, some people have mentioned *seeing* you at least, which is a good start. I told you your stitches were nothing to be wary about."

Levi had worn his hood up when entering the market, like usual, but he hadn't felt quite as much of a need to keep his face obscured. He'd even met eyes with a few people along the way, who smiled at him or nodded in greeting—and his eyes had been what worried him most. Like Ashmedai had guessed, because he was a creation of Braxton's, no one seemed to mind.

"Indeed," Levi said, lowering his hood completely.

"You're sure you're not mad at me for mentioning you to Grillo?" Daedlys asked.

"Not at all. Grillo is very kind and easy to work with. I've even befriended his son, Kenner."

"Marvelous! I'd hoped for such an outcome. It would have done you no good if you were still so shy come Festival Day. You're going to love every minute of it."

Levi had been so caught up in helping prepare for the festival, he sometimes forgot he'd get to enjoy it. "First, I need to survive the hunt. The king asked me to assist next week."

"He did? Ash must have taken a liking to you."

It was impossible to keep the fresh blush from Levi's face then.

Daedlys examined him with a crook to his smile. "I see…. Well, how fortuitous. I've been fixing Ash's sword belt. It's practically brand-new now. I imagine you're here for a belt and weapons yourself."

"Yes, please. Braxton said you can make any request as payment, or simply have me help around the shop, if you'd like."

"I have a better idea—you can be my delivery boy for the day."

"Delivery boy?" Levi followed Daedlys toward a wall of basic weapons and equipment. There were other shops more dedicated to weaponry, but Levi wasn't looking for anything fancy, and he'd always thought Daedlys's shop had the lovelier belt and accessory designs, with very fine stitching and embroidery like the tunic made from Emerald silk.

"Once we find you something suitable, you can deliver Ash's belt to him."

"I...." Levi's blush heated further. "I can do that."

"Here, I was just about to package it." Daedlys levitated a black belt that had been resting on a table in front of the weapons wall into his grasp. It was beautiful, meant for a longsword, and stitched in gold. It was always so strange to see Daedlys touch something, since he was see-through. When he held the belt out to Levi, it almost seemed to levitate still.

Levi reverently tucked the belt into his bag.

"What about you?" Daedlys asked. "Do you have any experience with weaponry? I'm guessing no."

"I'm a fast learner," Levi defended. "What do you recommend?"

"A dagger. Right-handed or left?"

"Um...." Levi honestly didn't know. "I use both evenly, I think."

"Then you can have two and grab whichever feels most natural in the thick of battle. I have this design for dual-daggers." Daedlys gestured to a dark brown belt, simple in the front, with a gold buckle, and a gold ring in back where it crossed and connected to twin sheaths that would rest on either side of Levi's hips.

There was a black version as well, very like the king's in some ways, but with silver accents.

"Could I... have that one instead?" Levi asked.

"Certainly. Then I'd say these daggers." Daedlys waved his hand at a set on the wall with silver accents and black grips.

"You're sure it's not too much for simply making a delivery?"

"For you? Never. Besides, I already have a dozen preorders for Brax's black crystals. Now—" Daedlys levitated the daggers into his hands as well and then spun them to hold them hilt outward toward Levi. "—I wouldn't be much of a friend if I let you take these without some instruction. Go on."

Levi accepted them, one in each hand.

"You'll not necessarily want to wield them at the same time unless you find you're well-suited for it. It could be useful on the hunt, however, since you're more likely to find yourself amidst multiple targets. Square your stance."

Levi did so, automatically putting his right foot back, left foot forward, and therefore holding the left dagger out as if to parry, and the right back, ready to strike.

"Very natural," Daedlys praised, floating to the side to give Levi room. "Give a thrust a try. Shift your hips as you strike and—"

There was a deer—a *second* deer charging from the left, as he stabbed forward with his dagger. He had but a moment to swipe outward with the second one, slicing the doe's throat as she charged, and then he yanked the right dagger from the buck's chest to drive both weapons forward, one in each deer, before their combined weight could topple forward and crush him.

"Fantastic! And you've no experience, you said? Braxton must be a wizard as much as an alchemist."

Levi blinked at the sound of Daedlys's voice, seeing that he had sliced and stabbed nothing but air. The deer had seemed so real. But there were no such creatures in the Shadow Lands anymore.

"You'll do fine on the hunt, sweet Stitches. Shall I secure the belt for you so you can wear it out?"

Levi lowered his arms and straightened his stance, unsure what to do with the daggers without anywhere to sheathe them yet. "Y-yes, please."

"You're going to look stunning, my dear, don't you worry."

Daedlys's touch was as strange as seeing him hold something, for it felt like a brush of wind more than any real weight, a cold presence wrapping the belt around Levi's waist and showing him how to tighten it with translucent fingers.

That was why Levi started shivering, he told himself, feeling a chill linger at the base of his spine, even after Daedlys stepped back to allow him to admire himself in a nearby mirror.

The rest had merely been another daydream.

ASHMEDAI INSISTED that he and Dreya walk and talk during their morning business to reach the festival site sooner, not wanting to miss his chance to see Levi. At first he thought he *had* missed him, for there was no sign of the young man, but then Ashmedai saw Grillo only just arriving, which was when he spotted Levi.

Levi wasn't coming from down the road but up the market steps, his hood back, bag slung across his body, and sporting a very handsome weapons belt in black with twin daggers.

Despite the different picture Levi painted from the hooded and hunched figure Ashmedai had first met, he also seemed distant, maybe even troubled—until his eyes met Ashmedai's and immediately seemed to pulse with purple light.

"What do you think?" Dreya asked.

"Hm?"

"About ensuring none of the advisors have a booth to man this year. Not only for me! We could all use a break. Especially Luccite. She works so hard, don't you think?"

"Absolutely. Whatever you recommend," Ashmedai said absently, offering a polite bow. "Now, if you'll excuse me."

Dreya seemed about to say something more but let him go without argument.

"Preparing for the hunt?" Ashmedai asked once he reached Levi.

"I thought it best. Also, Daedlys finished your belt." Levi reached inside his bag to produce the belt—black, like the one Levi had chosen for himself.

It was pure vanity to assume Levi had matched Ashmedai on purpose, but the thought made his smile widen. "Perhaps you could help me confirm there isn't any need for adjustments before you go."

Levi's cheeks flushed deep indigo, and his eyes flashed toward Grillo. But while it was obvious Grillo was waiting on Levi, the minotaur stood back, content to let them finish. Everyone else around the clearing between the houses and market steps were busy amongst themselves.

Levi's smile was sweet as he motioned for Ashmedai to turn around. The shadows were hiding in his eyes again, though—Ashmedai could see them—like swirls of deeper violet.

"Is everything all right?" Ashmedai asked. "If you'd prefer to not assist me—"

"I want to!" Levi exclaimed. "I-I mean… I very much would like to assist you. My mind was elsewhere before, but… I'd rather it be here."

"Are you sure?"

Levi paused a moment before answering, a pink tongue flitting out to moisten his blue lips. "Yes."

He stepped forward, not waiting for Ashmedai to turn but approaching from the side and boldly wrapping his arms around Ashmedai's waist. Levi clasped the belt closed with his arms still coiled around Ashmedai, and for the first time, Ashmedai realized how similar they were in height, for Levi's breath struck the side of his cheek.

The proper response would have been for Ashmedai to keep his face forward, but the delicate pressure of Levi's hands at his hips and waist wasn't causing a very *proper* reaction.

Ashmedai turned to meet Levi's eyes, caught in their amethyst glow that was a simple lean away. He licked his lips as he'd seen Levi do and overlapped Levi's hands on his waist.

"D-does that feel in need of adjustment?" Levi asked, breath still puffing lightly, but now on Ashmedai's lips.

Ashmedai helped Levi shift the belt until the sheath was on the correct side. "Feels perfect," he said, letting his fingers move to Levi's wrists and caressing the stitches on one and the smoothness of the other. Keeping hold of Levi's wrists, he caressed more insistently the one with stitches, like a question.

Levi gave a hasty, private nod, like he wanted nothing more than for Ashmedai to do as implied but didn't want to acknowledge the throng of people around them.

Covertly, between their bodies, Ashmedai lifted the still-stitched wrist and began to run his thumb and middle finger in slow parallel strokes like the first time, the pulse of shadow magic not unlike the deep purple shadows that occasionally clouded Levi's eyes.

Perhaps Ashmedai completed the motion a little slower than the time before, watching Levi's face instead of his wrist, and noting the way Levi's breath caught, high in his chest, with a quiver at his lips. Ashmedai slowed further, drawing the spell out for as long as he could, and he could have sworn a whimper left Levi by the end.

A crash forced a much louder gasp from Levi's lips—nothing dangerous, just a pile of lumber toppling nearby—and Ashmedai felt Levi start to tug his hand back. Then Levi relaxed, clearly not wanting their contact to end, and both their eyes fell to the wrist and fading shadows.

Smooth. Just like the other.

"Will I see you again tonight?" Ashmedai asked, releasing Levi with a linger of his fingers.

Levi's entire face looked indigo now. "Yes."

Ashmedai couldn't wait.

LEVI STARED at the tower ceiling above his bed. The hunt was tomorrow, and though he had trained with his daggers and was reasonably confident in his skills, he had never put those skills to practical use before—unless the daydream with the deer meant more than he knew.

The daydreams had persisted all week, usually just a flash of something he didn't recognize, a time and place he knew he had never been. The walks with Ashmedai had persisted too and were much more pleasant to dwell upon.

But dwelling was why Levi was still awake at such a late hour.

Defeated, he threw aside his blankets and rose from the bed. He could read, but learning something new about the world outside the barrier, or even just indulging in some of the more torrid tomes Braxton owned, wasn't appealing tonight.

Levi sat in the chair at his window, gazing toward the castle. There was a light on in one of the towers. He wondered if Ashmedai was awake too.

At that thought, Levi touched each of his smooth wrists. He wanted to ask for more stitches gone, but every time the desire occurred to him, they were at the tower door, and he didn't want Braxton to see.

With a wave of his hand, Levi created an illusion of Ashmedai before him, this time mirroring him in a chair beside the window, reading a nondescript book. Levi's illusions didn't include sound, or he'd mimic Ashmedai's voice as well to read him something. That would be far more appealing than reading to himself, especially when Levi's mind drifted once more to Braxton's romances. Some of them got rather heated, and imagining those scenes spoken aloud in Ashmedai's deep tones made the heat rise in Levi's cheeks.

Despite having no sound, Levi could do much more with just an image—like shed Ashmedai of his clothing. He didn't know what the king's body looked like beneath his garments, but he had often wondered....

No. Levi couldn't do that. Even if it would only be his imagination, it felt wrong to objectify Ashmedai in that way. The real thing would be preferable anyway.

Dismissing the image, Levi felt equally guilty considering pleasuring himself with the image of Ashmedai still so fresh in his mind, even though he'd already resisted the urge for days, after Ashmedai removed more stitches. The sensation was more than pleasant, it was... *pleasurable*. He'd noticed even more the second time than the first.

Levi had pleasured himself before. Not long after he first achieved consciousness, Braxton had told him to familiarize himself with his body, and Levi had done so. He hadn't expected to find pleasure when his exploratory touch inevitably led between his legs, but when he started to feel it, to harden and find his breath catching, he hadn't shied away. No bodily reaction could have been more natural.

He looked again at the castle in the distance and the light on in one of the towers. Oh, to know another's touch someday, rather than only his own.

Snatching up his cloak but not changing out of the nightshirt he wore to bed, Levi fled down the stairs as lightly as he could. He didn't know what he was doing, where he was going, but when he reached the bottom of the tower, his first stop was to ensure Braxton was asleep.

Braxton didn't bother locking the workshop at night, and the door was propped open, allowing Levi to easily peek inside without a creak. Breathing evenly, Braxton lay upon the bed set against the left wall. Beyond him, at the very back of the workshop, was a large black crystal, like the smaller ones, but as immense as the Amethyst gemstone in the market.

Levi had seen the black crystal before, when cleaning the workshop, but every time, he felt more unease being near it. He doubted the Amethyst gemstone, even being the Source Crystal, would make him feel that way, though he'd always avoided it when in the market square, afraid proximity would call more attention to his eyes.

Fleeing just as silently for the front door, Levi soon slipped out of the tower completely and headed down the road. Although night was not truly night, at least not much different than their version of day, the air felt colder as Levi walked, though that might have also been because he was in a nightshirt instead of trousers.

A short walk to clear his head and expend some energy would help him sleep. That's all he needed. But, as he drew closer to the top of the market steps and the more direct road at his left leading to the castle, Levi wondered if Ashmedai would admit him should he knock on the castle doors.

Shuffling up ahead drew Levi's attention to the right portion of the road, where the Emerald carriages came and went through the wood. Levi pulled his cloak tighter around himself as he stared, hoping he was imagining the sound—and the slowly approaching shadow from the wood's depths.

A figure began to emerge, and before Levi could take it in fully, he darted down the market steps.

What a fool he was to go walking at night! He knew enough stories and whispers of the demon to be aware that the twilight hours when the streets were empty was the likeliest time for people to disappear, snatched up by the demon itself, even if they were nowhere near the barrier. Bedtime stories to frighten children maybe, but then who was coming out of the wood?

The market was much darker at this hour, with fewer crystals on to brighten the way, and only a handful of lanterns, as well as a candle clock at the base of the steps near Gordoc's stall. It was very late, almost closer to early, an hour or two before Levi needed to be up for the hunt.

The shuffling came again, closer. Footsteps? They were coming from above, where whatever that was had come out of the wood.

Levi moved deeper into the market, swift and searching. There was no one around. He could go to Daedlys's shop, where Daedlys and Klarent lived above it, but there was no light on. If he roused them and they answered the door to harbor him, would he be putting them at risk?

The footsteps were coming down the steps!

The brightest point in the market was the square, illuminated by the Source Crystal. It might not be the safest place, but at least Levi could hide behind it. Hide he did, too afraid to peer around it and see what pursued him. Instead, he glanced over his shoulder at the castle on its hill.

The view here was closer but not as direct as from Levi's window. The tower with its light on was still visible, though. Ashmedai had to be awake. He was so close, yet so far....

As the shuffling drew nearer, Levi huddled in his cloak at the base of the Amethyst gemstone. There was a faint hum of power emanating from it, now that Levi was close enough to hear, but all he could focus on was the horror Kenner had described, with a maw large enough to swallow him whole.

"Who goes there?"

Levi gasped as a hand clamped down on his shoulder, and he sprung upright with enough force that the hood fell back from his head.

Yentriss.

"You. Like any other number of foolish children who think it might be fun to test the demon's patience." She sighed with what Levi could only describe as motherly disappointment. "Are you sleepwalking, or truly that daft?" She scanned down Levi's body, taking in the nightshirt beneath his cloak, bare legs, and simple shoes.

"I-I... couldn't sleep," Levi said, hanging his head. "I was startled when I heard you coming. I'm sorry. Do you usually patrol so late?" Or *early*, he reminded himself.

The lizard woman had a lovely glimmer to her green and gold scales in the meager lighting, almost ethereal in the shadow of the Amethyst gemstone. She wore a simple long-sleeved surcoat and trousers that gave a stately, soldierlike appearance. "Old habits." She shrugged. "I have deputies who patrol at times too. We never find anything amiss, mind you, other than wandering babes."

Levi hung his head lower. He hated being likened to a child, though he supposed he had been acting like one.

As he adjusted his cloak and tried to stand up straighter, the Amethyst gemstone was poised directly behind him, and he thought Yentriss's stare turned penetrating, enough that he quickly looked away again.

"None of that now," she said a little softer. "I haven't seen eyes the likes of yours in a long time, but you needn't hide them. If there was ever something sinister to that Amethyst, it was because of what the demon did to it, maybe even what our lost prince did to it, but Brax has proven he can make useful things from its power in the years since. We'll see if that proves true of you, but so far nothing has proven otherwise."

Levi looked up. Yentriss was a harsh woman, but there was a tenderness beneath her scales that could be earned, something Levi had only caught glimpses of when she smiled at Grillo or patted Kenner's head. He hoped he could earn it someday.

"Go home now," Yentriss said plainly, and Levi offered a hasty nod before heading around the gemstone to return to the steps.

He still couldn't be certain of where he would have gone had Yentriss not interrupted his stroll, but with a final glance at the castle once he reached the top of the steps, he knew where he'd wanted to be. Even as he turned for Braxton's tower, Levi wondered if Ashmedai would have let him in.

WHAT A fool Ashmedai was for thinking that inviting Levi to join the hunt would mean *more* time with him.

"Duck!" Yentriss called from the back of the line, and everyone knew to listen—for the rollhounds had been released.

Rollhounds were what had become of dogs and were still often kept as pets, mixed now with a sort of armadillo appearance and able to hurl themselves forward in their contorted form and even propel themselves into the air ahead of the hunters.

Ashmedai watched half a dozen land in front of where he led the charge, continuing forward hot on the trail of whatever scent they had picked up.

Some of the hunters were especially skilled in controlling the rollhounds, but the hunters' numbers weren't only based on strength. Some were adept at long-range weaponry, like Yentriss, others in magic, or simply useful with the natural affinities of their monstrous selves.

Myrra, for example, was a creature of massive size, even taller than Grillo, and seemingly made of stone. She could make the ground tremble and act as both deterrent and wall to direct their prey where they wanted them to go.

In contrast, Amuro, a second-generation-born citizen, and therefore one of the most mixed of chimeras, was faster than the rollhounds and could cast magic that seeped from him like mist to put their prey to sleep. He walked as easily on four legs as two, for his hindquarters were like a furred mammal, his arms like a lizard, and he had a tail like a rat, with an elongated face made from armored skin, the teeth of an alligator, and a mane of hair as full as a lion.

Those who volunteered for the hunt all had unique skills to contribute.

Like Levi—who was somewhere back by Yentriss, staying out of harm's way.

Ashmedai kept his hand on his longsword but didn't yet draw it, speeding between trees in pursuit of the hounds. Several other hunters kept pace with him, many were just behind, and even more were farther back with Yentriss and Levi, where Ashmedai could barely keep track of them, let alone start a conversation.

The days leading up to the hunt had mostly been the same, with Levi assisting Grillo, and then, upon his return, Ashmedai would walk Levi back to Braxton's door. It was never enough time.

Nor was there enough time during the chaos of the hunt.

"Jackalopes!" Pentelyn warned, using her many eyes to steer their direction as she flew above them. She was a harpy with a second set of eyes above the first. "Grouped to the right!"

Myrra lumbered ahead, veering right until she was at the forefront, and struck the ground with her mighty fists. The path ahead rumbled, and there was a scatter of winged creatures and glider monkeys—and, farther in the distance, a shift in direction of the jackalopes.

Everyone carried a warding crystal, and the collars of the rollhounds had been fastened with crystals as well to provide early warning if they neared the barrier. The hunt was often too chaotic to recognize how far into the wood they might have traveled, and people traversed the part of the wood inhabited by edible animals the least frequently, so as not to spook them more than necessary.

Ashmedai caught up to Myrra and passed her, with everyone hurrying onward at his heels. The jackalopes were in clearer view now as the rollhounds unfurled from their contortions to further herd them.

Half the jackalopes headed left as desired—the other half kept right.

Damn.

"I'll steer them back!" Pentelyn called as she soared overhead.

Ashmedai didn't like the hunters separating, but if they could cut off the wayward jackalopes fast enough, it would mean twice as much meat for the month ahead.

Then he remembered why he had wanted to invite Levi, and it wasn't only for his company.

A swift glance at a nearby tree, then back at the farthest row of hunters, indicated more than enough darkness. Leaping forward, Ashmedai dropped into the tree's shadow like submerging in a deep lake, reemerging in a blink where additional shadows existed behind Levi.

"Quick!" Ashmedai sprinted after him.

Levi whirled, tension gripping him as tightly as he gripped his newly acquired daggers—but then he smiled.

A shadow jump could be dangerous with so much uncertainty and moving bodies, but the risk had been worth it.

"Cast an illusion to block the way of the rightward-heading jackalopes," Ashmedai explained, taking hold of Levi's elbow to keep him moving forward.

"B-b-but what should I—"

"Whatever first springs to mind. Hurry!"

The panic that had once again risen in Levi gave way to resolve, his eyes focusing forward through the rushing hunters and scattering animals to where Pentelyn was quickly catching up with the jackalopes heading right.

Then the crystal on Pentelyn's belt flickered.

Levi flung his arms outward, fingers flaring, other than the thumbs and pointer fingers keeping their grip on his daggers. Light seemed to dance at his fingertips, but it didn't shoot forward to travel the expanse between him and the jackalopes. There weren't even any telling flickers where the illusion began to form. Suddenly there was simply a horse, not unlike Braxton's mechanical horses, but this one looked flesh, like Ashmedai hadn't seen in a thousand years. It was all white, rearing in warning in the jackalopes' path like a bright beacon in the darkness.

The herd stumbled to a halt and changed course in the other direction.

"Brilliant!" Ashmedai squeezed Levi's elbow. "What made you think of that?"

"I-I don't know." Levi smiled shyly.

As the two herds of jackalopes got more within range, Yentriss started firing with her longbow, taking out several with hardly any effort before their pace grew faster at the sign of imminent danger.

The jackalopes that had initially gone left were far enough into a clearing that Amuro dropped to all fours, sprinted ahead of them, and leapt into their midst, spreading his mist to put them to sleep. Those jackalopes were easy prey for the rollhounds after that.

The remaining section of the herd was scattering, running in between the hunters, so that even Levi would soon get the chance to show his skills with a weapon. Ashmedai didn't expect much, but as he released Levi's elbow and drew his sword, he became transfixed watching Levi dash forward without hesitation, whirling impressively with both daggers to fell one jackalope, then two.

Then three.

"Pentelyn!" Amuro's call pulled Ashmedai's attention away from Levi, and he searched for where the harpy had gone.

Only she was still heading *right*, following a lone jackalope that hadn't turned with the rest.

"I can catch it!" she called back, not bothering to look behind her.

Had she not seen her crystal's glow? But then, Ashmedai could no longer see it flickering, which didn't make any sense when Pentelyn hadn't altered course.

Then Ashmedai saw why—her crystal was on the ground, flickering against the trunk of a tree. She'd dropped it and didn't realize!

"Pentelyn!" Ashmedai cried louder than Amuro, but she didn't seem to hear him.

She was flying faster, aiming to get ahead of the jackalope. Ashmedai could see some of the crystal perimeter on either side of her, but too far away for her to notice. In front of her was nothing, or the remaining crystals must have all worn out, which meant there would be no way to know when she came upon the barrier, until….

Ashmedai didn't think; he simply dove into the nearest shadows, having only guesswork to guide where he might pop up that would be far enough in front of Pentelyn despite her momentum, yet not across the barrier where *Ash* would become little more than his namesake.

As the darkness that enveloped him returned to the sight of the wood, Ashmedai spotted Pentelyn coming right at him, just as the jackalope darted past his feet.

"Stop!" he commanded her, and the harpy jerked backward so suddenly she nearly fell out of the sky. Ashmedai spun, and it was only an arm's length behind him that the jackalope leapt—and never landed.

It disintegrated into particles of dust.

Before Ashmedai could turn around, he heard a thud, unsurprised to find that Pentelyn had landed, panting and staring in horror at how close she had come to disappearing.

Ashmedai sheathed his sword and pulled a brightly glowing crystal from his belt to drop behind him. He immediately returned his gaze to Pentelyn, hoping to soothe—

"Gazellians!"

He and Pentelyn's attentions both shot back toward the rest of the hunters. Gazellians were an edible and highly desired game, but they were also some of the most dangerous animals that inhabited the Dark Kingdom, no longer mere gazelles but bearing the hunger, fangs, and temperament of rabid wolves.

A dozen could be seen, heading parallel along the barrier from the opposite direction Ashmedai and the hunters had come from, meaning they were stampeding right for them.

The hunters dispersed like falling drops of water, giving as wide a berth as they could, with magic and weapons ready to defend, not attack, for a stray arrow now might draw the whole pack to devour whoever fired.

Which was when Levi's hesitation returned at the worst time, for he stood frozen, still too much in the pack's path, and one of the gazellians veered toward him with a snap of its jaws.

Ashmedai had as much time as he'd had to save Pentelyn, maybe less, so once again, he didn't think. He dove into the shadows, appearing out of Levi's own shadow in front of him, and stopped the gazellian with the only recourse he had left.

Arching his arms upward to summon every immediate shadow to him, Ashmedai became the very darkness itself and swooped forward onto the charging gazellian like a black wave. He never had and never would explain to any of his people what it felt like when he did that—not even to Braxton—because it was nourishment, like devouring something using bare hands and teeth. Because it tasted and felt incredible.

Because he hated how much he enjoyed it and longed for more the moment he reformed into his humanoid self on the other side, leaving behind an empty husk like the gazellian had been dead and decaying for weeks.

There was good reason Ashmedai preferred to use his sword.

The one consolation was when Ashmedai glanced behind him and didn't think Levi looked afraid or disgusted, even though Levi had never witnessed that part of Ashmedai's power before. Levi's expression was utter awe.

A few of the fleeing gazellians fell behind after being startled by Ashmedai's attack, and Yentriss struck them down with arrows without alerting those that continued onward. The hunters had many prizes in exchange for their close calls, though Ashmedai would never say it was worth it.

Once the dust settled and the hunters gathered closer to one another, the others noticed Pentelyn returning from where a brightly lit crystal still glowed on the ground, her own that she'd dropped blinking against a tree until she retrieved it. Amuro raced to her side, and it was clear in moments that everyone knew what might have been.

It was understandable to be shaken, but Ashmedai had never seen Pentelyn look quite so distressed, near tears as Amuro, her husband, gathered her close. She was usually as calm and seasoned a warrior as Yentriss.

"You're positively pallid," Ashmedai said, going to her swiftly. "You're all right, aren't you? No harm done, save a scare? You've had close calls before."

There was something Pentelyn didn't want to tell Ashmedai. He could see it in the way she avoided looking at him with any of her many eyes, though he'd known her since near the beginning, when she had been the first cursed-born child.

Amuro was the one who answered, gently holding her to his side. "Penny's pregnant," he said, drifting one of his lizard hands low over her stomach. "We're so sorry, Ash. We didn't want to say anything when there were already so many—"

"*Amuro*," Pentelyn hushed him.

"So many what?" Ashmedai pressed, but the pair looked at each other and kept quiet.

Ashmedai's people never kept things from him. Or at least, he had never known them to before. The recent years had been harder on everyone, and as Ashmedai had said to Levi, he had been far too much a hermit lately, other than to attend to obligations he couldn't ignore.

"Never mind. You needn't say anything you don't wish to. But being with child, and after a scare like that? You should go see Luccite immediately."

They both nodded, and Amuro said, "I'll take her there now. Thank you, Ash. Thank you for saving them."

Them.

Ashmedai would gladly lay down his life for any of his people, but the guilt that accompanied knowing he might not have gotten there in time was so much greater when it could have been two lives lost.

As the couple headed out of the wood, most everyone else was acting less spooked than they plainly were, starting to gather up the day's kill for skinning and butchering back in the city. Several of them passed Ashmedai strained smiles or fleeting looks, even with all the rollhounds returned to help keep guard. The people were terrified, and it was obvious something else was going on.

Ashmedai would need to call another city council meeting sooner than usual.

The only exception to the palpable unease was Yentriss, who never failed to maintain a clear head.

And thankfully, she was distracting Levi.

"You're good with those daggers," she said as Ashmedai approached them. "Long range can also be useful, but illusions might not always save you. I could teach you the bow, see if you have any aptitude, so you're even more prepared next time."

Ashmedai was going to cut in and say that he thought that a marvelous idea, only to watch Levi's expression go slack, his violet eyes drifting from Yentriss to stare at nothing.

"Levi?" she said sharply when he didn't answer.

"Hm?" Levi snapped back like coming out of a trance. "I'm so sorry, Yentriss. Yes, I would very much like to learn the bow from you. I think the hunt must have left me a bit jittery."

"Jitters will do you no better than paralysis," she said coolly. "We'll have to work on that. Ash," Yentriss said as she noticed him.

He smiled to be cordial, but responded with a subtle nod to dismiss her, to which she went off without comment to help the others.

Levi's gaze was drifting again.

"Levi?" Ashmedai took his hand.

Levi jumped. His eyes looked damp.

"Was it another daydream?"

"I-I…. Yes?" he answered, more like a question.

"What did you see?"

"I didn't. I mean... I don't think I saw anything, but after Yentriss offered to teach me the bow, I thought I heard another woman's voice."

"What did she say?"

"She said... '*Son*, there are many things you still need to learn.' I don't know why it's affecting me so much. I don't even understand why I'd imagine such a thing. Because Yentriss is Kenner's mother, and I never had one of my own?"

There was no easy answer, so Ashmedai settled on, "Perhaps."

Levi sniffled. "I've had others this week, even the other day before I gave you your belt. I didn't want to worry you. I was hunting deer."

"There are no deer here anymore."

"I know...."

Ashmedai wasn't sure what to say.

"I really did enjoy helping with the hunt for the most part." Levi mustered a smile. "It was thrilling. You were remarkable."

It had been a long time since Ashmedai had seen the most powerful part of himself as anything but vile. "I was going to say the same to you," he deflected. He meant it after all—Levi's illusions and his dancing daggers.

"I should get back," Levi said, "maybe catch up to Pentelyn and Amuro to accompany them out of the wood. It's later than I told Braxton. Will you...?" He gestured after the couple, looking hopefully to Ashmedai that he might join them too.

"I wish I could, but there is much I need to attend to here. Tomorrow?"

Levi nodded, wiping at a stray tear that streaked down past one of his lines of stitches. There weren't many on his face, though the most notable stretched outward from the edges of his mouth.

Ashmedai would have gladly wiped that tear away himself. He would have liked to keep hanging on to Levi's hand, which he still held. Since he had to let it go, he lifted it to his lips and kissed the back of Levi's fingers.

Indigo was becoming Ashmedai's favorite color.

ASHMEDAI DID have much to attend to, but not only helping the hunters and ensuring that the open part of the perimeter was replenished with fresh crystals. There were too many mysteries blossoming, and while he might need to wait for a council meeting to discover more about Pentelyn and Amuro's, another was that Braxton was clearly not being honest with him about Levi, and he couldn't decipher that mystery on his own.

As soon as everyone had returned to the city, Ashmedai headed for Luccite. Pentelyn and Amuro were just leaving, and although Ashmedai was curious and wanted to wish them well, he stayed hidden in the shadows. Once they were gone, he slipped into Luccite's shop, as undetectable as a gust of wind.

Luccite was both healer and alchemist, though with a different focus than Braxton, so her shop had any number of tools, potions, components, and tomes. And, since she could see so well in the dark with her slitted cat eyes, there was little need for brighter crystals as lights, keeping the atmosphere calming.

Ashmedai wished he felt calmer now.

The panther-like woman noticed him only after a floorboard creaked, her ears twitching just before she turned to look at him. She was especially short, one of the shortest in the kingdom, but though she had to look up a great distance to meet his eyes, that in no way diminished her presence.

"Ash. To what do I owe the honor so late? Concerned about Pentelyn?"

"Very, but that's not why I'm here. I need your assistance concerning Levi."

"The construct? Why not ask Brax? He made him."

Ashmedai strode closer to her, keeping his expression severe and his voice low, despite them being alone. "There is something Brax isn't telling me, and I don't know what or why."

Luccite's eyes danced with curiosity. "Then bring Levi to me."

CHAPTER 4

ASHMEDAI COULDN'T remember the last time the council hall had been so dissonant. What happened during the hunt had spread like brushfire among the people, and while the truth was simply an accident that thankfully hadn't turned into tragedy, the story being stoked was a twisted amalgamation of rumors.

The warding crystal had failed Pentelyn.

The barrier was closer than before.

Gazellians were overrunning the wood.

The demon had been spotted, devouring jackalopes and rollhounds alike.

What had begun as a normal, civil discussion had escalated, and nothing Ashmedai or his advisors shouted now seemed capable of calming the crowd.

A piercing scream cut through the noise like no lone voice had managed, causing many citizens to grab their ears and wince. Silence spread quicker than the din had begun, and the screaming ebbed.

Daedlys floated in the center of the rows of people, his banshee cry ending with a satisfied clearing of his throat. "Thank you. You all know I hate doing that, so please don't make me do it again. Ash." He nodded, sinking down from where he had floated above the crowd to return to Klarent beside him.

"Thank you," Ashmedai acknowledged. "Now please, I know many of you are frightened, but we must discuss this rationally, or nothing will be accomplished. Let me assure you all that Pentelyn's crystal did not fail her, it fell from her belt, the barrier is no smaller than it was a thousand years ago, and the herd of gazellians we encountered was unexpected but of normal size."

"And what of the demon?" Shevah asked before Ashmedai could continue, to which faint murmurs began to rise again that only diminished when Daedlys floated higher in warning.

"The hunters are all in attendance," Yentriss spoke up. "I saw no demon. Would anyone else care to say differently?"

Nervous people glanced at one another, but none of the hunters said a word.

Until Amuro ventured, "One thing you said isn't completely correct. The barrier might not be smaller, but the space we live in is, for we have spread and are still spreading. We are poised to spread farther much sooner than you know."

Nervous eyes glanced around once more, only this time Ashmedai noticed how no one would look at him.

"You revealed Pentelyn's pregnancy." Ashmedai addressed the couple seated in the front row. "Are you saying there are others?"

The persisting silence and wary glances said enough.

"How many?"

It had never been mandated that couples express their desire for children before seeking them, but in the past, since it happened so infrequently, a couple would often tell Ashmedai before they started trying, or immediately after they became pregnant, asking for his blessing. It hadn't seemed necessary to mandate doing so since everyone always did anyway.

How out of touch Ashmedai had become rang truer than ever before as more than a dozen hands hesitantly began to rise, expanding throughout the hall. Ashmedai's advisors, all in attendance save Braxton, looked as shocked as he was, but it was clear that many of those with child had been whispering amongst themselves and knew how many there were.

"Why did you keep this from me?" Ashmedai asked.

Slowly, the hands dropped.

Pentelyn, after patting Amuro's arm and taking a steadying breath, rose and stepped forward to address the head table—and Ashmedai directly. "My parents waited centuries to have me. There was a small influx of children after my birth, but there was always the fear that we only have so much room. We can't migrate to other cities, we can't expand farther outside the city without deforestation we can't afford, and in the years since the curse, there have only been a handful of accidental deaths.

"We don't die, Ash, but we still want to grow, to experience new things, to share our lives with others. None of us planned to have children all at once, it just came to a head, because some of us have waited even longer than our parents once did, and we don't want to wait anymore or feel guilty for wanting families of our own.

"We're so sorry," she finished, as if what she had expressed was anything anyone should feel guilty over.

"You didn't trust me enough to speak the truth?" That hurt worst of all, because of course Ashmedai could understand a desire for family, for companionship.

He spotted Levi in the usual spot at the back, though no longer hiding within his hood. The sight of him didn't only make Ashmedai think of his own desires but of how even Braxton had made himself a son.

"We trust you, Ash," Pentelyn said, and all the eyes that had been avoiding the head table returned there now to bolster her sentiment, "but you aren't all-powerful. We know you're trying. We know you hope to fix all that concerns us. But when we realized how many of us were pregnant at once, all these years of waiting for answers, for solutions, seemed so much more daunting. We felt trapped and didn't know what to say."

They hadn't wanted to worry Ashmedai, the way *they* were worried. It was everything he most feared and hated about the curse that tortured his people.

With a slight twitch of her wings and a solemn bow, Pentelyn returned to Amuro. The others remained quiet, the various couples who had revealed being with child sitting closer together or holding each other in whatever ways their forms allowed.

Ashmedai's advisors said nothing either. What could they say, when the burden to assuage the people fell on Ashmedai alone?

"If you trust me," he began, "then please, believe all I have said about the hunt. And know that you can always come to me with any concern, any request or news, and always be honest with me.

"However, I understand your fears over space and resources. I can't deny that the promise of so many more future citizens, and likely more and more to come after that, isn't sustainable as we are now." Ashmedai closed his eyes, hating how he had to admit what everyone already knew. "This should be a time of celebration, yet everyone is tense and guilt-ridden for wanting to bring new life into our world. I swear, I swear to you all, here and now, that we will find a solution. We will find the answers to keep our kingdom thriving."

When he opened his eyes, he still saw uncertainty.

"How?" a lone voice asked.

Klarent—sounding far meeker than Ashmedai was used to.

Clearly, Ashmedai had failed them already, because he didn't have an answer.

"My black crystals."

To everyone's cumulative surprise, Braxton had answered, wheeling forward from behind the head table to the spot they always left open for him.

A stir of movement from Levi proved he hadn't known Braxton was coming either.

"I am making enough for everyone," Braxton continued, "available through Daedlys's shop as many of you already know. While generally a tool of convenience, they will be a critical component in what I have planned."

"Which is what, exactly?" Luccite spoke from the other end of the table, leaning around Dreya to meet Braxton's gaze.

"To remove the threat of the barrier. I am close to making a breakthrough. Not decades or even years close—weeks."

A few hushed exclamations flitted through the crowd. Even Ashmedai had to take a breath, for despite his promises, he had feared such a thing impossible, or at the very least, a far distant goal.

"Won't that anger the demon?" Gordoc broached nervously from the stunned crowd.

Yentriss answered with a question like she had before, with nary a waver in her voice, "For all the rumors and stories, can anyone here say they have seen the demon since the night of the curse?"

It was an often-debated question, yet no one spoke up that they had.

"Then we will do what we must." She motioned for Ashmedai to retake the floor.

Ashmedai peered past her at Braxton. "Thank you, my friend. I suppose I can no longer fault you for missing these meetings if that is why you were absent."

A few members of the crowd tittered at the jab, and Braxton himself offered a rare smile.

"My people." Ashmedai stood to ensure he had everyone's attention. "Never believe you need to keep such things from me again. It is my duty, my privilege to serve and protect you. And it is only together, through Braxton's efforts, mine, and your own, that we will persevere. I am certain Daedlys will provide the crystals for valid trade."

Daedlys's proud nod wasn't necessary, since fair trade was the foundation of their close-knit society, but Ashmedai still appreciated the steadfast response.

"I also want everyone to enjoy Festival Day like never before, confident that your fears will soon be put to rest."

Not everyone looked convinced, but enough were assuaged by Braxton's certainty that their smiles and relaxed postures strengthened the faith of others.

"Let me say one final thing." Ashmedai smiled too. "Congratulations—to all of you."

The lighter note the meeting ended on made the previous pandemonium fade from memory like a fleeting nightmare. For once, instead of being stopped by Dreya, Ashmedai was swarmed by the pregnant couples, each hoping for a blessing now that the truth was out. He could hardly refuse them, for each new member to their community had always been a joy, even with lacking space.

Amidst all that, Ashmedai asked Luccite to stay, and made sure to catch Levi's eye so he would also remain. Dreya did linger, excitedly chatting with Luccite, who seemed somewhat agitated by the attention but didn't move away from her. Once the couples departed, Dreya left as well, and Levi came forward through the hall. His nerves appeared to have returned, tight in his shoulders. He kept straying his eyes to Braxton who, like Ashmedai, had been accosted by several people and had yet to leave.

"Levi, I don't believe you've met Luccite, have you?" Ashmedai introduced them.

Luccite extended a hand, covered in soft gray fur and with claws she kept retracted.

Levi trembled slightly as he accepted it. "M-Madame Healer. I suppose Braxton saw no need for us to meet, since I am not alive in the traditional sense."

"Feels like a normal pulse to me," she purred, lingering her grip on Levi's wrist, which made him blush with a bashful glance at Ashmedai, though there was no way for her to know what had transpired between them.

Levi glanced again at Braxton, but the alchemist was a good distance away, engrossed in discussion with Daedlys and Klarent, among others.

"I was hoping you might enjoy visiting Luccite's shop," Ashmedai said. He kept his voice moderate, not purposely low, but he also cast a subtle spell that pulled invisible shadows around them so their voices wouldn't carry. "She is curious to learn more about you."

Levi's astuteness was in no way dulled when he was anxious, for the continued aversion of his eyes proved he knew they didn't want Braxton to hear about this—or he was simply that nervous being near Ashmedai when Braxton could see them.

"N-now?" Levi asked.

"It doesn't have to be now," Ashmedai said. "How about tomorrow? You and Grillo are taking a break, aren't you? So he can build and repair a few stalls to better gauge how much more lumber he needs? You can tell Brax you've been asked to assist with other festival business."

"This is about festival business?" Levi cocked his head.

He *was* astute; he was also sweetly naïve.

"Yes," Luccite stepped in. "We were hoping you might assist with one of the booths, but we don't want to ask anything of you that you can't handle. A small examination would help me understand what you're capable of. Shall we say my shop at half past sunrise?"

Levi looked at Ashmedai, and it felt terrible to lie to him, so Ashmedai whispered a truth.

"I want to be certain you are always safe and protected, and there are some things Luccite knows that Brax does not. You could meet me at the top of the market steps. The carriages from Emerald should be arriving. We could see them together before continuing to Luccite. Will you come?"

The offer eased some of the tightness in Levi's shoulders. "Yes, I will be there."

Ashmedai would have risked a gentle touch, might have even kissed Levi's fingers again, but he didn't want to push Levi's boundaries with Braxton nearby. He said good night and watched Levi retreat to Braxton's side, where the discussion had just ended, and Daedlys and Klarent offered boisterous good nights as well.

Braxton nodded once more at Ashmedai before beginning to head for the exit with Levi beside him.

"You're right. Something is different about him," Luccite said. "A strong soul."

"A construct isn't supposed to have a soul." Ashmedai had known that from the beginning but hadn't been sure how to address it.

Luccite's catlike grin was as interested as ever. "Exactly."

A DISH shattered on the kitchen counter, falling due to Levi's foolish haste to be gone before Braxton questioned where he was going. Surely Braxton would come out of his workshop now.

Levi hurried to clean up the mess, taking deep breaths to keep from shaking too hard and inevitably breaking something else. To his relief, once he was finished, the workshop door hadn't opened. There was purple light coming from beneath it again.

Hoping to further calm his nerves, Levi poured his draught to take it as expected of him before he left. It never failed to make him grimace, but it did its job, clearing his mind to think of better things— like Ashmedai, concerned about Levi's safety enough that he wanted him to see the healer.

Levi was certain it wasn't only to ensure his safety while manning a festival booth, but he trusted Ashmedai's intentions. He trusted him implicitly. He didn't think Ashmedai could have sinister aims. The king was caring, selfless, attentive. He'd risked his life to save Pentelyn.

He'd risked his life to save Levi, though Levi hadn't realized the breadth of that until he was headed back home after the hunt.

There were so many wondrous people in the Dark Kingdom, but no one compared to the Shadow King. No one could ever compare to Ash.

The pulsing of purple light started to increase like the last time Levi had noticed it, drawing his attention from his straying thoughts. He wondered what the light was. Part of Braxton's experiments to weaken the barrier, certainly—but what exactly?

Before Levi realized it, he had set his empty teacup aside and traversed half the lower level toward the workshop door, drawn to that light almost but not quite as potently as he was drawn to Ashmedai. The increase in pulses seemed to hypnotize him.

"Help me in the garden, won't you?"

Levi blinked, and there was a woman in front of him—human with red hair.

Her face wasn't familiar, and yet… it was. Like her voice. Levi had heard that voice before, hadn't he? He hadn't thought he recognized it, but seeing her, he could almost remember *why* he knew her.

"Leander?"

The purple light vanished into sudden blackness, and Levi was left staring at nothing but the closed workshop door. He could hear rustling from inside and began to backpedal. He didn't fear Braxton, but in that moment, he wanted nothing more than to leave and make his way to Ashmedai sooner.

Levi was out the door and on his way to town before Braxton could leave the workshop.

He didn't understand what his daydreams were or what they meant, but he assumed Ashmedai was just as worried. Perhaps it was the stray souls lost over the centuries to the demon, finding a conduit through Levi. Perhaps it was Levi's mind trying to form a past for him when he had none. Dwelling on what-ifs made his pace quicken, and he tried to think of anything else.

The festival. The carriages from Emerald.

Ash.

Then all those things coalesced, for Levi was almost to the market steps, and he could see the half-built structures heralding the coming festival, as well as the Emerald caravan having just arrived from the main road into the wood.

Amidst the people waiting to see what the new shipment would bring was Ashmedai, though he wasn't looking at the carriages, black but sanded down to rid the wood of any Shadow Lands sparkle. He wasn't looking at the black mechanical horses that were almost indiscernible from flesh and blood.

He was staring down the road at Levi, waiting for him with a smile.

"You might want to stay close," Ashmedai said upon Levi's arrival, taking his elbow to tug him nearer. "The crowd can get a bit rowdy on delivery day."

The warmth and closeness of Ashmedai wiped all recent worries from Levi's mind.

While people who crossed into the Dark Kingdom would be changed into monsters like the rest, nonliving things held their form, which was why automated carriages were necessary. Levi hadn't been created yet the last time the caravan came through, though he knew how deliveries worked.

Dreya and Yentriss were at the head of the crowd, keeping eager hands from the carriages. Specific requests that had been approved during city council meetings would be divvied out first; then necessities, particularly any unplanned, would be given to those in need; finally, anything remaining or unexpected on the carriages would be posed to the crowd, given away if there was but one voice asking for it, but given based on need or lottery if there were many voices.

About half as many people as the number at most council meetings were clustered in attendance, but it still felt claustrophobic to Levi, and he was grateful for Ashmedai's sturdy presence—and the way Ashmedai's hand lingered on his elbow as if they were a couple on a stroll.

He was especially grateful for the support when the first carriage came to a stop in front of the crowd and proved to have several arrows lodged into its side.

"Highwaymen," Dreya said, as though dismissing the playful antics of a child. With a swift grip and yank on each of the arrow shafts, she removed them and tossed them to the ground.

Levi had heard the carriages were often attacked by highwaymen, but the doors were enchanted to only open upon arrival in Emerald and once they returned home. Highwaymen could batter the structure and horses all they wanted, and they'd never get at what lay inside.

The wood beyond the barrier must be full of cutthroats. Some even wondered if a thieves' guild had been built somewhere beyond the barrier, since it was a place most decent people feared to travel.

After getting everyone to quiet down, Yentriss kept her eyes on the crowd to keep the peace, while Dreya threw open the first carriage's doors to reveal the contents within. Each crate was marked according to what lay inside, and Dreya would excitedly call out the item, for Yentriss to more calmly call forward who could claim it.

A few disagreements on orders arose but were quickly squashed by Yentriss's glare or Dreya's mediating. For the most part, this monthly occurrence was old hat for everyone—they were simply excited for anything that had come from the outside world.

"Two dozen bolts of Emerald silk!" Dreya called when the carriages were nearly empty.

"Daedlys and Gordoc!" Yentriss announced, glancing at her list. "Even split. Colors to be bartered."

Levi hadn't seen Daedlys among the others. The translucent man was able to blend in easily just about anywhere, but his floating form was very apparent when moving swiftly. He might have been a glider monkey leaping from one tree to another, he moved so fast to get ahead of Gordoc.

"To be *bartered*, banshee," Gordoc huffed, rushing to catch up. "Getting there first doesn't give you first pick."

"I'm not sure you should get any," Daedlys said without looking behind him, "since you were so certain when telling shoppers there might not be any silk this month."

Gordoc's fishlike lips gawked in offense.

"Relax, gentlemen," Dreya appeased, prying open the lid to take stock of the contents. She had a funny little hat on again today, only this time it was more like a beret. "Seems there's an even mix. Green." She passed them each two bolts. "Blue." She passed out more, so on and so on through many colors of the rainbow—something else Levi wished he could see in real life instead of only reading about them or admiring pictures, but the sun was needed for that.

Dreya continued through many bolts of fabric, too many for Daedlys or Gordoc to carry, but they each had a small cart to load.

"Finally, one additional red and one cream."

"Red," Daedlys and Gordoc said in unison, following their declarations with menacing glares at each other.

"I require the red for a special order," Daedlys declared.

"So do I," Gordoc insisted.

"Gentlemen," Dreya said soothingly, "could you cut each bolt halfway and share?"

"No," they overlapped again.

Yentriss's sigh was audible even from where Levi and Ashmedai watched from the back, though some of the crowd had thinned, not waiting to see what might remain in the depths of the final carriage.

"Well then." Dreya held out a sideways fist, and within her grasp conjured two thin sticks like incense. "Whoever draws the long straw wins the red." She had enacted similar simple games to settle disputes, which Levi thought both ingenious and endearing.

Daedlys and Gordoc each claimed a straw, seemingly pleased with their choices, and when Dreya gave a nod, they both pulled.

Daedlys's was the long one.

"Red goes to Daedlys!" Dreya declared.

Daedlys shimmered in his preening almost enough to go invisible. Gordoc grumbled but accepted the cream.

"Just a few unexpected items for this month," Dreya said next.

She mentioned spices, scraps of leather, and several pieces of jewelry, most of which only had one person interested, though a cluster of arrows with green feathers were argued over and eventually awarded to a lottery winner.

"The last item is a music box with a white horse spinning inside." Dreya opened it for the crowd. The box was small enough that it only just filled her palms as she held it out, made of painted wood in green, blue, and white. Inside was indeed a white horse, rearing up on its hind legs as it rotated to a tinkling melody.

"For no bard is humble,
And no hero's flawless.
All that matters is the stories we tell."

"What was that?"

"Hmm?" Levi looked at Ashmedai.

"You were singing along to the music box."

"I was?"

Ashmedai furrowed his lovely black brows—then turned forward and called out before anyone else, "I'll take it!"

The crowd pivoted to look at them, hushing in surprise as they confirmed who was laying claim. Levi wondered if Ashmedai never asked for something of his own, or if the people simply hated to disappoint him, for those who had seemed ready to throw in their lot decided against it.

"Ash has it," Dreya confirmed. "The caravan will remain until the day before the festival to be loaded for the return trip. Thank you all."

The remaining crowd began to disperse. At the same time, Ashmedai started forward, still holding Levi's elbow, clearly meaning to claim the music box.

Levi planted his feet. "I had another daydream."

Ashmedai stopped with him. "Just now?"

"No. I mean, I don't think so. It was earlier this morning."

"What did you see?"

"The woman I heard during the hunt. I know it was her because she sounded the same. She had red hair like me."

"Like the boy from before?"

"Only she was human. She said, 'Help me in the garden, won't you?' And then… Leander?"

"Oleander? There was a flower called that once."

"That must have been it…." It all felt like a dream, like Levi could almost remember, almost understand, but truly grasping the meaning was just out of reach. He glanced shyly at Ashmedai, feeling small with those beautiful white-on-black eyes studying him so intently. "Do you think there's something… broken in me? Is that why you want me to see Luccite?"

"Not broken." Ashmedai tightened his hold on Levi's elbow and lifted his other hand to gently cup the side of Levi's cheek, his long nails tickling pleasantly at the edges of Levi's hair. "Nothing about you is broken, Levi. You're simply a mystery needing to be solved. Come, let's get your music box." He smiled, showing off his many fangs, which was almost enough for Levi to miss what Ashmedai had said.

"*My* music box?"

"You know its tune and made an illusion of a horse just like the one inside. Clearly it is meant to be yours."

Levi had wondered where the idea for a white horse had come from during the hunt, but he couldn't possibly have seen something like it or the music box before. "Do you think I can see the future?"

Ashmedai chuckled. "In this kingdom, anything is possible."

Daedlys was rearranging his cart with his keen telekinesis as they approached the carriages, Gordoc already heading away in the direction of the market, wearing a pout. Once Levi and Ashmedai reached Dreya, she was waiting to hand Ashmedai the music box with a smile.

"Enjoy it," she said. "Oh, and… have either of you seen Luccite this morning? She's usually here for delivery day. She's the only one who loves seeing what Emerald sends each month even more than I do."

"Preparing for us, I'd imagine," Ashmedai said. "We have an appointment with her."

"Ah. Tell her I missed her," Dreya said and turned to close the carriage.

With little ceremony, Ashmedai began to present the box to Levi, only to hesitate and call out to Daedlys. "My friend, would you examine this for us?"

Daedlys had just finished levitating the final bolt of fabric into place and floated over to them. "Of course! Let's have a look." Like anything Daedlys held, the box seemed to hover on its own as he turned it and opened and closed it again, inspecting it closely. "Beautiful, to be certain. Are you interested in the type of wood or—"

"No." Ashmedai stopped him. "I only wondered if it might be homemade for a specific owner rather than from a shop."

"Mass-produced," Daedlys said with a shake of his head, handing the box back to Ashmedai. "There's a shop's stamp on the bottom, but the detailed craftsmanship tells me there weren't many made. Perhaps it was the last of its stock."

Ashmedai nodded thoughtfully and then gave the box to Levi.

Levi felt his cheeks flush as Daedlys's eyes fell on him, and the banshee smiled like he knew something unspoken.

"Why, Stitches, my dear, I've been meaning to ask—why haven't I seen you wearing that new tunic yet?"

Levi gave a start big enough that he almost dropped the box. He gripped it tighter in response, eyes wide as he searched for an answer.

"I hope to see you in it soon." Daedlys beat him to it. "You'll look positively radiant." He winked and floated back to his cart to begin wheeling it away.

"Tunic?" Ashmedai asked.

It was rare that Levi wanted something just for him. He felt guilty and selfish for taking the tunic at all, just like he had when wishing to be closer to Ashmedai than Braxton was.

Because he wanted Ash for himself too.

"It's too much." Levi dropped his eyes. "Too special."

"Then someone special should wear it." Ashmedai's fingers grazed Levi's hand, and Levi looked up, caught in the eyes he adored. He shifted his grip on the box so Ashmedai could take the hand he had touched, and Ashmedai kissed the knuckles like before.

Levi didn't think his cheeks could feel any hotter.

Almost everyone else was gone now, only Dreya and Yentriss remaining, but they were on the other side of the carriages. They wouldn't notice. No one would notice.

Levi leaned toward Ashmedai.

"Lauffy!" Dreya yelled after one of the departing citizens, and Levi and Ashmedai snapped away from each other.

Had Ashmedai been leaning in too?

"Well...." Ashmedai softly lowered Levi's hand and let it go. "Perhaps you'll wear your new tunic to the festival?"

For the king, Levi would do anything. "Perhaps."

Ashmedai took Levi's elbow again and led him from the caravan to the market steps.

WHEN THEY arrived at Luccite's, Ashmedai could tell Levi had never been inside this shop. He looked around in utter awe, pausing to breathe in the unique scent of mixed oils, poultices, and spices. Levi didn't have his bag today, so he still held the music box, which only added to the mystery—because how could Levi recognize a horse or a tune from something out of a shop in the Emerald Kingdom?

"There you are," Luccite greeted them from a stool before one of her shelves, which, since she was on the third step, made her almost Ashmedai's height. Her eyes went to the music box. "What is that?"

"Oh, um... a music box from the Emerald carriages," Levi explained. "Ash got it for me."

Luccite tsked. "The one time I miss delivery day, and for *you*, and you swipe something I might have actually thought worthy of collecting. My loss, I suppose."

"You collect things from Emerald?" Levi asked.

"I collect things from all over," Luccite said with a gesture at a few of her fuller shelves. "Emerald is simply the only source these days."

Ashmedai walked with Levi as he studied the shelves more closely. Mixed in with the usual healer and alchemical paraphernalia was the occasional trinket of foreign craftsmanship, like an elven-made clock from the Diamond Kingdom, or a dwarven mortar and pestle made of stone from Ruby.

"Dreya sends her regards," Ashmedai remembered to say.

"Silly girl." Luccite's ears twitched. "We see each other every day."

"You're also an alchemist?" Levi asked, nodding at items he must have been used to from Braxton's workshop.

"Of course."

"Why don't you and Braxton work together?"

"We both work better alone," Luccite said, at last descending the steps of her stool. "Besides, I focus more on maintenance and occasional procreation. People might not get sick here, but they can still get injured. Brax is the inventor, interested in technology over biology—other than you, I suppose. He spent centuries trying to perfect you. Well, *you* are solely unique. The other constructs didn't come close."

"What were they like?" Levi asked as though he'd often wondered but never had the nerve to ask.

"You know the horses that draw the Emerald carriages?"

"Yes."

"The horses have more personality. Come on now." She motioned for them to join her in the back behind a curtain she parted. "We'll want to keep this private in case anyone else comes in this morning."

Levi's awe turned to apprehension, palpably felt through Ashmedai's maintained grip on his elbow. Ashmedai switched his grip to his other hand so he could smooth the first up and down the small of Levi's back.

"You have nothing to fear," he said. "Luccite simply wants a look at you. Perhaps what we discover can explain your... daydreams." Ashmedai felt Levi sag into his touch. It would have been so easy to loop his arm around Levi's waist and embrace him properly, but now wasn't the time.

Behind the curtain was where Luccite treated and examined patients, where the walls were covered in bookshelves with even more tomes, jars, and tools than in the main shop. A table was in the center, padded for comfort and adjusted low to accommodate for Luccite's short height.

"Sit, please." She gestured Levi toward it. "I won't ask you to fully undress, but I do need you to remove your tunic."

Levi had started to move forward, completely out of Ashmedai's grasp, but he froze and looked back nervously.

"Would you like me to leave?" Ashmedai asked.

"*No.*" Levi's eyes sprang wider than when Daedlys had mentioned the tunic. "I-I-I...." He let himself trail off and took a long, cleansing breath. "I... would prefer you stayed. I've just... never been undressed in front of anyone but Braxton before."

"It's an exam," Luccite assured him and then smirked in a way only a cat could, "not a courtship."

Once the tunic was removed, the deep indigo Levi had turned, a common enough sight by now, proved to travel farther down his neck and chest than Ashmedai might have guessed.

Levi placed it and the music box beside him on the table as he sat, his eyes staying fixed on his hands clutched in front of him. It wasn't only the blush making Levi indigo, as some of his patches of skin were deeper blue than others, just as some were lighter, proving how he had been made from different parts.

Each piece was affixed to another with stitches, the sizing and shape complementing one another to make a cohesive whole. The stitches weren't any more unsightly to Ashmedai on Levi's arms and chest than they were on his face—or had been on his wrists. They were simply part of him.

Levi's form was slender but well-muscled, and despite the stitches and azure color, he looked very human—or half-elven, Ashmedai supposed, since Levi's ears had a slight point. He was hairless and smooth, and Ashmedai had to resist the urge to move forward and touch Levi in a way that definitely wouldn't be seen as *examining* over courtship.

Luccite got straight to work, letting Levi know everything she was about to do before she did it, though otherwise not making comments. For the most part, she checked physical things, like Levi's breathing, his reflexes, his heart—which caused Levi to squirm, since she listened to it with one of her sharp feline ears pressed to his chest, and the fur must have tickled. All Levi's reactions were normal for anyone living.

Eventually Luccite tried several colored powders on Levi's skin, rubbing streak after streak on the back of his hand, gauging his reactions, but Levi had none.

"You eat and drink normally?" she asked.

"Yes."

"You have a sense of taste? Of flavors?"

"Yes."

"Do you sleep?"

"I do, but I don't dream."

"Yet you have daydreams?"

"I… I think that's what they are."

"Hmm." Luccite stood back, scrutinizing Levi closely, and raised a hand, which slowly began to form a ball of pure white light above it. "Finally, I'm going to cast a rune on you to test something special. You won't feel anything other than slight warmth emanating from where the rune hovers."

"To test my magical affinity?" Levi asked.

"We already know you have magic. A small amount, but some. This is something a little more complex to… understand your soul."

That caused Levi to sit up straighter. He had relaxed more and more during the exam, occasionally casting Ashmedai timid yet grateful glances, but for the first time, he seemed visibly excited rather than nervous.

Luccite took the ball of light and used it to draw in the air in front of Levi's chest a vertical line with two shorter lines branching from its top, and then a circle between the branches. It glowed brighter at first and seemed about to change color, then suddenly began to rotate through many colors, one after the other, faster and faster, every color of the rainbow. It even seemed to change shape into different runes, like a circle with a vertical line through it, then a circle with a horizontal line through it, then a jagged line that went down and up and down again. All of it cycled so quickly, it was like the flicker of a candle, until it suddenly vanished—gone in a blink as though snuffed out.

"Huh," Luccite commented as her arm dropped.

"What does it mean?" Levi asked.

"It may take further investigating," Luccite said cryptically. "For now, I think it best if I speak with Ash privately."

The disappointment was clear on Levi's face. He wanted answers too, but there must be something very daunting about the rune's reaction if Luccite wanted to talk to Ashmedai alone.

With a solemn nod, Levi got down from the table and replaced his tunic. After he reclaimed the music box, he went to Ashmedai. "I guess I'm still a mystery."

"One I think we can solve. As for manning a festival booth"—Ashmedai took on a livelier tone, not wanting to completely neglect the ruse they had begun this on—"I think we can agree you can handle just about anything, but I do have something in mind for you if you're interested. Do you know about Klarent's booth?"

Levi answered with a wavering, "Y-yes."

"Would you be willing to perform?"

"M-m-me?" he stuttered more. "With what?"

"Your illusions. You could tell a story with them, or simply give a light show. The crowd's attention would mostly be on them, not you. What do you say? Only if you feel up to it. You are allowed to say no to me."

Levi had come so far with beating his shyness, but *beating* one's proclivities wasn't always the answer. With Levi, though, Ashmedai had seen the way he enjoyed entertaining Kenner and being amongst other people. If it was something Levi wanted, he should be able to work toward it.

Those same thoughts appeared to be swirling through Levi's mind as he considered the request—did his desires outweigh his fears? When he had his answer, he looked at Ashmedai with a confident smile.

"I think I'd like that."

"Wonderful. Why don't you check in with Klarent about a time? Perhaps he and Daedlys will even have some suggestions for how you can use your illusions. I'll see you soon."

Levi nodded a farewell to Luccite. "Thank you again for the music box," he said to Ashmedai, dithering a moment before finally lurching forward and pressing a tender kiss to Ashmedai's cheek.

He hurried away before Ashmedai could properly respond, but where those lips had touched felt warm, and Ashmedai reached up to feel the spot with his fingers.

Luccite wore her usual sly smile when he turned to her.

"Well?" Ashmedai asked.

"One soul—*many* bodies."

"We already knew that." Ashmedai frowned. "Brax used alchemy to create and animate constructs, in this case many pieces to create a better whole. The mystery is *why* Levi has a soul."

"You're not listening." Luccite shook her head. "He has one soul and many parts, yes—but parts that were all once attached to bodies with souls of their own. The pieces aren't from replicated constructs, Ash. Levi was made from multiple *real* people."

CHAPTER 5

ASHMEDAI DOVE from shadow to shadow to traverse the market bustle as quickly as possible. Up the steps and down the path toward the wood, he was a mere blink of movement to anyone who might have seen him.

Levi should still be at Daedlys's shop—which meant Braxton was alone.

Exploding into the tower with all the force of his swirling shadow magic, Ashmedai must have looked like a storm incarnate. He marched across the lower level with such mad determination, he hardly noticed how he had left the door half off its hinges and upset pieces of stray parchment to flutter like a tornado was raging through. When he reached the workshop door, he threw it open with just as much force.

"Brax!"

In some ways, the space echoed Luccite's shop with tools, potions, components, and tomes, only rather than neat shelves and tidy organization, everything was scattered about haphazardly and a bed rested against one wall.

The ceiling was low, making the entire room seem like a cave, especially since it was made from stone, with candlelit sconces as well as crystals glowing. Table upon table was also loaded with more of Braxton's black crystals, or unknown items covered by tarp. At the very back of the workshop, where Braxton sat facing away from Ashmedai, was a larger black crystal that towered nearly to the ceiling.

"Levi," Braxton growled as he used his wheels to pivot his chair, "I have repeatedly—Ash? What on earth—"

Ashmedai didn't bother continuing forward. He saw the shadow cast by Braxton's chair, dove into the one cast by the door, and appeared directly in front of his friend to hover with a menacing flex of shadows that covered Braxton in darkness.

"Who is he?" he roared.

Not a twitch or ripple of trepidation touched Braxton's expression. "We have been over this. Levi is not—"

"He is not a construct," Ashmedai snapped, but though Braxton still gave no sign of being cowed or afraid, Ashmedai saw how the shape of the shadow he cast over Braxton was twisting, growing, and he pulled away with a sharp intake of breath and desperate tamping down of his anger. "You made him from real people. Don't deny it."

The shadows calmed, and Braxton sat taller. "What if I did?"

He displayed no remorse or appeal for forgiveness. That should have made Ashmedai angrier, but it zapped the remaining ire from his heart, leaving him numb. "How? Each piece still looks human or elven. *How* did you do it?"

With the same calm detachment, Braxton wheeled around Ashmedai. "When people first enter the barrier, there is a delay before they begin to change into one of us. Most, once they see it starting, go mad and flee. You know this. Isn't it better that they are not disintegrated, their parts wasted?"

"There haven't been any new people in…." Ashmedai trailed off before finishing his thought, the full horror of the situation solidifying. "There have been new people. You just made us think otherwise. Were all your constructs real, living beings?"

"Of course not," Braxton retorted with a sweeping gesture at the workshop. "They were made here, from cloned material, as I told you. And that is why they were failures. They had no true spark of life. It took years to assemble nonaffected parts from people who had crossed into our lands and perished—decades, centuries, to ensure that the parts matched enough with minimal alchemical manipulation to create Levi as flawlessly as he is. And I know you agree with me, Ash. You think him flawless too."

It was almost an accusation, but now wasn't the time to get sidetracked by Ashmedai's feelings for Levi. "How could you? You mutilated people who might have been talked down to join our community."

"Talked down?" Braxton huffed. "These people were not going to be talked down. And even if they could have been, most were villainous highwaymen, and we would have run out of room for new citizens long ago and been in far worse shape than we are now. At least this surge of new offspring comes as late as it has, when I am finally ready to free us from this nightmare. I have played my part to get us here, Ash. Just like you did."

That was an accusation, enough that Ashmedai leaned away from Braxton, feeling a sharp twist in his gut.

"I did what I thought was right," Braxton said more softly, remorseful maybe for his comment but not his actions.

"You think what you did was right?"

"To buy us more time, I would do worse. But if it disturbs you so, rest assured, I have no need to continue. Levi was a success. And I did not create him purely for companionship or assistance around the tower. Levi is one part of the whole that will change everything." Again, Braxton gestured around the workshop, like all the answers lay within it. "What I learned by creating him is all I need to finally solve this. Trust me."

For a thousand years, Ashmedai had, but he still felt haunted by the ghosts of Levi's past. "His soul is someone else's."

"Someone who died. Does it matter?"

"He's been having flashes of that life."

"What?" Braxton moved closer to Ashmedai with a scrunch of his brow. "His draught was supposed to prevent that."

"Draught?"

"Something to keep any memories from surfacing. It must not be enough. I told him it would help him acclimate and feel more comfortable here. That wasn't a lie."

"But it is a lie. It's all a lie!"

"Do you want to tell him the truth?" Braxton volleyed back. "The memories are from his mind, his head, not a jumble from other parts, but those memories are still fractured. If you tell him, it might bring more to the surface in a way he won't be able to handle."

"He deserves to know."

"That he was a coward so terrified upon entering our lands and starting to transform that he fled, and I was barely able to save half of him before he disintegrated, let alone the head now resting on his shoulders? Does that sound like a pleasant bedtime story?"

When Ashmedai had rushed from Luccite's shop to confront Braxton, he hadn't truly considered who Levi was, only that Levi was someone other than the seemingly brand-new soul who looked upon everything he encountered with wonder.

Including Ash.

Losing that seemed a far worse fate than death, but who was Ashmedai to decide for Levi? Worse was that no matter how he looked at the situation, there was no answer that wouldn't hurt Levi in some way. Which left Ashmedai with one final question.

"You swear you didn't make him from parts of Cullen?"

"Ash...." A somber sag of pity overtook Braxton's expression. "Even if it hadn't been a thousand years since then, you know there was nothing of Cullen left."

Ashmedai had thought hearing that and truly believing Braxton meant it would wound him deeper than anything else he had learned today. When it didn't, he wasn't sure what to feel.

"How many?" he asked.

"Bodies? A dozen. Maybe two dozen over the centuries."

"And you swear none of them were savable?"

There was still something similar between Braxton and Levi besides the matching color of their hair—a certain way about their mouths, even though Levi's was stitched. But if Levi's eyes were what made him look like Cullen, then that was also the part of Braxton that looked the least like his creation.

Cold blue.

"I did save them, Ash. I made them Levi."

Ashmedai didn't know what to say. He couldn't punish Braxton for what he had done. People weren't punished in the Dark Kingdom, because no one committed crimes. At worst, altercations would require mediation, separation from one another, or just time for people to calm down. Easy for a small community with only so much space. They literally couldn't afford to commit atrocities against one another.

Ashmedai had never considered atrocities against outsiders, even if most were highwaymen.

"You swear you will never do anything like this again?"

"I swear." Braxton nodded, and while his eyes could be cold, when his heart was in his words, as it seemed to be now, Ashmedai couldn't doubt him. "This is almost over, my friend. You know that everything I have ever done these thousand years has been to correct what happened that night. For *you*." Braxton reached for Ashmedai's hand, a rare act, any seeking of physical connection when Braxton usually kept his distance. He was trying to comfort Ashmedai, to reassure him, as any friend would.

Ashmedai blinked the sting of tears from his eyes and placed his other hand atop Braxton's. "I suppose I should let you get back to ending our curse. I have never wanted that more than I do now."

Braxton pulled away with a somber smile. "I couldn't agree more."

As Ashmedai left the tower, walking slowly this time to gather his thoughts, wounded was indeed *not* how he felt. Levi wasn't Cullen. He was someone, some unknown traveler or vagabond who had tread into a cursed wood and panicked, and now he was someone new. Shouldn't he be allowed to continue being who he'd become?

The sounds and extra lights from the budding festival grounds alerted Ashmedai to how far he had walked before he realized it. Beyond the black carriages from Emerald, workers continued to build stalls and prepare for Festival Day.

Among those workers was Levi.

He had a bag now, probably lent to him from Daedlys to better carry the music box. Luccite was with him, as well as Dreya, talking animatedly as usual, probably to recruit them for some task or another.

Although, whatever they were discussing, Ashmedai couldn't help noticing the way Dreya's attention was mostly focused on Luccite, a subtle flush to her cheeks and an extra bounce to her usually drooping ears. She kept finding little ways to touch Luccite, and every time she did, her hair leaves rustled.

A myriad of recent instances flashed through Ashmedai's mind, and he could have kicked himself for not realizing sooner. Dreya was constantly mentioning Luccite lately, or asking after her, and whenever Luccite draped herself like the cat she'd become, Dreya never minded being what Luccite leaned upon.

Dreya fancied Luccite, and Luccite might just fancy her back, given the way her ears twitched and how she looked up at Dreya from her shorter stature with rapt attention. Maybe Ashmedai hadn't noticed before because of his increased seclusion until recently, or maybe his eyes were simply more open because he knew what it felt like to want someone for the first time in centuries.

Taking in Levi's sweetly stitched face, his wavy scarlet hair, his eyes that glowed with a violet light all their own, the truth was, Ashmedai was glad he wasn't Cullen.

LEVI TRIED to follow what Dreya was going on about, but her words seemed more hurried than usual. Something about new preserving methods for the meat from the hunt, and did Luccite have any ideas, or could Levi ask Braxton if he had any? Levi didn't think new methods were necessary, but Dreya had seemed eager to find something to discuss when she spotted them.

No—when she spotted *Luccite*, because she wasn't really talking to Levi; he had just happened to be with Luccite when Dreya appeared. Levi had hoped Ashmedai would still be with Luccite when he finished with Daedlys and Klarent, but the king had already left. Luccite had decided to accompany Levi then to find out all she had missed from delivery day.

What amazed Levi now was realizing that Dreya wasn't the only one acting strangely—Luccite was too. Levi had only just met the healer, but he thought Luccite's reaction earlier when Ashmedai passed on Dreya's regards had been strange, almost like she would have blushed if she weren't covered in fur. She also seemed to be hanging on Dreya's every word with that same anxious but admiring expression.

"Any other suggestions you might—"

"Your help, please!" someone interrupted Dreya's rambling. It looked as though two half-built stalls were encroaching on the same corner, and their owners didn't look happy about it.

Dreya's ears flattened to her head. "Sorry, Lucc. If you'll excuse me." She almost forgot to acknowledge Levi, looking much more forlornly at Luccite as she left.

Luccite stared just as longingly after her.

"You and Dreya have known each other for a long time, haven't you?"

"Hm?" Luccite turned to Levi, and a ripple seemed to run from her shoulders down her spine with a shifting of muscle and fur beneath her robes. "Your point?"

"Well… you're not courting. Why? You're clearly interested in each other."

"Pfft."

The way Luccite looked away with an accompanying squirm made it so obvious that Levi had guessed right, he had a sudden feeling of dread drop deep in his stomach, wondering if he was that obvious around Ashmedai.

"I was here in the beginning, you know, a dwarf once," Luccite said. "I'm an old woman compared to anyone born of this place, and Dreya is barely thirty."

"No offense, Madame Healer," Levi said with a brewing smile, "but I hardly think age matters when everyone here is unaging once they reach adulthood. I myself am less than a month old. Do you think me less of a man?"

Whether a defensive comment or a telling one, whatever Luccite was about to say stalled on her tongue—and she smirked as she spotted something behind Levi. "Others certainly don't."

Levi turned to see where she was looking and found Ashmedai. For a strange, wonderful moment, Levi wondered what the king would look like in sunlight. Moonlight still framed him beautifully, making him almost shimmer like the glittering trees.

"Roped into anything new?" Ashmedai asked when he reached them.

"Hm?" Levi looked around, remembering that he had been talking with Dreya—and Luccite, who seemed to have disappeared. He spotted her heading back down the market steps, though she wasn't at all subtle in the way she glanced toward Dreya before departing. "I don't think so. Dreya was mentioning something, but it seemed more a ruse to talk to Luccite than to employ either of us."

"You noticed too?" Ashmedai's smile seemed more somber than usual as he looked at Luccite descending the steps, and then at Dreya across the festival grounds. "I hadn't realized, but it seems so obvious now that there's an attraction there."

Being in Ashmedai's presence again, Levi couldn't take his eyes off him, not even when white-on-black captured his own inferior violet. Perhaps it was the curve of Ashmedai's white cheek, the silkiness of his black hair, his long neck, or the fangs in his smile. It was all those things, Levi supposed—pieces making up a radiant whole.

"I asked Luccite why she's never pursued anything with Dreya," Levi said.

"And?"

"She said she's too old."

Ashmedai released a quiet huff. "I'd say that's fear talking more than belief in those words. Plenty of couples here have already proven that age means nothing if two grown people are of the same mind."

"Exactly. What a blessing that I do not think, act, or look *my* age." Levi smiled.

A similar flash of a wider smile stretched Ashmedai's face, but he seemed distracted, his mirth only fleetingly genuine before it strained. "It is rare for new love to blossom. Perhaps my advisors need a helping hand. Maybe at the festival."

"A subtle steering in the right direction, you mean?"

"My shadows can steer as well as any guiding hand. They'd never even know," he finished in a whisper.

The clandestine proposal seemed equally devious and delightful to Levi, just like Ashmedai's smile—before it faded again. "I'd say that is a worthy cause to assist you in, my king, but is everything all right? You seem… sad. Is it something Luccite said?" Levi had almost forgotten what they had been up to earlier. "Is it about me?"

Ashmedai looked ageless, without the hint of a smile. He always looked ageless, but like this he seemed frozen in time.

After a swift look around at the mild bustle of workers, Ashmedai suddenly seized Levi by the shoulders and dragged him behind one of the finished stalls, pressing him up against the wall and causing Levi's pulse to quicken. Levi had rarely if ever seen Ashmedai use force before. He was always one to be gentle, even when agitated. To feel such force used on him didn't frighten Levi, even seeing that he and Ashmedai were completely hidden from prying eyes.

The close quarters, the firm grip on his arms, the flash of Ashmedai's white-on-black eyes catching the light from the moon above, only made Levi feel more blissfully captivated.

"You, Levi, are very special," Ashmedai began quietly, like a furtive echo on the wind. "Never doubt that. I spoke with Braxton and…."

"Yes?"

Ashmedai looked frozen again, lost. His grip loosened, but he didn't release Levi. He looked down, gathering his thoughts or maybe his nerve before he met Levi's gaze again. "If you could dream up a different life, would you? What would you want your life to be if you could have anything your heart desired?"

For the longest time, the thought that Levi could *choose* hadn't even entered his mind. He was Braxton's and would always be Braxton's, content to stay sequestered in the tower or hide within his cloak when he was asked to venture outside.

Now, given the choice, all he wanted he had before him, because he had either already acquired it or believed it was just within reach.

So, he reached.

Levi shrugged Ashmedai's hands from his shoulders to grasp the king's face and kissed him. He didn't think this was what Ashmedai meant by his question, but it was all Levi wanted. A queer sense of having wanted this before, something similar to this, stirred within him like… like one of his daydreams, a feeling that he had wanted this and not been allowed to take it, not without staying hidden like he had always been hidden. So he had resisted his desires and been so lonely because of it.

It didn't make sense, but Levi could have sworn that even before he'd been created, he had known want, to be something other than what he was, to have someone he thought he could never have, someone like Ash… and in that moment, claiming Ash was all he could have asked for.

Levi boldly slid his tongue past Ashmedai's teeth, feeling the barest scratch of their sharp points, and shivered all down his body. He wondered if Ashmedai could feel the prick of stitches at the corners of his mouth, but if he could, he didn't seem to mind.

Ashmedai kissed back with a force as great as what he had used to pin Levi behind the stall. He kept Levi pinned, pressing into him as a turn of his head guided the path of their tongues and pushed their connection deeper. It was all so warm, heated, almost feverish, and every slow coil of Ashmedai's tongue made Levi want more.

His hands shook as he lowered them from Ashmedai's face to slide around his neck and pull him closer. He felt Ashmedai cling just as tightly, wrapping strong arms around Levi's waist and pressing their bodies flush. That was how Levi felt—*flush*—with no desire to lose the building heat in his stomach that made him press into Ashmedai harder and whine between their lips.

Ashmedai smiled like a contented shark when they pulled apart.

"C-can that… be my answer?"

As wide as Ashmedai's smile had been, the way it sank made him look like he might weep, and Levi wasn't sure why, because Ashmedai said, "Yes. Yes, it can. Keep taking your draught, Levi, and your daydreams should fade. Nothing else matters." He cupped Levi's cheek almost reverently. "Not as long as you are you."

Levi had thought he would be more curious about Luccite's findings, especially if Braxton had been consulted in the end too, but hearing Ashmedai say that... he couldn't imagine a better answer.

Like many times before, Ashmedai walked Levi home. If smoothing stitches felt too intimate in front of the tower, then stealing another kiss there would be impossible. Therefore, Levi snuck one while they were halfway down the path, feeling content enough afterward that parting from Ashmedai wasn't nearly as bittersweet.

THE NEXT day, Levi didn't even mind that he started his morning by heading into the wood again with Grillo.

Well, he started by taking his draught. He didn't need daydreams. He didn't like them anyway and was glad when Braxton said that the new batch of draught should be stronger. Whatever those visions were seemed far less important than the coming festival or when Levi would next see Ashmedai.

This would be their last trek into the wood, Grillo had said, and Levi was surprised to find he felt saddened by that. He wasn't as wary of the wood or nearing the barrier as he'd been in the beginning, and looked around at the surrounding trees in pleasant wonder as he and Grillo traveled to where they would gather lumber.

There were several glider monkeys following them today. Since Levi and Grillo used the same path each time, the monkeys had grown used to them, bolder. Occasionally one would even drop down into the lumber cart. The monkeys stopped following, however, when the first of Levi's crystals began to flicker.

Clever creatures.

Levi and Grillo turned left. They would be going farther today, having cleared most of the trees in the first area they utilized.

"Would you like to assist with building the final stalls?" Grillo asked, close at Levi's side. "I also need to add a stage to Klarent's, as you know. I hear you'll be up there yourself at some point."

"I will," Levi said with a dip of his head. "And I would be honored to assist you. I am sure construction will be far easier than performance."

Grillo chuckled. "Klarent roped me in too, so you won't be alone."

"Really? What is your talent?"

"Poetry reading," Grillo answered with a wink. "Don't tell Yen. I wrote it for her."

The sweet sentiment of romance—still strong in a long-standing marriage between Grillo and Yentriss, the promise of it budding for Dreya and Luccite, and the progress of Levi's own with Ashmedai—filled him with a warmth almost as blissful as being in Ashmedai's arms.

Almost.

"You and Yentriss were married before the curse?" Levi asked.

"We were. I was a carpenter. No surprise there, I'm sure. And Yen, naturally, was a soldier. We were peaceful with the other kingdoms, so it was more a precaution against highwaymen. Most days she was a city guard, walking the streets. Since I was often out on the streets myself, working on various projects, well, how could I possibly ignore the seemingly indifferent, statuesque guard?"

He smiled with a fondness that again warmed Levi's heart.

"What about you?" Grillo asked. "Your talent for the festival?"

"Oh! Klarent asked me not to tell anyone, since it's part of his performance too, but I can say it involves my illusion magic. Ash said the crowd will be more focused on that than me. I hope he's right."

"I'm sure you'll do splendidly, and Kenner will be pleased. Rest assured you'll have a few friends in the crowd with my family."

"You and Kenner, perhaps. I don't know if Yentriss likes me very much."

"Nonsense. She acts tough with everyone. Save me, of course. Just you wait. She'll be a blushing mess after my performance." Grillo laughed again, and Levi chuckled with him.

He wondered how a blush would present itself on green and gold scales.

"She's always been serious-minded," Grillo went on, his mirth lessening as he was drawn into memory, "but I suppose the curse enhanced that with the scales she grew like natural armor. When the curse first happened, there were many people who tried to flee. We lost dozens, and Yen was crucial in trying to prevent more, but she could only do so much. She saw more citizens… erased than anyone else. She and Ash."

Levi had grown so used to the people here that he hadn't considered how many more there might have been if history had gone differently. "That must have been very difficult."

Grillo smiled again, never without one for long. "And that is why we celebrate what we have each year instead of mourning what we lost."

They reached another edge of the barrier, and Levi set down the glowing crystal where there was a gap in the perimeter. He pulled out a second as they veered once more toward their destination. By the time they stopped and Grillo started felling trees, Levi had no crystals left, though there was a larger gap near them that made Levi wary.

There were no glider monkeys here. No jackalopes or gazellians either. There weren't even tracks to indicate there ever had been animals near these trees. The stillness was eerie, but Levi tried to keep his mood light by thinking of the next time he would see Ashmedai.

The king would walk Levi home again once the day's work was done, and Levi had every intention of stealing another kiss.

Grillo was onto a particularly large tree that, even for the minotaur, would take several minutes to topple. Levi knew better than to wander, content to organize the cart with the lumber they had so far, but when he looked up, scanning the nearby trees, he noticed an area close by with disturbed dirt. Perhaps there had been animals through here.

Curious, Levi moved toward it. The earth was definitely disturbed, dug into, maybe even freshly, or something had been recently buried there. By a rollhound perhaps? While mostly domesticated, there were some in the wild.

The area seemed distorted in a way. Levi knelt to better inspect the upturned dirt, reaching out to gently smooth some of it aside. Was that… cloth?

A boom startled Levi, and he looked back to see the large tree on the ground. Grillo was wiping the sweat from his brow and started to move toward Levi, heading slightly north and around the trees to come up parallel to him.

"Last one. I don't know about you, but I am starved—" The sound cut off abruptly from Grillo's lips, his body going rigid and eyes snapping wide as he looked to his left… and howled.

His arm up to his elbow had vanished.

"Grillo!" Levi rushed to him, not thinking of his own safety or how close he too might be to the barrier. He grasped Grillo's still-whole arm and pulled with all his might to drag the sizable minotaur from where the barrier must be.

It was horrifying and fascinating to watch where Grillo's arm had been, the wound seemingly frozen, not yet bleeding, only to suddenly gush and make Levi's head feel woozy. Never had he been so grateful that Kenner wasn't with them.

Struggling to not let the gory sight fell him like the trees, with nothing else to stop the bleeding, Levi tore his tunic off over his head and swiftly began to bind it around the stump.

Grillo stared in mute shock as if the pain had also been frozen—but then he howled far louder than before as that too caught up to him.

"*Grillo.*" Levi forced the minotaur to look at him and not the missing arm. "We must get you to Luccite. Can you make it?"

It was awful to see such pain and fear on the face of a man usually so strong. Grillo nodded, pulling on a brave face despite feeling what must be agony, and held a shaky hand to the already blood-soaked tunic, applying more pressure with a grimace.

Levi looped his arm through Grillo's uninjured one, supporting the small of Grillo's back to better catch him should he pass out or stumble, and swiftly led them back down the path, leaving everything else behind.

CHAPTER 6

ASHMEDAI STORMED into Luccite's shop almost as explosively as he had Braxton's tower the day before—only to stumble to a stop and stare.

Levi was pacing back and forth in front of the closed curtain, presumably with Grillo and Luccite behind it, and he wasn't wearing a tunic.

His bare torso caught Ashmedai off guard, even though he'd already seen it. Like Levi's face and hands, his upper body was covered in stitches, connecting different parts or covering where organs had been replaced internally. Only now Ashmedai knew that each part was from a different person who had once been alive and had the misfortune of crossing into their territory.

The parts were all blue, changed by the alchemy that had given Levi life, but although they matched enough in size and shape to create a trim, well-muscled figure, some were darker or lighter blue as a nod to the different shades of original skin Levi had been made from.

His head had been from one person, though, with only patches of skin here and there replaced on his face. Who had he been, Ashmedai wondered?

Levi turned in his pacing and spotted Ashmedai, looking both overjoyed and full of grief at once. They moved in tandem toward each other. Levi looked so distraught, with damp eyes and hurried steps, that it seemed the most natural thing in the world for Ashmedai to accept him into his arms and hold him.

"It's all my fault," Levi sobbed into Ashmedai's shoulder. "I-I was distracted. If only I'd had one more crystal. It was all my fault!"

"Slow down," Ashmedai soothed him, gently petting the soft waves of Levi's hair. "You were not the cause. I am sure you did everything you could. You acted swiftly to bring Grillo here, just as you should have."

Ashmedai had been at the castle, but word traveled to him quickly about how Levi and Grillo had burst forth from the wood and down the market steps to reach Luccite with nary an explanation—save Grillo's bloody stump.

"I-I saw… what looked like something buried by an animal and went to investigate," Levi said with a sniffle, nuzzling his face into the crook of Ashmedai's neck. "Since I was safe, Grillo arced too widely to join me, not knowing the barrier was close. If I'd had one more crystal…."

"Stop that. You couldn't have known."

"But I failed the first thing that had ever been asked of me outside of Braxton giving me errands, and it cost Grillo his arm."

Ashmedai didn't know how else to comfort Levi, so he simply shushed and stroked him, hugging him tighter. The way Levi hugged so fiercely back warmed Ashmedai, but he wished he could do more to prove to Levi it had been an accident.

Then a stray thought stuck on what Levi had said. What would an animal have buried in the wood?

The door burst open even more wildly than when Ashmedai entered, admitting a determined Yentriss and a frightened Kenner. For a moment as the door swung closed, Ashmedai saw the crowd gathered outside that he'd also had to push through.

Yentriss held Kenner's arm as they rushed inside, but she barely gave Ashmedai or Levi a glance, merely pushed the boy toward them, muttering a brief, "Ash."

Ashmedai nodded and motioned the boy to them as Yentriss slipped behind the curtain.

Ashmedai meant to release Levi and kneel before Kenner to offer the boy comfort, but Kenner saw their embrace and sought his own by joining them, flinging his arms about their legs and pressing his face to Ashmedai's side.

"All will be well," Ashmedai soothed him and then lifted his eyes to Levi to impart the same sentiment. "It was an accident, but one Luccite can fix, because Levi got Grillo here quickly."

Levi smiled despite his damp eyes.

"They said… the demon… ate Father's arm." Kenner sniffled.

"The demon did no such thing," Ashmedai said.

"Tore it off?"

"Magic took your father's arm, Kenner, not a monster hiding in the dark."

The boy wriggled away, and Ashmedai reluctantly withdrew his hold on Levi as well, who looked comforted at least as he wiped the remaining tears from his eyes.

"The demon's still out there, isn't it?" Kenner asked.

A bench rested against the wall, and Ashmedai led Kenner there. They sat, and Levi joined them, with Kenner between him and Ashmedai. "Some think it is."

"Wasn't it scary when you chased it into the wood?"

It was always difficult answering questions about that night, so Ashmedai did his best not to. "What's scary is any of my people getting hurt, but look how calm I am. Need you fear if your king does not?"

The tears that might have formed in Kenner's eyes never fell. He seemed satisfied with that answer and leaned against Ashmedai, while also reaching to grasp Levi's hand. Levi accepted it firmly.

This was what Ashmedai wanted from his people, for them to always feel safe with him and with each other, especially the young. He just wished that wasn't put to the test by tragedy.

A few minutes passed with little said before Yentriss exited from behind the curtain. Levi tensed and immediately released Kenner. When Yentriss approached, Levi stood, looking like he thought he needed to run to escape her wrath, yet showing no signs that he would.

Yentriss's face was as stony as ever—until it cracked with emotion and she lurched forward to hug Levi.

Levi froze, clearly not sure how to react, but as he slowly lifted his arms to return the embrace, all Ashmedai could do while looking on was smile.

"You saved him," Yentriss said.

"I-I-I—"

"You saved him," she affirmed, releasing Levi and straightening to return her countenance to calm resolve. "Who knows what might have happened if Grillo had been alone? He told me what happened. It wasn't folly. A whole line of the perimeter needed to be replaced, and the barrier curved in a way you couldn't have predicted, but your quick thinking got him here before too much blood was lost. For that, he will live. Thank you."

If further dissent rose in Levi, he didn't speak it.

"Come, Kenner." Yentriss turned to her son. "You can see your father now."

The boy hopped off the bench in excitement, fears banished now that all was truly well. Luccite stood proudly at the curtain, her robe faintly stained with blood. As she held the curtain open for Yentriss and

Kenner, Ashmedai saw Grillo on the table. He looked weak but alert, his arm regrown from Luccite's efforts, though it almost seemed as though he'd gotten a donation from his wife, since the new arm was covered in scales.

Grillo's eyes didn't meet Ashmedai's. They centered on Levi, and before the curtain closed, he offered a grateful smile.

Levi sagged back onto the bench, stunned, maybe, but content.

Good—because now Ashmedai had to ask, "You were parallel with Grillo but perfectly fine. The barrier curved?"

Levi turned to him, sliding closer across where Kenner had sat as if automatically drawn to Ashmedai. "I must have been a mere reach of my hand from the same fate."

"Can you show me where this happened, where you think something was buried?"

Fear filled Levi's eyes. "We left everything behind. It should be an easy trail to follow. But… isn't it dangerous?"

"We won't get too close. I would let nothing happen to you."

Ashmedai reached for Levi's cheek, adoring as he was of its curve and indigo hues. There were the least number of stitches on Levi's face, only at the stretch of his mouth and, more faintly, at his cheekbones and brow. Ashmedai stroked along the stitches beneath his thumb, and it seemed only then to dawn on Levi that he wore nothing but trousers, for he hunched like he wanted to hide his nakedness while under Ashmedai's scrutiny.

Slowly, observant of any sign that Levi might not want what he was about to do, Ashmedai dragged his fingers down Levi's jaw to his neck, where there were perhaps the most prominent stitches, and then farther down between his clavicle and slightly to the side where a long, angled line stitched over Levi's heart.

The heart must have belonged to someone else once, but it was Levi's now. Levi's mind caused it to beat. Levi's will directed its yearnings. It belonged to Levi, though Ashmedai wouldn't mind the chance to share it.

Shadow magic sprung from Ashmedai's fingertips before he'd even consciously begun to conjure the spell. With no refusal or look of discomfort from Levi, Ashmedai drew the line of dark, pulsing magic along the slanted stitches, down and up again, feeling Levi shiver with every stroke.

Levi heaved closer, forcing Ashmedai's whole hand to flatten over his heart. The final cleansing of magic left smooth skin that was all Levi's.

"You smell like lilacs…." Levi whispered.

Their lips were left so close that there was nothing to do but sigh into the space between them until their mouths met. They weren't somewhere private, not even as private as behind a festival stall, since someone could come out from behind that curtain anytime. The kiss remained chaste, but Ashmedai looked forward to when he might next feel Levi's warmth with a deeper embrace.

"Come," Ashmedai said. "We'll get you something to wear and hurry into the wood before too much time has passed."

Given the crowd outside, waiting to hear word, once Ashmedai informed them that Grillo was well, it took but a moment for someone to offer Levi a cloak. Others joined them to help rebuild the lacking perimeter and bring back the supplies.

Ashmedai knew he couldn't sense the barrier, but when they reached the site of the accident, being so close to it left his skin prickling and his hair on end, like there was a coming lightning storm. Crystals were placed where the perimeter needed it, while Grillo's axe, cart, and the remaining lumber were gathered.

Levi frowned, looking around at where the new crystals had been set. "Maybe I imagined it. I could have sworn the upturned dirt was there—" He pointed beyond the bright line of glowing crystals. "—but that's impossible, and everything looks smooth now. Maybe the hole was somewhere else. I can't remember anymore. I'm sorry."

"It's all right," Ashmedai said, not wanting Levi to blame himself. "In all the chaos, it's understandable if you got turned around. We'll look a little longer and then head back."

They looked and looked, but by the time the others were ready to head back, no disturbed dirt had betrayed itself. All that marred the ground was a bit of Grillo's blood.

The last thing Ashmedai would ever want to believe was that the barrier could *move*, as some of the rumors among his people speculated, but today, he wasn't sure what to believe.

Braxton was at the edge of the path when they exited. It always seemed surreal to see him outdoors when, obviously, to get from the tower to the council hall, he had to traverse the distance somehow.

Braxton couldn't shadow jump like Ashmedai, but he certainly appeared out of nowhere when it suited him.

"I heard there was an accident," Braxton said, more to Levi than to Ashmedai, showing honest strain in his expression. "Are you hurt?"

"No, Master," Levi said, not immediately realizing he had fallen into old habits. "I-I mean… no. Only Grillo was hurt, but he is going to be fine."

"What happened?" Braxton lightly gripped Levi's forearm.

Levi explained, the same way he had to Ashmedai, though without the tears and self-deprecation.

"And? What did you find buried?"

"Nothing. We couldn't find the spot I saw." Levi hung his head. "Perhaps it was an animal track that got covered. Perhaps it was nothing. I'm sorry. I wasn't prepared enough. I didn't bring enough crystals."

"Levi, no one expects you to fill a sack so full it's more of a burden than the lumber." Braxton stroked down Levi's arm, once again in recent memory showing a rare act of intimacy. Ashmedai thought the quick flick of Braxton's eyes meant he might have finally noticed the missing stitches on Levi's wrists, though he said nothing. "The important thing is how you acted quickly to save Grillo's life. Soon, the threat of anyone losing a limb or worse will be but a distant memory."

The others helping with the supplies had all started to drag their feet while continuing down the road, listening in on what Braxton might say.

"In the meantime," he called, noticing their glances, "I can provide as many additional warding crystals as would ease the people's minds, along with the dousing crystals already in production. I'll make sure Daedlys receives a fresh supply."

That appeared to placate everyone, but Ashmedai couldn't say he felt the same.

"We should head home," Braxton said to Levi. "You've had quite the day—and could use a change of clothes." The borrowed cloak covered Levi but was not the most functional of garments.

"I'll see you soon?" Levi asked of Ashmedai.

"Of course. Rest well," Ashmedai said. With a controlled expression, he nodded at Braxton, who nodded back, and Braxton and Levi headed for the tower.

Ashmedai had never been so conflicted in all his years ruling over the Shadow Lands. Braxton cared what happened to Levi; that much was apparent. Braxton's concern, his thankfulness that Levi hadn't been harmed, was far too genuine. Even so, Ashmedai couldn't shake the feeling that something else was going on in his kingdom.

Knowing that, and not wanting to accuse his friend of anything he couldn't prove, left Ashmedai wondering if he had made the right decision to not tell Levi the truth.

ONCE, THE thought of being stopped by almost everyone Levi passed on his way through the market would have terrified him, but the day after Grillo's accident, Levi wasn't stopped to be gawked at or ridiculed. People stopped to praise him and thank him for saving Grillo's life.

No one blamed Levi for the lost arm. Blame fell on the barrier, on the demon, and though Levi wished he could have prevented the accident, he was starting to believe it when others said it wasn't his fault.

"The hero himself," Luccite greeted as Levi entered her shop. She had on a teal robe today that complemented the hue of her gray fur.

"I wouldn't say that." Levi glanced aside.

"I would," a deep voice countered, and Grillo appeared from the back room, walking strong and confident as ever, and having used his new arm to push the curtain aside.

"You're up!" Levi rushed to him. "So soon?"

"A night's rest under our good healer's supervision was all I needed. Besides, we still have work to do. I hope you weren't planning to skip out on helping me finish the stalls and Klarent's stage. I'm still getting used to this thing." He flexed the fingers of his lizard hand.

"I am happy to help. You're not... angry with me for not having a crystal between us that might have spared you all this?"

The expression that touched Grillo's human, but also bull-like, face was one Levi had seen before, for Kenner—a father's expression, gentle and patient. "You did your duty. I had no reason to think a crystal would have been needed between us. In the end, you saved me." He held out his new arm, and Levi grasped it by the wrist. "Thank you, my friend."

Friend. Levi supposed he had several now, but it still seemed miraculous to hear it.

"There will be no stall-building today." Luccite breezed by them, looking especially small when compared to Grillo, since she was only half his eight-foot height. She plucked a small vial filled with green liquid from one of her tables and handed it to Grillo. "Take a sip from this twice a day until it's gone to help the new arm adjust. If you feel any unfamiliar pains, see me immediately. And take at least today and tomorrow off from carpentry. The festival is enough of a ways out that you can rest."

"Yes, ma'am. I guess I better let my wife know I'll be a loaf about the house for a while." Grillo turned to Levi. "I'm sure Kenner wouldn't mind if you came for a visit, and I hear Yentriss owes you some bow lessons. Unless you'd prefer to let Dreya find other work for you the next couple of days?"

"Oh...." Levi had never been invited to someone's home before, but he also enjoyed being around the other festival workers. "Maybe I'll do both."

"And how are you feeling?" Luccite asked Levi.

"N-nothing new," Levi said, not wanting to say more and risk sparking Grillo's curiosity. Levi hadn't had any daydreams since Braxton started increasing the dose of his draught, which he decided was a good thing, even if it tasted bitterer than ever. "If I am ever feeling off, Madam Healer, I know who to see. You are a wonder."

Luccite dismissed the praise with a wave of a furred hand. "Mutation manipulation is an old pastime at this point, what with all I've done to ensure our people can procreate. Good thing we have so many regenerating species." She indicated Grillo's arm.

They turned to go, but Levi stopped as he considered what she'd said. "Does that mean you knew about all the pregnancies?"

"Not all of them," Luccite said with a smirk. "Many couples asked for my assistance decades or longer ago, just to be sure they'd have the opportunity once they were ready. I never realized they'd *all* be ready at the same time."

Amuro and Pentelyn entered just then, as if summoned by the observation. Pentelyn had a visible bump from her abdomen, either newly popped or something she had been hiding before now.

"On that note, my next patient has arrived." Luccite ushered the couple inside. "Good day, gentlemen. Keep me informed."

Levi walked Grillo out but parted from him to finish an errand for Braxton, having promised to visit Grillo at home soon. Levi's bag was filled with more black and white crystals to deliver.

Daedlys's shop wasn't far from Luccite's, but as Levi approached, he saw a sign hanging from a hook on the door—Be Back Soon. Levi resigned himself to return later, only to catch the faintest melodic sounds coming from inside as he turned to go.

Someone was singing.

The haunting tune, not yet words but simple humming, drew Levi forward, and he tried the door. It was unlocked, and though Levi knew better than to enter where he was being asked to wait, he slipped inside to hear the song better.

Klarent wasn't visible, likely somewhere in back or in the apartment above, but it was clearly his voice as the humming turned to lyrics Levi thought he might have heard before.

"Beyond the dense, dark wood
Lies lands forever night;
Shadows fall—and claw—and rend
To see to travelers' end.

"Oh lands possessed by demons' thrall,
The Shadow Lands take all.

"The king once sold his soul
To rule forevermore;
Twisted form—he stalks—and lures
To further grow his horde.

"Oh lands possessed by demons' thrall,
The Shadow Lands take all.

"Beware beyond the wood
For monsters made of men;
Darkness falls—and out—they come....

"To make you one of them," Levi lightly sang the last line with Klarent. He felt nauseated, like his body was fighting itself.

"Levi?" Klarent appeared with a startle. He must have heard the unintended duet. He didn't look angry—Levi didn't think he had ever seen Klarent angry—but he did appear as though something had upset him. "Were you listening? We got it all quite wrong, didn't we?"

"We?" Levi asked, still immobile by the door, unsure if he could keep down his breakfast or that morning's draught.

"That was an old Emerald fable," Klarent said.

Levi blinked at Klarent for several moments before he realized what that meant. "*You're* from Emerald? But I thought you were an original inhabitant when the curse struck."

"Close enough." Klarent moved to a small sofa against the wall and slumped onto it, prompting Levi to push through his nausea and join him. "The curse had only been active for about a year when I came exploring to see if the tales were true."

"You're one of the people who crossed the barrier and was changed?"

"Indeed. I was always a scholar, so I wasn't afraid. I was… fascinated, especially when I began to take on my new form." As Klarent lifted his fingerlike hand tendrils, Levi could see the honest pride in Klarent's eyes for what he had become.

Which made Levi even more curious. "May I ask…?"

"What did I look like before? Very strapping." Klarent sat up taller. "Same height, mind you, and similar frame. Brown hair. Blue eyes. Proud, square jaw. I prefer the tendrils." He winked. Klarent had no hair anymore, but his eyes did retain a certain navy hue, though they were large without pupils, almost like Daedlys's black pits.

"Did you leave family behind?" Levi asked.

"Parents, siblings, friends. I still miss them, but they're long gone now. I think that's why my focus became history. I had a large family once, all of us quite close, and I wonder sometimes what their descendants might be like."

"You must have been so lonely when you learned you couldn't leave here."

"Meeting Lyssy helped," Klarent said with a wriggle of his face tendrils, which Levi knew was his way of smiling.

It made sense why Klarent had appointed himself the kingdom's chronicler if he was an outside scholar wanting to learn all he could. In Levi's few weeks of life, he had only heard the tale of the demon from the mouth of a child. He'd been too anxious to ask it of anyone else, let alone one of the most knowledgeable, but now he felt compelled to understand.

"What really happened the night of the curse?"

Klarent sagged lower into the sofa, though this time, almost wistfully. "The old king had passed away, and Prince Cullen longed for direction. No one can truly say they know his state of mind at the time, not even Ash, a newcomer to Amethyst, who had befriended Cullen."

"Did Cullen summon the demon?"

"No one truly knows that either. Perhaps. Perhaps the demon simply was. All anyone can be sure of is that Ash was there when the people needed someone to lead after Cullen vanished. Without him, everything might have fallen into chaos."

"I didn't realize Ash wasn't originally from here," Levi said, finally relaxing into the sofa.

"Diamond, I believe, in a valley beyond the Sapphire Kingdom, which is nearest to us. Diamond is the primary land of the elves. Or was once. Who knows now, a thousand years since?"

Levi frowned at the map those words created. "Sapphire is closest? Then why do the carriages only go to Emerald?"

"They used to go to Sapphire too, but a couple hundred years ago, their people stopped loading them. No one knows why. So, Brax stopped sending it there." Klarent sighed, seeming far away despite being able to recite anything about the history of the kingdoms with nary a pause for pondering.

"Klarent?" Levi broached softly. "What made you sing that song today?"

"I was thinking of home," Klarent said, followed by another deep sigh, and then he closed his eyes. "I'm pregnant."

"*What*?" Levi leapt to the edge of his seat. "Truly?"

A slightly more agitated flurry of mouth tendrils preceded Klarent's response. "Daedlys doesn't know. It was an accident. We'd discussed it, planned it for years, though we hadn't told anyone we were finally going to go through with it. When it was revealed that a good dozen or more people were already pregnant, we decided to wait... only it seems we made that decision too late."

There was no visible distention of Klarent's belly, and honestly, Levi wasn't sure how pregnancies worked between the various species and genders, but it still seemed such a miracle to look upon his friend and know that a new life was growing inside him. "This is wonderful!"

"Is it?" Klarent scoffed. "So much is unknown right now, and we decided to wait. What if Lyssy is angry?"

"With you? Over this?" Levi couldn't help but smile, because he knew Klarent and Daedlys better than he knew almost anyone in the Shadow Lands, and their devotion to each other was unconditional. "Never."

The orange hue of Klarent's skin seemed to darken a few shades at the apples of his cheeks and partway down his tendrils. "What if Ash is angry?"

"How could he be? Ash said at the council meeting that he never wants anyone to think that way again or to keep such things from him. This is good news." Levi took Klarent's hand, and the tendrils of his fingers coiled up Levi's forearm to wrap tight. "It's you and Daedlys, one of the most inspiring couples in all the Dark Kingdom. I am sure your child will be miraculous, and soon there will be no worries over barriers or lacking space. Unknown though the future may be, Braxton has assured it."

One thing Levi never doubted was that if Braxton put his mind to something, he was certain to achieve it.

"Thank you." Klarent took Levi's other hand to wrap it in tendrils too. "I think I needed to hear that. All that mess with Grillo had me returning to old fears. But then our sweet Stitches saved the day, didn't you? And now you have again."

Levi felt his cheeks warm, and the warmth spread further through his chest. Here was yet another example of romance persevering—a potent and ageless love bringing new life into the world.

"What are you two conspiring about?"

Levi and Klarent lurched away from each other at the sudden return of Daedlys.

The banshee held a bag overflowing with thread and trimmings, presumably from one of the other shops. On top was some particularly beautiful gold lace ribbon.

"Just festival business," Levi said, but as he stood, he turned his back on Daedlys so only Klarent could see him mouth, "*Tell him.*" Then Levi spun back around and presented Daedlys with the bag slung over his body. "I brought another shipment of crystals. I can pick up supplies later. I'm… off to visit Grillo," he lied, though it was only a white lie, since he had seen Grillo before coming here.

Daedlys's black eyes seemed to bore into Levi, so Levi wasted no time making scarce to avoid being questioned. He paused after the door closed behind him, listening in to see if Klarent would take his advice.

He had only faintly been able to hear Klarent's humming before, and even with the pair closer to the door, Levi caught but a few muffled words—until an exclamation of obvious joy dangerously close to being as loud as one of Daedlys's screams signaled all would be well.

Which was when Levi looked out into the market and spotted Ashmedai.

All would be well indeed.

"YOU LOOK like you have a secret," Ashmedai said as he and Levi strolled through the market.

Levi hunched but maintained his smile. "It's not mine to tell, I'm afraid, but it's a good thing. I'm sure you'll find out soon enough."

Knowing someone else's secret further proved how much Levi had become part of the community. Ashmedai didn't mind having to wait to learn it.

They hadn't mentioned a destination, merely started walking as they talked, heading away from the market steps—which meant they soon reached the Source Crystal at the center of the square.

They paused at its base. The Amethyst gemstone was as hefty as the man-sized black crystal Braxton had in his workroom, though it towered taller since it rested on a pedestal, so wide with its various jagged edges that most people would have been unable to wrap their arms around it and touch their fingers together. Unless they had tentacles, and of course some citizens did.

Seeing Levi so close to it, Ashmedai thought the glow of Levi's violet eyes seemed to pulse with the Amethyst's powerful light.

In truth, Ashmedai hated this crystal but not its color. He loved the color. He would just rather enjoy it on Levi without a painful reminder as the backdrop.

"Would you like to continue our stroll by the lake?" Ashmedai asked.

"I'd love to," Levi said.

The Black Lake was reached by continuing to the very end of the market and down a small set of steps onto the beginning sands of the beach, which was otherwise hidden by the ravine walls the market was built into. It didn't truly look like a ravine until one reached that descending curve in the rocky walls, leading around to the hidden beachfront and the deep lake that was otherwise entirely enclosed.

Without any visible flowing water in or out, the lake could have been stagnant, but underground rivers kept it fresh. Some mining was done, but they had never tried excavating too deeply, especially in the caves under the water, assuming somewhere beyond would be unknown edges of the barrier they couldn't risk stumbling upon.

Many unique creatures lived in the lake's depths, safe enough that fishermen and swimmers weren't unheard of, but although snow and frigid temperature never touched the Shadow Lands, it was still technically winter and too cold for the beach, so the area was empty.

The temperature was about perfect for a thunderstorm, however. Ashmedai hadn't noticed, but the cloud cover had increased, and it looked like rain soon. He ignored the threat for now, not wanting his time with Levi to be cut short.

"You never ask me to smooth any more stitches," Ashmedai said.

"Oh, I...." Levi glanced at his feet. He did that often, turned shy and fumbled for words. The difference was that, now, he eventually looked up and smiled with confidence. "May I be honest?"

"Always."

They were nearly to the shoreline, and as they skirted it and the faintly lapping tide, movement caught Ashmedai's attention—then Levi's a second later.

"Ah!" Levi jumped, scrambling to grab Ashmedai's arm. The last wave had carried a family of moth crabs onto the shore.

They looked like giant spider-legged crabs, but where they got the first part of their name was often overlooked, until they spread their wings and took off toward the rocks.

"You have nothing to fear," Ashmedai said, hushed and close beside Levi. "Moth crabs are harmless. Just about a hundred times larger than a housefly."

"Housefly?" Levi looked at him, and because of his clinging, their mouths were but a hair's breadth apart.

"Never mind. You were saying?"

Levi took a steadying breath but didn't move away. "When you smooth my stitches with your magic, it feels… pleasant. Too pleasant. Intimate."

Ashmedai had assumed as much given the way Levi gasped and flushed during the process. "Do you not like that feeling?"

"I like it very much."

"Then why don't you ask for more?" Ashmedai grinned, because in that moment, he could have given Levi anything.

Levi shifted against Ashmedai and took one of his hands. He brought it upward to rest upon the stitches of his right cheekbone.

The pulse of violet shadow magic Ashmedai brought forth was almost the same color as the dark depths of the lake, with hints of the brighter violet in Levi's eyes.

"Lilacs…." Levi said with a shiver.

"Hm?"

"You smell… no." Levi's nose crinkled. "It's not you, but…." After he trailed off, before Ashmedai could lower his hand, Levi drew it over to the opposite cheekbone. Ashmedai did as was silently requested, calling on his magic once more to smooth the stitches to flawless skin.

As before, Levi shivered, though his eyes seemed to clear with realization. "It happened before, yesterday, when you healed my heart."

"What happened before?"

"I thought I smelled lilacs, but it wasn't you. You smell lovely, but more like… sandalwood. The lilacs were a daydream… I just didn't realize it."

Ashmedai felt his expression slacken, much as he hated to lose this good feeling.

"It felt like I was somewhere else," Levi continued, "with lilac bushes all around me."

"You're sure?" Ashmedai pressed. "But your draught…."

"It was working. I hadn't had a daydream in days. But I think, when you make me whole, they grow stronger."

Because smoothing Levi's stitches made him more one person, and his mind remembered the last time it had been the sum of its parts.

"Would you like me to stop?" Ashmedai asked.

"No." Levi clung to him, lifting Ashmedai's hand toward the stitches through his brow. "I thought I didn't like the daydreams, that I didn't want them. I can't explain why now, but… I want to see more."

Guilt clawed into Ashmedai's chest. He couldn't refuse, and so he smoothed those stitches too, and Levi smiled wider.

"Yes. I first started having the daydreams after you fixed my wrist. They scared me then but… I want to know. I need to know. Please. I can almost hear a busy street, but I know it's not the market." He closed his eyes, those beautiful violet eyes, lost to whatever he was remembering.

Ashmedai obeyed, but he wasn't sure if he was ready to lose Levi's unique smile with stitches at the corners of his mouth. Instead, he brought his hand downward, but he had already gotten the stitches across Levi's heart that might have been reached by untying the top of his tunic, and the stitches along Levi's neck seemed so final, as those were what had first connected the real him to his other parts.

That left places that were harder to reach, that Ashmedai would have to seek with blind hands—unless he undressed Levi right there on the beach.

The prospect was far too tempting.

Holding his breath for a moment, maybe because Levi was too, Ashmedai gripped the fabric at Levi's waist and twisted his fingers to coil the tunic upward. Soon he felt the cool skin of Levi's stomach.

Ashmedai reached beneath the tunic, letting the fabric fall about his wrist, and felt his way to a line of stitches beneath Levi's navel. He smoothed them with tender strokes of his magic.

Then he did the same to a line above Levi's navel.

Then to some around the small of Levi's back.

Then to some up the middle of Levi's back.

Then carefully around the curve of each shoulder where Levi's arms connected to his torso.

By the end, Levi was flush against Ashmedai, with deep, shuddery gasps leaving him. Ashmedai had started to pant too, awed by the indigo in Levi's cheeks and the parting of his equally dark lips. Sprinkles started to fall on them from the coming storm, and Levi's eyes were bright with excitement.

"What can you see?" Ashmedai asked.

"I-I don't know how," Levi said in wonder, "but I think it's Emerald."

All Ashmedai wanted was to keep giving Levi pleasure, because he knew the truth of the daydreams was not something to smile about.

He stroked with his hand, still beneath the tunic, down Levi's back until he reached another edge of fabric. Ashmedai didn't know where all Levi had stitches below the waist, but most of what remained had to be there.

Boldly, Ashmedai dipped his fingers into Levi's trousers, following the gentle curve of his backside to a line of stitches that connected Levi's left leg. He followed that line, first along the outer thigh up Levi's hip, and then... *inward*.

Levi's eyelids fluttered, and if he still saw Emerald behind them, that didn't seem to matter, for all he moaned was, "*Ash*."

Before Ashmedai's hand could fully reach between Levi's legs, Levi convulsed with an arch upward and proceeded to sag in such a telling way that the sated look in his eyes wouldn't have been needed to know what happened.

Ashmedai was tempted to reach between Levi's legs anyway. He wanted to touch him, to feel what he had helped cause and spur Levi toward even more passion.

A spark of blinding lightning heralded an almost instant and deafening crack of thunder. The rain started in earnest, and Levi laughed.

"I guess the moth crabs were being prudent when they sought the rocks." Levi held out a hand toward the falling rain. "I kind of like it."

He was marvelous, peerless, a true vision of ignorant beauty, as if believing he was in the eye of the storm, even though his hair was plastered to his face and thunder and lightning raged all around him.

"Levi...," Ashmedai said, his words nearly lost to the wind picking up speed, "I lied to you."

"What?" Levi let his cupped hand fall. "Lied about what?"

Ashmedai withdrew from Levi. "Your daydreams are more than I admitted. Braxton made you from parts of people—real living people. You are not a construct. Your dreams are memories. From this part of you." He hesitated to reach for Levi's cheek but allowed himself that much, feeling bolstered when Levi leaned into his touch. "Your mind persists.

"When I confronted Brax, he said that telling you the truth might cause more harm than good, and I foolishly listened. He swears all the people were lost causes, swears he will never do such a thing again, but... I should have told you as soon as I knew. I'm sorry. I'm so sorry. I feared losing you. It was selfish."

Levi had yet to deny Ashmedai, but when he lifted a hand to take hold of Ashmedai's wrist, surely he would tear the hand from his face.

Instead, he held it there.

"You asked me what I wanted, if I would choose another life."

"I should have—"

"You were trying to protect me, and in the end, you still told me the truth." Levi drew Ashmedai's hand from his face, but not to brush it aside. He brought it to his lips and kissed the back of it. "Thank you."

The swell of love Ashmedai felt was more than he would ever believe he deserved.

He crushed Levi to him. "Are you all right, knowing this?" Ashmedai asked, wet lips brushing Levi's equally damp ear.

"I don't know. I'm a bit of a mess, though… elsewhere." If the chill of the storm hadn't been causing Levi to shiver, Ashmedai might have missed his renewed blush.

"*Oh.*" Ashmedai pulled back, having forgotten what his shadow-touch had caused. "I should help you clean up. And we need to get out of the storm. Would you like to see my castle, Levi?" He hadn't invited someone to the castle, other than Dreya, who had more so invited herself, in longer than he could remember.

Levi's eyes glittered through the rain like beacons leading home. He gave an emphatic nod, and Ashmedai whisked Levi into his arms and toward a large enough shadow for them both, diving inside with Levi clinging to him.

CHAPTER 7

THE DAYDREAMS were memories. That should have been Levi's first assumption, not thoughts of premonitions or some connection to people outside himself. Memories made more sense. He had experienced the things he was seeing, smelling, feeling—or at least the head on his shoulders had.

The castle was even more remarkable than Levi could have guessed. It was beautiful from the outside, even in the distance, black and glittering like the Dark Kingdom's trees, but even more so, as if it was speckled with precious stones. Levi hadn't known Ashmedai could take someone else into his shadows, but when the blackness swallowed them, there was no accompanying fear of the dark. Levi felt comforted, like being swaddled as a babe in a warm blanket.

Light had returned, revealing they were suddenly out of the rain, already inside the castle. They'd reappeared from a circle of shadows Ashmedai must always keep there, for the furniture had been arranged just so with a bright white crystal glowing that caused a large portion of the floor to be completely cast in darkness, like a shadow entryway.

The room was a study, decorated in reds and blacks like Ashmedai's clothing. Everything was either gold or brocade or silk in the same deep colors Ashmedai wore. This room must be his favorite, with a massive candle clock, large black bookshelf covered in tomes, and a chair resting beside a window that looked upon the city. The study was in one of the castle towers, maybe even the one Levi looked at and pondered over when he saw a light on.

"Come," Ashmedai said, leading Levi from the room into a high-ceilinged hallway.

The simple command reminded Levi why he already had and still felt uncomfortable in his trousers. The rain had helped, but now they were in a dry, cozy space.

With some of his memories returned more succinctly, Levi had a vague sense of feeling shame when he had pleasured himself in his past life. He didn't know why. He didn't even feel shame having released in the king's presence, because he could tell Ashmedai had wanted to give him pleasure.

Levi wanted to do the same in return.

Now, after their brief trek through the castle, Levi was in a vast washroom, reached after having entered a bedchamber with similar coloring to the study. Levi assumed it was where Ashmedai slept—*if* he slept—and this was where he bathed.

There were oils and warm running water that Levi used to clean himself once Ashmedai left him. An ornate mirror was on the far wall, gilded like so much Levi had seen of the castle. It was floor length and reflected Levi in his entirety as he walked toward it, clean now, but still naked. His clothing was soaked from the rain.

When Levi first explored his body, he had noted every line of stitches. So many of them were gone now, leaving but a scattered few. Patches of skin and body parts were often a different shade of blue, but where Ashmedai had smoothed the stitches away, those parts matched in hue now, making Levi an almost unified azure.

His skin had been peach-colored once, light like cream, and his eyes... he couldn't remember, but maybe they had been blue instead of violet. His hair had still been red, though.

Focused on his body's reflection, made from different people, Levi wasn't sure what he felt, or if he was okay with the thought that, once, he had been someone else. All his parts had been different someones', but only his mind, his head, remembered its former life and, in some ways, got to live on.

It made Levi more aware of each of his parts and where his remaining stitches connected or covered him. It also made him enjoy even more the places where stitches had been removed, because he was becoming his own man in more ways than he'd first realized.

He supposed the only thing that truly disturbed him after learning all this was whether remembering more would erase who he'd become.

"Levi? Are you all right in there?"

Levi turned back to the washroom door. A long black robe hung on the back of it, made of some sort of plush fabric that looked wonderfully warm and inviting. "Coming!" he called and, leaving his wet clothes draped over the edge of the tub to dry, donned the robe to exit into Ashmedai's bedchamber.

"Prrp!" An unfamiliar noise sounded from behind Levi—but he had only just turned away from facing that direction.

Slowly, on edge with his hand still on the handle to make his exit, Levi peeked over his shoulder.

A ghostly form hovered directly in front of his face, shaped like a medium-sized, longish-haired cat, but translucent with the faintest pale glow. It was see-through like Daedlys, but whereas Daedlys's black pits for eyes had become a source of comfort for Levi, these were bright, haunting white.

"Ah!" Levi yelped and leapt backward to escape the phantom cat, but since he had already turned the handle, the door gave way, toppling him out of the washroom—and into Ashmedai's arms.

"What happened? Are you—?" Ashmedai began, with strong hands holding Levi steady. He darted his eyes beyond Levi, and instantly, the concern on Ashmedai's face faded to amusement. "It's only Aurora, curious about you, I bet. She's a cathom."

Feeling his heart in his throat, Levi let that sink in as he sank against Ashmedai. The hands at Levi's elbows slid up his arms and around his back to offer comfort, though Levi felt foolish for needing any.

Just a cathom, what had become of cats the same way dogs had become rollhounds. The phantomlike felines were wholly domesticated and safe, but although Levi had known they existed, he'd never seen one, since they tended to be indoor pets.

He'd also never known Ashmedai had one.

"Rora, you've startled our guest." Ashmedai clicked his tongue, calling her closer. "Apologize, won't you?"

Gently, Ashmedai shifted Levi in his arms so he still held Levi, but Levi now faced the washroom door. Aurora floated out. Her movement was like Daedlys's as well, but while his lower half ended in a wisp instead of feet, she had all four paws. They seemed to find traction on the very air, pulling her forward like she trod on solid ground.

She *was* on solid ground. Or rather, on a countertop, walking about and demanding to be petted, her fur pure white save where there were tufts of brown at her ears, paws, the end of her tail, and part of her chest. He remembered how soft her fur was when he reached out....

But what his hand touched was no normal cat on a countertop. Aurora was still hovering, still translucent, and though she bucked up into Levi's petting, there wasn't fur beneath his hand so much as a sensation like sifting his fingers through the softest silk, cool but not cold to the touch.

Levi huffed a jubilant laugh, not only because Aurora had turned out to be a sweet creature, but because he remembered, "I had a cat!" He laughed again and stroked Aurora more confidently. The cathom began to purr and rolled over in midair, so Levi stroked along her back.

"Another daydream?" Ashmedai asked.

"Yes. I can't recall the cat's name, but she was very like Aurora. Slightly longer hair. My mother's cat. She was always very sweet with me."

As Levi attempted to scratch lower toward the base of Aurora's tail, she whipped up and darted away with another "Prrp!" and disappeared right through Ashmedai's bedchamber door.

"She has the run of the castle," Ashmedai said, "and likes it that way. She's not used to company, other than Dreya, but I think she likes you. I found her after I first moved in. She was hiding in a closet, not knowing yet that she could pass through walls. I don't know who she belonged to, if anyone from the castle, but she's been mine for centuries."

Only then, as Levi turned in Ashmedai's arms to face him, did he realize the king was dressed as he was—in nothing but a robe.

Ashmedai's robe was red but otherwise identical to the one Levi wore. Behind Ashmedai, his kingly clothing was draped over a tall wingback chair in front of a fireplace that hadn't been lit when Levi went into the washroom, but now it blazed, casting golden light along Ashmedai's white face.

Without his usual high-collared tunic, Ashmedai's clavicle and a small peek of his chest was visible. At first Levi thought he saw scars, but they were more like protrusions, ridges, three distinct rows of them one beneath another across Ashmedai's chest, and possibly a fourth where Levi couldn't quite see.

He wondered where else Ashmedai had ridges.

"I-I… left my clothes by the bath," Levi said. He and Ashmedai were still closely met in the center of the room, but no longer touching, and yet, being so near each other made Levi's breath pick up. The desire mixed with the denial of contact made him want to push the robe from Ashmedai's shoulders.

"That's fine," Ashmedai said—answering Levi's *actual* comment, not the thoughts in his head. "You'll likely need to borrow some of my clothing anyway. I can return yours tomorrow. Would you like to pick something out?" The king gestured behind him, beside the fireplace, where a large wardrobe rested.

Levi normally saw Ashmedai in the same—or similar—outfits of red and black brocade with gold trim. He couldn't imagine wearing something like that himself, but surely Ashmedai had softer things, casual things to drape himself in when he lounged here alone. Levi wanted to see that. He wanted to know Ashmedai as he was when he was his most private self.

"Levi?"

Levi hadn't meant to, but his hand had reached of its own accord to touch those fascinating ridges. They were too symmetrical to be scars. They almost felt like bone. Ashmedai had claws after all, however delicately he used them, as well as points on every tooth. Levi had read about many creatures of myth, all of which someone in the Dark Kingdom had emulated after the curse, sometimes a combination of several. He didn't know what Ashmedai was supposed to be.

"More of my strangeness," Ashmedai said quietly, referencing an old conversation about how they both had trouble accepting who and what they were.

Levi answered with the sentiment he had finally taken to heart. "No such thing in the Shadow Lands." He flattened his hand over the ridges, mimicking how Ashmedai had covered and smoothed the stitches over Levi's heart. Feeling Ashmedai shiver, which was far too tantalizing an act from the Shadow King, Levi found his nerves strengthened.

He lifted his other hand to the opening of Ashmedai's robe and drew both sets of trailing fingers downward, parting the soft fabric as he went, until he reached the tie at Ashmedai's waist. The king made no move to stop him, so Levi undid the tie and pushed the robe from Ashmedai's shoulders like he'd envisioned.

Similar ridges to what arched across Ashmedai's chest were also along his ribs, as well as lining his elbows and knees, usually in three or four parallel rows. None crossed over the flat of his stomach, but some curled up around his hips, fading downward where they pointed in a tantalizing V.

Ashmedai's cock was also ridged, with fainter but clearly there lines, especially visible with how he was hardening.

Levi wanted to touch every one of them.

"I want to pleasure you as you did me," he said, beginning to untie his own robe.

"I-I barely touched you," Ashmedai sputtered, like it was no great feat, though for Levi, he had never known anything as blissful.

"You can touch me now," Levi said, letting his robe fall to join Ashmedai's on the floor.

Levi had never been bare in front of anyone but Braxton, and then, it was always clinical. Where once he would have been frightened, now, those nerves were pure anticipation. He watched Ashmedai reach for him with what Levi still felt was undeserved reverence, yet from the king, he knew it was genuine.

The first touch was simply along Levi's cheekbone and then down his neck over his heart. Ashmedai seemed to be tracing all the places where he had already smoothed away stitches, mimicking how he had touched Levi beneath his clothing in the rain, only now nothing encumbered him.

Finally, once every other part of Levi had been gifted a caress, and they were both hard, Ashmedai reached between Levi's legs. Gentle claws found Levi's cock, and the soft underside of his fingers curled firmly.

Levi gasped and bucked into his grip. "M-may I... touch you too?"

It seemed words failed Ashmedai, but he nodded.

Levi's hands had a roughness to them, the hands of someone who had worked hard over many weeks. He thought that might make them unpleasant against the preternatural smoothness of Ashmedai, but the king shuddered with every stroke along the lines of his beautiful ridges. Ashmedai was so warm, both his touch on Levi, turning into rhythmic strokes, and his cock in Levi's palm.

"I want my mouth on you," Levi husked when they were both panting.

Ashmedai laughed, more like a startled eruption. "I... don't mean to doubt your desires but... do you know what you're doing? What *we're* doing?" he corrected, for he clearly didn't mean to imply he doubted Levi's skills, only that he wondered if Levi was aware of what this type of intimacy meant.

"I'm not a child, remember?" Levi removed his hand from Ashmedai to still Ashmedai's strokes on him. "I've only been this version of me for a short time, but I know what I want. And… I've read a few romances in my studies." He glanced aside at the admission.

"Brax has romances in that tower?"

"He's not completely cold."

"I feared I was becoming cold," Ashmedai admitted, drawing Levi's eyes back up to meet the haunting white-on-black that Levi had never quite been able to perfect when conjuring illusions of Ashmedai in his room.

This was no illusion.

"All I feel from you, my king," Levi said, "is warmth."

Levi kissed him, unprepared for how the closeness of their bodies brushed their cocks together. He loved those ridges as much as he loved Ashmedai's claws and sharp teeth, but especially after feeling them on his skin.

A shaky breath puffed from Levi against Ashmedai's mouth in the aftermath of their lips and tongues entwining, and he fought the urge to rut forward. He had released too swiftly once before and had no desire for that again.

The large canopy bed behind them was perfectly aligned for Levi to back Ashmedai toward it, and he did, slowly, carefully, guiding Ashmedai where he wanted him to go. The curtains of the bed were also red and black brocade, tied to their posts but capable of shielding Levi and Ashmedai from everything but each other. For now Levi left them tied and pushed on Ashmedai's chest for him to drop down onto the edge of the bed.

Ashmedai had always been a vision of beauty, but with his arms extended to support him and his back arched, the toned muscle down his torso tightened, making every one of his ridges more prominent. Levi could barely contain how much he wanted to descend upon the offering laid before him.

Visions swirled behind Levi's eyes, like what he remembered from their first kiss behind the festival stall. Levi hadn't known this with another man in his former life, but he had wanted it, craved it desperately, and been denied. Been… unable to reach for it. Now nothing stood in his way, and Ashmedai, Shadow King in all his naked splendor, was better than any wayward daydream.

Levi lowered himself to his knees between Ashmedai's white thighs. Whenever Levi blushed, his skin turned indigo, but Ashmedai's pure white tones took on a faint rosy pink. That telling hue was in his cheeks now and slightly down his chest, but also along the inside of his thighs and pulsing from his ripe cock.

With saliva rapidly building, Levi bent forward and eagerly took Ashmedai into his mouth. A plaintive whimper left them both like a harmonizing chorus. Levi descended farther, hollowing his cheeks to increase the suction around Ashmedai's length. He took Ashmedai in as deep as he could, until Ashmedai's tip touched the back of his throat and Levi's nose was pressed to Ashmedai's belly.

Ashmedai was hairless here. He was entirely hairless other than his eyebrows and the long black hair on his head. Levi was mostly the same, but above his sex were dark curls that didn't match his red waves. That thought might have saddened Levi, to think that so little of him was *him*, but all that mattered now was who he was today and what he had in his grasp.

Levi licked the underside of Ashmedai's cock, only to bob down once more with added saliva and suction to ensure Ashmedai felt this.

The haggard moan the king released was wonderful encouragement.

On the next bob, Levi paid close attention to Ashmedai's ridges, working his tongue between each groove. He hadn't been sure where to place his hands, but with his confidence increasing from every wanton whine pulled from Ashmedai's lips, Levi spread his fingers across Ashmedai's inner thighs and squeezed as he quickened his pace.

"L-Levi…," Ashmedai uttered brokenly. The blankets on the bed were completely black, outlining Ashmedai's body starkly and how his clawed nails gripped the fabric like he might tear it.

Levi hastened, massaging the ridges up Ashmedai's hips while his tongue massaged the ones on Ashmedai's length. He bobbed and sucked Ashmedai down as obscenely as if he could swallow him whole. He could feel such glorious heat through Ashmedai's skin, and he wanted to feel more spill down his throat.

"Levi!" Ashmedai cried sharper, one hand starting to lift as if to reach for Levi, but then it twisted into the blankets again.

Even more of Ashmedai's white skin was flushed pink, and when his eyes closed and fluttered briefly, Levi could have sworn Ashmedai's white pupils went black like the rest.

"I-I—" Ashmedai tried to speak, tensing all down his body, his neck arching backward and mouth falling open, so that Levi knew how close he was and doubled his efforts to bring Ashmedai there.

When Levi felt the heat he'd been waiting for, he swallowed and licked the remnants from Ashmedai's skin.

Ashmedai slumped heavily onto his arms but kept himself propped up, breathless as he gazed down his body at Levi in apparent wonder. "You are so… beautiful…."

"Me?" Levi dropped his eyes but raised them swiftly again to not miss one moment of Ashmedai lying there rosy and spent. *You're* beautiful."

A twitch at Ashmedai's lips seemed to say he didn't believe that, so Levi vowed to prove it to him.

He swooped upward from between Ashmedai's knees and climbed onto the bed, crawling atop Ashmedai and straddling his hips. Their cocks brushed each other again, Levi's firm and heavy, with Ashmedai's wilted but twitching with promise. Seated in Ashmedai's lap, Levi grasped the king's face in both hands and kissed him. The taste of Ashmedai still lingered on Levi's tongue to share, and he did so boldly.

"I love your ridges," he said between fevered peppering of more kisses to Ashmedai's lips. Then to his cheek. Then down his neck. "I love the way they feel against me. I love the way *you* feel against every part of me." To make that clearer, Levi toppled Ashmedai backward, Ashmedai's arms giving way to lay him flat upon the blankets. Like that, Levi could truly touch all of Ashmedai, spread out atop him, kissing and writhing.

Wanting so much more than a shuddery outcome in the rain, Levi was close to bursting, and after mere moments of squirming and pawing and tasting Ashmedai's skin, Ashmedai was there again with him.

"*Yes*," Levi mewled at the firm presence of Ashmedai against his hip. "I want more. I want you. I want us to both find release again. Please."

IT HAD been so long since Ashmedai had known any kind of pleasure, let alone something as potent as having Levi beg for more after having his mouth on Ashmedai and drinking him dry.

Already Ashmedai knew he could easily join Levi in a second tumble over the edge, and the thought of doing so together was stirring. Levi seemed so desperate, so fervent and passionate, his hands constantly moving over Ashmedai's skin, and his thin hips wriggling and thrusting to find any kind of friction.

Ashmedai wanted to hold Levi there atop him and rut upward until his mind went blank from the exertion, but they could do better—slower—and draw this out to both their hearts' content.

The way they were now, Ashmedai's legs hung off the end of the bed, and Levi was scrunched to keep from tumbling backward. That wouldn't do.

Seizing Levi by the waist, Ashmedai ceased the young man's wild writhing and rolled them with a firm toss of Levi onto his back. He immediately scooped Levi into his arms again and hefted him up the bed with barely any effort, for to him, Levi weighed but a trifle.

Levi's eyes showed only a thin ring of violet now, they were so blown black, and he was one deep shade of indigo save the inside of his lips, pink and panting.

Ashmedai leaned over him but kept his weight on his own hip, sliding his cock alongside Levi's to share the existing and still-pooling wetness between them. Levi seemed to recognize Ashmedai's intent to make this last, and his franticness settled. He lay back to enjoy what Ashmedai offered, trembling at the slick, slow slide of their lengths. As Levi's hands reached upward to spread across Ashmedai's chest, still seeming so in need of touching him, his arms quaked.

Ashmedai felt it too, stimulation on the verge of being too much, but right now it was perfect. To that end of heightening each sensation that much longer, he kept their pace slow, but drew inward on the power of his magic and brought it to the edges of his skin—not only into his fingertips but everywhere.

"Tell me... would you like all your stitches washed away?" Ashmedai asked.

Levi's eyes widened, taking in how Ashmedai was glowing with dark violet pulses. "N-n-not all," he stammered. "Some? I'll finish too quickly again if you do too many," he ended with a bashful smile.

"Then I will leave my favorites until a time when you are ready," Ashmedai said.

Levi's eyes bulged briefly, surprised perhaps to hear that Ashmedai had favorites among his stitches. He did, for they were part of how Levi looked when Ashmedai first knew him. Ashmedai understood, however, the desire to have them gone.

He let his magic wash over Levi like a silk sheet but kept the true power only in his touch. With each smoothing of a set of stitches, he timed a thrust of his hips and pressed a kiss to Levi's lips.

Once.

Then again.

Then *again*.

"Ash…." Levi gasped, appearing to glow purple too with the magic around them.

In sync with Ashmedai's downward motion, Levi thrust upward to meet him, writhing once more with his hands braced on Ashmedai's chest, along the ridgelike grooves that Ashmedai had always thought made him more alien, foolish as that may be in a land where everyone was unique.

When all that remained were the stitches in Levi's smile and around his neck, Ashmedai stopped, though he didn't stop the deep rocking of their hips, their cocks wet and throbbing. Rather than rein in his shadow magic, Ashmedai continued to spread it outward, caressing Levi with it in ways no skin contact could.

The shadows were part of Ashmedai, an extension of him, and through their undulating across Levi's body, Ashmedai felt what they did to Levi and shuddered at how much more it made him feel touched in turn.

The shadows had no tangible shape but could be anything and everywhere, seeping from Ashmedai's skin like the sweat beginning to sheen on him. They held Levi's limbs like extra hands, cloaked Levi like soft fabric, and coiled around Levi's cock tighter than the slide of Ashmedai's thrusts.

Levi's breath caught then, his body tensing, so very close to releasing, and in that moment, Ashmedai slipped his shadows *inside* Levi too.

"Ah!" Levi cried, followed by the same sag and delighted smile touching his face as had happened in the rain.

Renewed by the added heat from Levi between them, Ashmedai pumped harder, faster, and let his forehead drop to press to Levi's, until a great flickering of meandering dark and light, of shadow and sparks, tolled Ashmedai's end again too.

The shadow magic dissipated, and with it vanished the mess between them, as Ashmedai fell onto his side, not wanting to drop his full weight on Levi. He didn't want to stop touching him either and snuggled close against Levi's side.

"Leander...," Levi breathed quietly, his eyes falling closed.

"Flowers again?" Ashmedai asked, equally hushed.

"No... not oleander. My name. My name was Leander." Levi's eyes opened and seemed to flash with the echo of memory.

"You remember more?"

"So many things, like a puzzle struggling to form a picture. My mother. Our cat." Levi laughed. "My little brother...."

An entire family, Ashmedai thought, shifting to prop himself up on his hip. "The boy you saw?"

Levi nodded, looking at Ashmedai like he wasn't quite seeing him. "Emerald isn't the kingdom you remember. None of them are. I had to hide being a half-elf. So did my brother. Our mother is human. Our father... he left to find the elves, his people, and never came home. I had to hide other things. My magic. My... desires."

"Why?" Ashmedai asked, disturbed to hear such news when the kingdoms he recalled were far freer and never would have denied someone who or what they were.

"Something... would happen if I was found to love men, or have magic, or be part elf. I... I can't remember what, but I think I was sent away."

"And found your way here," Ashmedai said, seeking Levi's hand between them and lacing their fingers, "where Brax made you into something new."

Levi's smile was somber but didn't dissolve. "I'm not angry with him. I understand why he didn't tell me the truth. But I am not his. He may be my creator, but I want a life of my own. I had a life of my own, yet even in Emerald I lived with my mother, too afraid to be alone, or maybe for my brother's sake. Maybe both. Don't all children eventually leave home?"

Ashmedai looked away down the length of the bed. He supposed *he* had, but home wasn't something he could quantify anymore outside a millennium in the Shadow Lands.

"You were from Diamond, Klarent said."

Ashmedai's attention snapped back to Levi.

"He told me he was from Emerald," Levi continued, "and that you were new to Amethyst when the curse struck."

"Yes…," Ashmedai answered sluggishly. "I was passing through, visiting, and… I found reason to stay."

"The prince? Klarent said you were friends."

Even now, in bed with the most exquisite creature Ashmedai had ever known, the mention of Cullen wounded him like the sharp point of a blade.

"I'm sorry," Levi said, reading Ashmedai's emotions easily since they must be plain on his face. "His loss still hurts you deeply."

"It's… difficult for me to talk about," Ashmedai said.

Levi nodded again, and it was clear he had no intention of pressing for more, but although Ashmedai felt that familiar ache that had been carved into his heart since the moment Cullen was gone, he also owed Levi some of the truth.

"You remind me of him," he admitted, smiling when Levi's eyes flashed upward. "His eyes were violet too, and like you, he was sweet, soft-spoken, but fiercely loyal to the people here. He just wasn't certain of what he wanted out of life."

Levi cuddled closer against Ashmedai, as if to say he didn't mind the comparison. "If you don't like talking about him, what about your life before coming here?"

"That's even more difficult to discuss, I'm afraid."

"Did you leave home because you were unhappy?" Levi asked.

"More so lonely."

"You didn't have friends? Family?"

"Many had left home long before to explore other lands. Those that remained became reclusive. Hermits." Ashmedai huffed. "I was almost allowing myself to become that here. Until you," he finished with a renewed lessening of the weight in his chest, something only Levi had managed in hundreds of years.

"The people love you," Levi said. "I've never understood why you seem to think you don't deserve that devotion."

"I don't," Ashmedai said without falter. "There are still things you don't know, Levi, things I'm… not ready to share. I'm sorry." Again,

Ashmedai looked away toward the end of the bed. He felt a stir of guilt that they were lying here when *lying* remained a barrier between them.

"It's all right." Levi's gentle fingers touched Ashmedai's cheek and tilted his face back to him. "I can't imagine there is anything you could tell me that would change this feeling blossoming in my heart."

Ashmedai placed his hand over Levi's. He wished he could believe that.

He wanted to….

"If the curse is truly to be lifted soon," Ashmedai said, "and one day, I can walk with you in the sun," *and my penance is over*, he thought, "then perhaps I will tell you everything. Until then, know that there is nothing in this world that has ever felt as precious to me as you."

The joy in Levi's eyes made the violet color sparkle in a way Ashmedai had always hoped to have directed at him but never seen—until now.

Until Levi.

They leaned toward each other in tandem, lips connecting like practiced repetition, like reflex. The simple press and then push for more, with Levi's tongue being the first to seek a breach, was all Ashmedai had ever wanted.

THE SMILE remained on Levi's face, perpetually stretched and beaming, even as he entered the tower. The rain had stopped, and although Ashmedai had offered to walk Levi home, they'd only made it as far as the edge of the residential area before they were cornered by Dreya.

Levi fell back against the tower door. He wasn't even sure of the time. What he had shared with Ashmedai seemed to fill some great emptiness that had been inside him—as Levi and Leander, much as there were still many missing memories to reignite. He knew love between men wasn't accepted in Emerald, which seemed so strange, since here love between anyone was celebrated, and those who chose to remain alone were celebrated too.

For that reason, much as a part of Levi ached for what he'd lost—a mother, a brother, even a family cat—he couldn't imagine being anywhere but where he was as this version of him, fully realized into someone who would no longer be shunned or denied his true passions.

"Are those Ash's clothes?"

Levi gasped, eyes darting upward from where they had been distant during his musings. Braxton had appeared from his workshop and was already halfway toward Levi.

As Braxton wheeled closer, Levi knew he had to answer, for he had borrowed a pair of trousers, a shirt, and a doublet far more fanciful than his usual clothing, in Ashmedai's signature red and black.

"I-I… got wet from the storm and—"

"You don't need to lie to me, Levi."

The sharp dismissal made Levi snap his mouth shut with a click of his teeth. Much as he had become his own man, Braxton still had the power to make him feel small. "I did get wet. *We* did. We went back to Ash's castle."

Braxton stopped in front of Levi, his expression tight but unreadable as he eyed Levi from head to toe and finally settled on his face. "I assume fresh clothing wasn't your main priority."

Levi didn't know how to answer that.

"Don't look so fearful. Only a fool would not have seen this coming, the way you act around each other, how much time you've been spending in each other's company. You've brought him back to the world of the living." Braxton smiled, though it was a strange, malformed expression, like something else pretending to be a smile.

"You don't disapprove?" Levi asked.

"Ash has secluded himself for too long. He deserves someone who can be everything he ever wanted."

Braxton had never spoken of such things before, and Levi still wasn't certain how to react to it. He shifted on his feet. "Then why do you seem so angry?"

"Levi," Braxton said, gaze unblinking and words sharp with consonants, "I couldn't ask you to be anything other than what I made of you."

The air was as tight as Braxton's expression, almost impossible to breathe, until the moment Braxton's eyes shifted focus and he began to wheel away.

"I'm not taking any more draught," Levi called after him, unsure why he felt the urge to rebel just then. "I don't need it anymore."

Braxton answered without looking at him, "On that we can agree."

CHAPTER 8

THE ARROW released with an audible slice through the air. Levi's muscles ached from how many times he had already loosed one at Yentriss's instruction. At least this time he didn't miss the target. Its coloring from the outside in went black, blue, white, and finally red for the center circle.

Levi's arrow struck the outside of the blue.

"Better," Yentriss said, though her tone still sounded dissatisfied. Embracing Levi before and being thankful that he saved her husband in no way meant she was going easy on him.

They were in the backyard of Yentriss and Grillo's home. It was spacious but with each section efficiently utilized—some for farming, some for training like the archery target, and a smaller space clearly set aside for Kenner to play in.

As Leander, Levi had practiced the bow, but he had always been better with his daggers. He would hunt just outside the city, most of which was illegal poaching, but it was the only way to ensure his family had enough to eat, when they otherwise rarely left the house for fear of being caught for what they were.

It was memories for Levi now, not daydreams, for when something came back to him, he remained aware of his surroundings. He thought he remembered his mother—no, his father—trying to train him to better understand what he was doing wrong with the bow. He couldn't picture his father's face, but maybe because it had been so long since even Leander had seen him.

"Can we play yet, Mother?" Kenner called from the back stoop.

Yentriss had told him he couldn't come into the yard until she and Levi were finished, since he was likely to distract Levi—especially since he held their young rollhound puppy in his lap, who was also eager to play. The boy had been watching them with impressive patience for near an hour now.

"Just a moment," Yentriss called to him without looking back. "If Levi can hit the center, you can play with him all you like."

It was a challenge, but also motivation, because Levi was sore but determined, both to show Yentriss he could learn as he had never been able to show his father, and to spend time with the boy who had befriended him and reminded him of his brother.

"Take a moment to relax," Yentriss said before Levi could lift the bow again. "Loosen your muscles. Roll your shoulders. Breathe."

Levi did all of it, even closed his eyes as he took in several breaths. When he opened his eyes again, he could see Kenner in his periphery, literally bouncing on the stoop in anticipation while the rollhound licked his face. He was one of the youngest members of the kingdom, from one of the oldest couples, a pair who had been married before the curse.

It made Levi wonder.

"May I ask… what made you and Grillo wait so long to have Kenner? I know many couples have done the same, but you're both so natural and tender with him, it seems something you would have wanted sooner."

As Yentriss glanced at her son, Grillo came out the back door with a tray of mugs. He handed one to Kenner, sat beside him on the stoop to wait, and petted the rollhound's floppy ears. There was that secretive smile again that Levi saw so rarely on Yentriss's stern face.

"Who says we didn't?" she answered. "But want isn't the same as function. We literally couldn't have a child in the beginning. After that, given my station among the people, allowing others to grow their families first seemed the more honorable choice. After a time, I… started doubting I would be a fitting mother. Grillo fought a very long time to rid me of those fears.

"He said our love was so overflowing that spilling over into something new could never diminish it, and if I could love him so potently, I should never doubt I would be just as adept at loving a child." Her eyes, green and gold like her scales, shimmered as she looked back at Levi. "Don't get me wrong, parenting is not easy, but with patience and practice, like anything else, as long as you want to succeed, you can find a way."

She faced Levi squarely, putting her family at her back, and was once again a coolly collected soldier. "Now, what do you think the problem is?"

For years Leander hadn't known the answer, because his father left before he could finish teaching him, and though he'd known the basics, he could never figure out what he was doing wrong.

Without picking up a new arrow, Levi reset his stance and mimicked loosing one once more, watchful of his posture and hold on the bow. When he released the string, he tilted slightly to the left.

"I'm not keeping the bow vertical."

"Very good. So, fix it."

Easier said than done, but even if Levi failed this attempt, he knew he could try again. He nocked another arrow, steadied his breathing and his aim, and focused the brunt of his efforts on not tilting the bow when he released.

The arrow arched from him with that same audible slice, and this time, while not perfectly center, it struck just inside the red.

"You did it!" Kenner cried, proclaiming Levi's jubilant satisfaction before it fully registered.

Levi turned with a wide smile, watching a twitch of that same satisfaction on Yentriss and rich excitement from both Kenner and Grillo, who left the stoop to join them. Kenner practically flew across the yard with the rollhound bounding after him, while Grillo, carrying the tray of drinks, moved more slowly.

Kenner threw his arms around Levi's legs with the usual enthusiasm, and when he next hugged his mother, praising her for being such a good teacher, Yentriss ruffled his hair with affection only so many got to see.

"Well done!" Grillo added as he reached them, looking first to Levi and then to his wife, whom he leaned toward to give a congratulatory kiss. The rollhound darted all around their feet, leaping and occasionally tightening into an armadillo-like ball, unsure of why everyone was so happy but uncaringly blissful to be part of it.

Witnessing it all brought forth an equal sting of yearning and a pleasant warmth. Levi missed his family, and he knew he always would, but he was comforted in knowing he had another one here with many new friends.

And a flourishing love all his own.

IN TRUTH, it was rare for Ashmedai to walk from the castle to wherever he needed to go. There were enough familiar, constant shadows in the

Dark Kingdom that he could simply jump from one to the next, avoiding his citizens whenever he wasn't in the mood to offer a mustered smile or chat about the mundane.

He felt guilty for thinking of time with his people like that—like a chore—but whereas they had all grown accustomed to this life and thrived over the centuries, the passing years had made Ashmedai more ashamed of what had brought it about.

This was the first morning in so very long that he wanted to walk.

He had gotten into the habit of walking Levi home, but yesterday had been the first time when Ashmedai began to do so starting from the castle steps. They hadn't made it far before Dreya appeared as though she was the one with shadow magic and whisked Ashmedai away, but at the start of the walk, Ashmedai had seen his kingdom with clearer eyes, and he wanted that feeling again.

The lack of companionship, since Ashmedai began his trek alone, lessened the experience, but not so much that he wanted to turn around or leap into the nearest pool of darkness. He was thankful for his quick thinking in asking Dreya yesterday if they could skip today's morning meeting.

The residential area had rows upon rows of buildings, some apartments with homes stacked atop one another, others simple houses with yards for play and gardening, or even a few larger yards for farming. One boon the curse had granted them was that every inch of the soil could bear fruit.

It was midmorning, and the streets were bustling with activity. Neighbors chatted, people left their homes headed for the market, many worked on extensions or repairs for their homes, or were out in their gardens. If the people hadn't been monsters, the homes all at odd angles as if no right angle could exist in the Dark Kingdom, and the plants effervescent with colors that glowed, the scene might have been like any happy kingdom.

Ashmedai wondered, waving and smiling at his people as he moved through them, if the other kings and queens of today walked among their citizens as he did. He supposed not, given what Levi had said, that the other Gemstone Kingdoms were very different from how they'd been a thousand years ago. That gave Ashmedai some trepidation over how they would be received once the barrier fell and they were free, but he couldn't let the decisions of other kingdoms sway what his own people needed.

"My king!" a female voice said in surprise.

Ashmedai was passing a quaint farmhouse about midway through the residences. Shevah had just come outside, carrying her babe on her hip.

Since Shevah was first-generation born into the curse, her mixed parentage had resulted in a top half like a Gorgon and a bottom half like a spider. Her wife was also first-generation, from a centaur and a sphinx, and had ended up with her top half quite human looking, and her bottom half like a lion.

Therefore, the babe was a beautiful hodgepodge—with sleek fur like a lion, spider legs, the buds of snakes forming for her hair, and despite the fur on her face, a very human visage.

"Why, Shevah," Ashmedai said with a reverent bow at the babe, "she's growing quite magnificently, isn't she? Forgive me, I'm a terrible king, but I believe I've forgotten her name."

Shevah laughed, her white eyes darting downward at the attention toward her child. "It's quite all right. You've been very busy. This is Eris. She's three months now. The drawback of her getting mummy's legs, though, is she's already capable of skittering across the floor. Would you like to hold her?"

Ashmedai had recently blessed the births of many of his people's coming children, but he hadn't held Eris yet, not even when she was first born. He hadn't held a babe since Kenner, and even then, only briefly.

"I would be honored," he said and took the offered child.

Eris's spider legs tickled as they kicked at the exchange, not because she wanted to escape, but simply getting used to the feeling of moving them. Ashmedai had no trouble holding her securely, and once he had her safe in his arms, he marveled at the way she marveled at him. Shevah had no irises, but the babe did, bright blue, though the whites of her eyes glowed like her mother's, making her young gaze quite entrancing.

She had never known "normal." Neither had Shevah or her wife. They had only known being monsters in a monstrous land, cursed with forever night, yet they would never see their existence as a curse, other than the threat of the barrier and memories of the demon. To them, to Eris, humans, elves, and dwarves were the strange ones.

"Are you all right, Ash?" Shevah asked.

Ashmedai looked up, realizing he'd gotten misty-eyed gazing at the babe. "Yes. Apologies. Your daughter reminded me how blessed we are with what we've been given." He always used his claws with care, but he was especially careful to only run the back of his fingers along the babe's sweet face.

She cooed at him, staring at the fangs in his smile like she might reach for one and latch on, finding them fascinating instead of frightening—like Levi.

Ashmedai passed the babe back to Shevah and thanked her for the chance to hold Eris. Shevah wished him well and continued through town. A great weight seemed to have been lifted, more in the act of holding that child and not shying from his own people than even lying with Levi. Ashmedai knew, however, that his change in perspective was *because* of Levi.

Levi made his penance feel more like deliverance.

Bright giggling caught Ashmedai's attention from the neighboring house—Grillo and Yentriss's house. It was also a farmhouse, for when Grillo wasn't busy with carpentry, he grew vegetables.

It was Kenner giggling, no doubt, but Ashmedai smiled wider as he moved around the house, for the boyish giggling was not only accompanied by Grillo's voice but by Levi's.

"Keep left!" Grillo called cheerfully over the laughter. "Mind the moss-berry fruit!"

Ashmedai rounded the corner, bearing witness to a chase. Levi had summoned the vision of a serpentine dragon about the size of a hawk that was flying after Kenner without need for wings.

Levi gave chase too, as did the family's rollhound puppy, but Levi kept his dragon closest at Kenner's heels, until he suddenly thrust the dragon that much faster ahead to move through Kenner, whose steps stuttered in surprise when it appeared in front of him.

Levi scooped the boy up while he was distracted and spun a still-giggling Kenner in a circle before depositing him on the ground. The rollhound yipped excitedly, formed into a ball, and proceeded to roll right into their feet, where it toppled out of its ball form onto its back. They laughed again.

Ashmedai could easily imagine how Levi must have played this way with a brother.

"Ash!" Grillo called. The minotaur sat on the back stoop, looking weary but far better than he had while staying at Luccite's. His lizard arm moved as naturally as his original one as he used it to push himself up to his feet.

Levi and Kenner turned to see Ashmedai as well, and Kenner gave a joyful wave while Levi smiled, not displaying nearly as much of the bashfulness that used to infuse his every expression.

"Yen went to the festival grounds, if you're looking for her," Grillo said, though his grin said he didn't truly think that's who Ashmedai was after.

"Merely out for a walk," Ashmedai said, continuing leisurely into the yard, "and pleased by the company I've found. Are you well, Grillo? You look it."

"Another day's rest needed, is all, and I'll be back to work."

"Are you missing stitches?" Kenner drew Ashmedai's attention to where the boy was looking at Levi, as if only just having noticed the changes in Levi's face.

"I suppose I am," Levi said. "Ash has been helping me get rid of them."

"Rid of them?" Kenner wrinkled his nose. The dragon had been dismissed, which had the rollhound sniffing about in search of it, but Kenner was focused on Levi. He reached up to grab Levi's collar and tugged him down to his level. "Why? Don't you like how you are?"

Levi floundered, glancing at Grillo, and then at Ashmedai, before returning to the boy. "It's not that exactly, but…."

"But," Ashmedai broke in, finishing his forward motion to reach Levi and Kenner, "sometimes we need to have the freedom to change the things about ourselves that don't quite feel like us. Do you understand?"

Kenner released Levi but kept his scrunched brow. Then his eyes brightened. "I'd want wings like Penny! Do you think her baby will have wings?"

"Perhaps," Ashmedai said with a chuckle. "We'll have to wait and see, won't we?"

Levi came toward Ashmedai and there was a moment of uncertainty, filled with fluttering nerves, like neither knew what should happen next. The shrinking space between them seemed to say that a proper greeting was called for, and by the time Levi reached Ashmedai, the answer was clear.

They kissed, the same as in Ashmedai's bed, light and sweet, though with a lean inward like the promise of everything they longed to share again.

"Are you looking forward to the festival, Levi?" Grillo asked as he came nearer, not commenting on what he'd witnessed but likely not surprised. "You can help me finish those stalls tomorrow. Then the event is just around the corner."

Levi smiled, echoing all of Ashmedai's recent joys in the expression. Their hands found each other as reflexively as their lips, lacing tight with neither having to glance down, as Levi answered, "I can't wait."

LEVI STARED at himself in the mirror, wearing the violet-colored tunic made from Emerald silk. He had tried it on numerous times since being gifted it from Daedlys, but ever since the king learned of its existence and asked if he might see it at the festival, Levi had wanted to save it for just this occasion.

The silver threads that edged the bottom, long sleeves, and oversized hood all seemed to sparkle in the light. The draping of the uneven hem, like a skirt but too short to be worn modestly without trousers, gave the garment a formal appearance, ideal for a special occasion.

Levi had originally claimed a basic leather belt to accompany the tunic, but he thought his weapons belt, black with silver, along with the black and silver daggers, completed the outfit in a more elegant manner. He wore a black shirt beneath, black trousers, and black boots. With his wavy red hair as neatly styled as he could manage, and although stray curls tended to fall into his eyes, he thought he looked almost....

Like a prince.

Levi knew that if he looked out his window, he would see the lights of the festival glistening, even this early, turning what had simply been structures the night before into the dazzling carnival they were intended to create.

He made a point to not look. Levi was excited, but he and Ashmedai had promised to attend the festival together, and he didn't want to experience any of it without his king.

Instead, Levi's eyes fell to the music box he had placed on his windowsill. He had played it often lately, remembering more and more of the melody's words each time. The stamp on the bottom of the painted green, blue, and white wooden box with its rearing horse inside said Jafari's.

Levi remembered the shop. He remembered wanting to purchase one of the boxes for his brother when they were first on the shelves, but his family had very little to spend on frivolities. He'd been saving for one of the boxes nonetheless, from odd jobs, while still looking for where he might apprentice, even at his older age. He should have completed an apprenticeship by now, though he couldn't quite remember by how many years. His mother had been too nervous to let him work much outside the home for fear of him getting caught.

He had been caught anyway, for... his magic, he thought? He couldn't quite remember that either, but every day another memory surfaced, though there was no way to know how much time had passed between then and now.

Levi lifted the lid of the music box, and it began to play its tinkling melody, the chorus of a folktale, *The Ride-Along Bard*.

> *"For no bard is humble,*
> *And no hero's flawless.*
> *All that matters is the stories we tell."*

Levi thought it might have been one of his favorites, but it certainly was now since the box had been a gift from Ashmedai.

Upon descending the tower steps, Levi found the main living area empty. There was no draught left out for him and no sign of Braxton, other than the faintest of dark purple light pulsing from beneath the workshop door. For once, Levi felt no draw toward it, but at risk of being pulled in against his conscious mind, he turned away.

Soon he'd leave this place as his home and go... well, he knew where he wanted his next home to be, though he felt foolish for assuming he would be granted the honor of living in the castle after only one visit. The days since then had been filled with responsibilities keeping Levi and Ashmedai busy, though they had stolen a moment or two—a kiss or mildly heated embrace—but the chance to truly be together again hadn't yet come.

Wherever Levi ended up next, he knew he would be happy so long as he could still call Ashmedai his.

He reached the front door and, against his better judgment, looked back. The pulses from the workshop had stopped, at least for now. Levi didn't know why, but he felt like he had wounded Braxton somehow, despite not yet telling him he wanted to leave. For that, for leaving Braxton, he was sorry. Braxton had lied to him, but he was still Levi's creator. His father.

That meant something to Leander too.

"Braxton," Levi called. "Daedlys asked me to stop by his shop this morning. After whatever he needs of me, I plan to stay at the festival for the remainder of the day. Do you need anything?"

For the first several moments, Levi assumed no answer would come, but then, very faintly, a single word came in reply.

"No."

"Goodbye then," Levi said, and when this time there was no answer even after several beats, he left.

In no time, Levi could see the lights of the festival making the distant city sparkle like never before. Levi did his best to not look too closely at any of the spectacle just yet, and hurried from the path down the market steps.

The festival spilled into the market, especially with decoration on existing stalls, mentioning Festival Day specials and food or wares that had been saved for just this occasion. Still, Levi tried to not look at any of it and headed straight for Daedlys's shop.

"Daedlys!" he called as he entered. He couldn't avoid the splendor of Festival Day once inside. Daedlys had decorated the shop in an assortment of violet crystals like firefly lights, and various swaths of sheer and glittering violet fabrics.

Only then did Levi realize that most of the lights he'd seen from the festival grounds, even if only briefly, had also been violet, in honor of the Source Crystal that was the heart of the curse. He'd nearly forgotten that today was a day for celebrating that color, and by wearing his new tunic, Levi had inadvertently dressed exactly as he should.

"Stitches!" Daedlys appeared, floating in from the back. His robe was black like usual, but even he sported a few trimmings in violet today. "I'm so happy you could help me before heading out to enjoy the festival. I have a very important errand for you."

"'Tis my honor. I'm sure you and Klarent are both very busy preparing."

"Indeed. I have much to set up out front yet, and my door will be open all day and night. Plus, my poor frazzled husband is already at his stall, practicing, though it's hours until you two perform. I told him all that stress can't possibly be good for the baby."

Levi smiled at the mention. He had discussed the pregnancy with Klarent and Daedlys many times since first learning of it, but to his knowledge, they hadn't yet shared the news with many others. "You reminded me, but I haven't had the chance to ask. Klarent told me a little of who he was before the curse. May I ask the same of you?"

Even for a banshee, Daedlys never looked haunting to Levi. He was cheerful and full of vigor, yet for once his countenance wavered, which was the opposite of Levi's intention. "I… was who you see before you—a thriving shop owner. Just with a little more punch." He tapped Levi's chest with a fist which, like usual whenever he made contact, was different from the sensation of touching something solid, like a ripple of cool water bowing against Levi.

Levi was hesitant to ask more, but his curiosity won out. "You don't have family here, though, do you? Besides Klarent."

"That's because, originally… I was from Diamond."

"You were?" Levi asked more excitedly. "You're an elf? Did you know Ash?"

"Oh no, I came here years earlier, and Diamond is a large kingdom. Honestly, I was almost planning to move back home before the curse. I'd heard they had a new ruler who was bringing more peace and prosperity than ever before. There were rumors that she made anyone who lived on her lands immortal. No one could die from old age or illness anymore. It was a tempting prospect, not only for my own sake, but…." Daedlys drifted off, his black eyes looking deeper than ever.

Levi didn't prompt further but waited to see if Daedlys would offer more on his own.

"To be honest, the years before the curse weren't the best for me. I was lonely, successful though I may have been. I came to Amethyst… after my wife died in childbirth."

Levi didn't mean to gasp.

Daedlys smiled somberly. "I think that's the real reason Klarent was so hesitant to tell me when he became pregnant. It had taken so long for me to be ready again, and then we went and decided to wait. Fate often has other plans."

"Yentriss told me something similar," Levi said, "that she waited so long to have Kenner because she was afraid she wasn't ready. But is anyone ever ready for what life brings them?"

"Not in my experience." Daedlys chuckled. "I never got the chance to go home, but then the curse came, and I was stuck, while also getting exactly what I'd wanted. No one here gets sick or grows old. And then, well...." His smile returned with a more genuine bend.

"Klarent," Levi said knowingly.

"I'd given up on finding love again, and then a stranger laughed at my jokes and wriggled those tentacles my way and everything felt new. Tragedy is common for everyone from time to time, dear Stitches, but I like to believe we all end up exactly where we are meant to be. And hmm... it seems I may need to come up with a new nickname for you." Daedlys's hand, which had dropped from the tap on Levi's chest, returned to brush that same cool sensation across his cheek, where stitches had been but were no longer.

Levi felt a blush heat the skin beneath Daedlys's caress.

"On that note...." Daedlys moved toward the front counter and waved a hand to cause a medium-sized ebony box wrapped in red ribbon to float up from behind it. "The reason I asked for you for this errand isn't merely because Klarent and I are busy. Only you can deliver this particular package." He lowered the box into Levi's hands. "It is to be brought to the castle straightaway."

"For Ash?" Levi asked.

"Unless someone else has been living there." Daedlys winked. "Make sure he opens it as soon as it's in his hands. Very time sensitive. Go on now. I'm sure I'll see you later."

Words failed Levi other than to offer a harried thanks, and he rushed from the shop, eager to see Ashmedai and know what the gift contained.

Still, to reach the castle Levi not only needed to traverse back up the market steps but *through* the rest of the festival. It would be impossible to not look at anything, but he tried regardless, keeping his eyes squinted and moving swiftly.

"Are you trying to injure yourself?" Yentriss's firm voice scolded just as a hand clamped down on Levi's shoulder.

His eyes popped wide of their own accord, and he realized he had been about to plow headlong into a post not quite as brightly decorated with crystals as others and therefore almost invisible with his eyes half-shut. "N-no, I... I'm sorry." Levi turned to her, still trying to keep his head bowed and his eyes not focused on anything. "I just don't want to see the festival until I'm with Ash. I know it's silly, but—"

"Plowing forward without looking where you're going is not the answer. Hold still," she commanded, and Levi looked up at her with another start as she placed both scaled hands on either side of his face. A warmth spread from where her fingers touched, and when she lowered her hands again, the lights around Levi seemed dimmer.

He looked about in surprise. The grounds looked like they had yesterday, with more people about and just as many stalls, but no decoration or added lights.

"You can conjure illusions," Yentriss said simply. "I enchant the mind. I don't do it often, mind you, but you'll see what you want to until after you've reached the castle. It'll wear off then, so don't look down the road again until you're ready. Understood?"

Levi spun back to grin at her with boundless gratitude. "This is brilliant! Thank you so much!"

Yentriss shrugged. "Useful for when Kenner has nightmares. And Grillo," she added with a grin of her own. "Now go."

No longer needing to rush blindly but still eager to reach Ashmedai, Levi continued toward the black multispired fortress that evoked almost the same wonder and sense of magic as its inhabitant.

One lone toll of the bell was all it took before the doors opened.

Levi's breath caught, not only because Ashmedai looked as beautiful as ever in his usual black and red brocade, but because of how his eyes shimmered and his mouth dropped open with a shudder, his chest heaving—purely from the sight of Levi.

The silk violet-colored tunic had clearly been the right choice.

"Special delivery," Levi said.

ASHMEDAI STARED at himself in his floor-length washroom mirror. "Oh Daedlys, you old busybody," he muttered, taking in each line of the elegant draping and fine stitchwork. "I'll have to think of a proper way to thank you."

The new tunic, made from *red* Emerald silk, matched Levi's violet one perfectly, though Levi's silver trim had likewise been replaced with gold from glittering lace ribbon.

It wasn't Ashmedai's normal style, since he tended toward high-collared garments that covered his ridges. This tunic dropped into a deeper V, where ties held it closed. With the black undershirt and trousers Ashmedai had already been wearing, the matching attire to Levi's would leave no imagination anymore as to their relationship should anyone not yet have guessed.

Ashmedai didn't mind, and before leaving his bedchamber, while he hadn't intended to don his sword belt today, given how well it would also match Levi, he secured it with his longsword about his waist.

"Shall we?" Ashmedai called as he descended the central staircase to the foyer, where Levi was waiting by the doors and spun toward him.

Ashmedai would swear he heard Levi gasp.

Then Ashmedai nearly gasped, because Aurora was there, and Levi was holding a small squishy red ball.

"Where did you get that?"

The wonder and adoration on Levi's face fell to amusement. "Oh, Aurora brought it for me. We've been playing fetch. There's more around here somewhere. It seems she has quite the collection. She keeps bringing me more. Is… that all right?"

Ashmedai's expression must have been utterly dumbfounded, but he eased Levi's trepidation by laughing. "Quite all right. Just don't ever tell Dreya. You little rascal," he added to Aurora, scratching the top of her head. Since she wasn't fully solid, she adored his clawlike nails and pushed up into the firm scritches. "So?" Ashmedai spread his arms, facing Levi. "I think Daedlys outdid himself. What say you?"

"You are breathtaking, my king." Levi reached for Ashmedai's hand, and Ashmedai marveled at the grand gesture when Levi kissed it like a true courtier. "To call you beautiful is never a strong enough word."

"You know you needn't ever call me your king," Ashmedai reminded him.

"I know. But I would call you mine," Levi said with his sweet smile.

The scene was far too much like a fairy tale to be marred by all the painful memories of this day swirling in the back of Ashmedai's mind, so he kept those thoughts quiet. "That you can," he said and leaned forward to kiss Levi properly.

"Prrp!"

Aurora's chirp was heard so near their heads that they lurched apart, only to both begin laughing. She darted between them, prancing through the air.

"I believe Rora approves of our attire as well," Ashmedai said and took Levi's arm, "or she's upset she's losing her playmate for the day. Shall we?"

Together, they began the short trek into town. The festival lights were always a joy to witness, still made up of crystals, like most lighting in the Dark Kingdom, but smaller ones and so many more of them, all strung together and covering every square inch of the stalls and larger buildings. Ashmedai had seen it all many times before, but he had been looking forward to watching the experience unfold across Levi's face.

Levi looked entirely entranced as they drew closer, but then Ashmedai had to wonder.

"You already saw most of it, didn't you? On your way to the castle?"

"I tried not to look too closely, and then Yentriss was kind enough to enchant me to see it as it was before," Levi said without tearing his eyes from the sight. "I wanted to experience this for the first time with you."

Ashmedai held onto Levi's arm a little tighter, since he feared his companion might trip, focused as he was on everything *but* the path they walked.

Most of the buildings, whether residential or businesses, had the Shadow Lands shimmer sanded from their wood, like the carriages to Emerald, but not for the festival. All the added stalls and new construction sparkled, accentuating the vibrancy of the lights. The only unique item was the addition of Braxton's black dousing crystals littered amongst the rest.

Moreover, sounds that had seemed muted and distant from even only a few paces away were suddenly amplified the moment Ashmedai and Levi crossed onto the grounds—a spell to ensure that anyone who eventually returned home to sleep wouldn't be kept awake at all hours.

Levi must not have noticed before, or honestly hadn't heard the difference after Yentriss enchanted him, for as the new noises erupted he clung to Ashmedai in surprise at how loud it suddenly was.

"Chicken skewers!" a vendor cried.

Items had a cost during Festival Day, but food and activities were free from bartering. Ashmedai nodded to the vendor and snagged two skewers, handing one to Levi, who marveled at it with the same level of fascination as he was everything else.

The hunt had provided a good amount of the food being consumed today, and plenty more had been saved and prepared to keep everyone's bellies full of unique fare.

"Go on," Ashmedai said when Levi continued to stare at his skewer.

"Did he say chicken?"

"Yes. There's a live one back there." Ashmedai pointed behind the stall, where one—no, three live chickens, actually—attempted to fly away in fear of being the next offering, but tethers around their necks prevented them from getting far.

They didn't used to have the ability to fly, Ashmedai recalled, though they also didn't used to have scales.

"Aren't *chickens* what they were called before and outside the Shadow Lands? Why didn't their name change like so many others?"

Ashmedai shrugged, taking an easy, tearing bite with his teeth. "They still taste the same."

"Ash! Levi!" A familiar voice found them just as Levi took his own eager bite, and through the crowd appeared Dreya.

A somewhat *tipsy* Dreya, Ashmedai thought, given she was without her customary hat and the leaves of her hair looked especially ruffled, as if a storm had blown through and she was the lone casualty.

Dreya latched on to Levi's arm while he was attempting to finish his bite, causing him to end up with a rather large mouthful of chicken.

"Best day of the year!" Dreya tittered, dragging Levi forward so that Ashmedai couldn't quite latch back on to his arm. "Months of hard work finally pays off, and we can enjoy ourselves. I hope the festival meets all your expectations, Levi. You're one of the reasons these stalls are standing, after all."

"Oh, Grillo did the difficult work," Levi dismissed with a duck of his head. "I merely handed him planks of wood and the right tools as needed."

"Pfft," Dreya huffed her own dismissal. "Every contribution, no matter how small it may seem, leads to the glorious celebration you see before you. Enjoy it! And accept your praises. You're practically a celebrity now." The scrunch of her face with a conspiratorial glance at Ashmedai—though that may have still been the drink shining through—

made him wonder if she meant Levi's celebrity as savior of Grillo or romantic gossip.

Dreya tripped just then, as a performer pranced past them, kept on her feet only by Levi's quick reflexes. Various entertainers were about, leaving only a narrow walking path. Ashmedai could tell Levi was surprised by some of them.

Myrra, for example, being large and made of stone, was a striking figure to be playing a lyre, though Jedic, a Gegenees with six arms, made perfect sense as a juggler.

"Urg." Dreya swooned slightly. "I've been conjuring last-minute requests all morning. I need a snack." She eyed Levi's half-eaten skewer.

Ashmedai plucked a popover from another passing vendor and handed it to Dreya before she could divest Levi of his first festival fare. She bit into it ravenously. She must have celebrated her hard work with more drinks than food, though he did recall that using up too much of her magic at once made her more susceptible to inebriation. Either way, she'd earned it.

The first opening of the festival grounds after the initial corridor of vendors and performers was an area for dancing, with a band playing off to the side. On the other side of the dance floor, Ashmedai spotted Luccite.

He caught Levi's eye and nodded toward the catlike woman, who hadn't noticed them but was watching the dancers with what Ashmedai took for longing, hopping on both feet to get a better look whenever someone taller shifted in front of her. Dreya hadn't released Levi yet, and they did owe these women some friendly scheming.

"Miss Dreya." Levi turned to her, having finished his skewer and not missing a beat of what Ashmedai had in mind. "Would you care to dance?"

Dreya had likewise devoured her popover and answered teasingly, "Won't the king be jealous?"

"I'll steal him away in time," Ashmedai said, nudging them out onto the floor.

The dance was a lively one, with several pairs rocking and spinning and twirling each other about in well-known choreography. Ashmedai was surprised, however, when Levi expertly led Dreya through the same steps, holding her close to prevent her tipsiness from causing any jumble of feet.

With a widening grin, Ashmedai ducked behind a stall and jumped from the shadow there to one behind another stall across the way. He snuck up behind Luccite in two short strides.

"Would you grant your king a dance?"

Luccite spun with what might have been a startled hiss. "*Ash.* Where…?" Her slitted eyes narrowed at him in suspicion.

"Come now." Ashmedai held out his hand. "It seems all you're missing is a partner."

Luccite's lips curled, but rather than argue, she took his hand and allowed him to pull her onto the dance floor, grasp her waist, and lead them into the same rhythmic spins and timed weaving to the music.

By now enough of the citizens had recognized their king had joined them and were spurred to join the dancers as well, always quick to follow his example. Hermit though Ashmedai had been of late, he never missed Festival Day, for he knew how much it meant to his people.

Luccite was a bit stiff and difficult to lead, despite the natural grace afforded her by being a cat—though she was also a good head or two shorter than him—but it wasn't long before her distrustful smile turned to something genuine. The song hit a bridge where all the instruments dropped off save the ones keeping rhythm, a signal for a very specific set of movements that involved one partner lifting and spinning the other through the air.

Ashmedai did so with Luccite easily, and she erupted with a rare giggle. The rhythmic beat continued for a second lift and spin that Ashmedai knew would culminate in final uproarious percussion that ended the song, and he eyed their surroundings, spotting Levi and Dreya and catching Levi's eye again to ensure they both spun their partner in just the right direction.

He lifted Luccite, and after their twirl and subsequently setting her down, she and Dreya were back-to-back as the song ended to wild applause.

"Dreya, I believe it's time I stole your partner." Ashmedai turned a stunned Luccite just as Levi did the same with Dreya, and they pushed the women toward each other. "You can take mine."

As Ashmedai anticipated, the musicians didn't pause before continuing into a softer ballad to allow the dancers a break. He pulled Levi to him and quickly spun them away before any dissention could be spoken.

Ashmedai naturally started to lead, and Levi's footing didn't stutter as he shifted roles to follow. They watched Dreya and Luccite fumble with overlapping words at first before Dreya, her tipsiness proving useful when it came to squashing nerves, seized Luccite by the waist and let the music take them.

"Do you think it'll be enough?" Levi asked, gazing at them fondly.

"If we see them straying, we'll just have to intervene again."

When Levi turned to look at Ashmedai, it seemed to only dawn on him then that they were dancing, close and slow to the gentler song. There were still steps to follow and mild spins, but this type of dancing reminded Ashmedai of the calm tide of the Black Lake.

During the song, Levi rested his head on Ashmedai's shoulder, and it was easy to imagine that, although they were surrounded by other couples, the dance floor was theirs alone.

"What else would you like to see, my darling?" Ashmedai asked.

"Everything," Levi said.

Beyond the dancing was a row of stalls for games such as archery, ring toss, and Hoodman's Blind. At the bottom of the market steps was a larger open area for Prisoner's Base, where two teams were equally set on stealing the other's flag, positioned at opposite ends, and if someone from one team touched someone from another, that person became a prisoner in need of rescue. The flag was the prize, but another way to win was to imprison everyone from the opposing team.

Ashmedai and Levi played each game above the market at least once, but when they made it down the steps, Prisoner's Base was in midsession. The red team was almost entirely captured, but the guard they had set up at their flag was Grillo, who stood his ground.

"*Ash*," Levi hissed, grasping Ashmedai's arm.

He looked where Levi indicated and saw what the blue team had yet to notice. Kenner, on the red team with his father, had snuck onto the other side of the field and snatched up the blue flag.

"The boy has it!" someone cried, and all the blue members spun to give chase.

Kenner bolted for his side of the field, far too small and nimble for anyone to catch him. He made it across the line with a narrow miss of a hand trying to slap his shoulder, but his feet were too quick.

"I did it!" Kenner dropped the flag and threw up his arms in triumph.

Grillo raced toward him, happily scooping up his child and setting him on his shoulder for the other members of their team to applaud. Kenner looked overjoyed, especially since he'd outdone a team of adults.

Ashmedai smiled to think that next year there would be a multitude of new babes, and in the years to come Kenner would have many playmates closer to his age.

Ashmedai was going to ask Levi if he wanted to join the next game, but when he looked, Levi had wandered toward the subsequent row of stalls bearing wares from various vendors, including Daedlys in front of his shop, and Gordoc, who had set up a stall directly beside Daedlys. The rivalry never ended with those two, since they sold similar items, each displaying garments of Emerald silk as well as an assortment of jewelry and accessories.

"There's my Stitches!" Daedlys declared.

But Levi's eye had caught a silver ear cuff with an amethyst stone on Gordoc's stall. Ashmedai could imagine its elegant coiling design looking quite fetching adorning the curves of one of Levi's half-elf ears.

Levi looked cornered, however, when he realized the cuff was not part of his friend's wares.

"What trade would you ask for this, Gordoc?" Ashmedai breezed past Levi and plucked the cuff from the stall.

"For you, my king?" Gordoc's fish lips puckered and then spread into a smile. "No trade at all. It's Festival Day! *Your* day. I can allow our protector to claim one item with my compliments. You too, Levi. I wouldn't have a stall at all if not for you and Grillo, and I do have the *best* items in the kingdom."

"Pfft." Daedlys crossed his arms. "That's subjective, but I suppose the cuff isn't hideous. If anything catches your fancy here, sweet Stitches, you can accept it as my personal gift."

Levi looked over the assorted items once more. He seemed to understand that Ashmedai had chosen the cuff as a gift for *him*, because what caught his eye on Daedlys's stall was a simple but equally elegant gold circlet with a ruby at its center.

"I know you've never worn a crown," Levi said to Ashmedai as he picked it up, "but I think this would look quite lovely on you, Ash, if you like it."

For Levi, Ashmedai would adorn himself in anything. "It's perfect. And we'll be certain to let anyone who asks know we found these items at the *two* best stalls in the market," Ashmedai added to appease the competing vendors.

First he secured the cuff on Levi's right ear, and then Levi placed the circlet atop Ashmedai's brow, where the drop of the ruby rested comfortably on his forehead.

"I'll admit," Daedlys said with a wink, "looks like the perfect *match*."

Ashmedai tugged a corner of his tunic and said, "Thank you."

It was only then Gordoc seemed to recognize what Ashmedai's outfit was made from, and he crossed his arms to mirror Daedlys. "You're getting the next round of drinks, banshee."

Daedlys laughed. "Deal."

They took their time after that exploring other stalls, trying other foods, even tried a few ales, meads, and wines, though in moderation since Levi had a performance later. Eventually they returned to Prisoner's Base to play a round.

Hours passed like minutes, and still so much more of the festival was left to be enjoyed.

"Is that the time?" Levi glanced at a candle clock on the wall of one of the stalls. "We better hurry. I can't be late for Klarent's opening act." He grasped Ashmedai's hand and began to speed them back up the market steps.

Klarent's stage was at the end of the row of smaller gaming booths but twice the size of normal stalls, even sporting a violet-colored curtain as the backdrop.

"You're assisting Klarent, is that right?" Ashmedai asked, keeping hold of Levi's hand even after they reached the stage and could see Klarent behind it, mostly hidden by the structure, muttering to himself in practice.

"It was all his idea," Levi said, "but I hope you like it."

"Give Klarent my best. I'll be watching from right up front."

Levi squeezed Ashmedai's hand, and before letting go he leaned in to gently kiss Ashmedai's lips.

The light, contented feeling in Ashmedai's chest persisted as he moved in front of the stage as promised, where a small crowd was gathering.

"Aren't you the fetching pair?"

Ashmedai turned, amazed to see Braxton wheeling toward him. If Braxton had seen Levi, then he'd also seen them kiss, which shouldn't have made Ashmedai feel a flutter of guilt, yet there it was.

"All Daedlys's doing," Ashmedai said, indicating his tunic.

"I'm sure."

Ashmedai moved to stand beside Braxton, still with a clear view of the stage. "I don't remember the last time you attended Festival Day. It is good to see you here, old friend."

"And you… old friend. It felt a worthy night to celebrate." Braxton motioned for Ashmedai to lean toward him and whispered, "I've done it."

"You're finished?" Ashmedai asked in his own fervid whisper. "You can…."

"Very soon. Only one small component remains, and then it will be time." Braxton leaned away, bringing his voice back up to normal volume. "Perhaps then you will spare me a walk by the Black Lake, if I am so lucky." He tapped his chair. "Maybe even in the daylight."

"Attention!" Klarent's voice drew Ashmedai back to the stage. "Please, join me for the inauguration of a brand-new celebration of creative talents, beginning with a reading from my newest historical account, and accompanied by young Levi's masterful illusions."

Applause sprang up as Klarent took center stage with a low bow and Levi gave a smaller bow from his position in the corner. The crowd quickly grew from a small gathering to a bustle of bodies, and Ashmedai shifted to make room.

Braxton was no longer beside him.

Before Ashmedai could look for where Braxton had gone, Daedlys took up the empty space.

"I truly am a miracle worker," he said with a perusing glance down Ashmedai's body.

"Indeed you are." Ashmedai chuckled. "Thank you again, friend."

"My pleasure." Daedlys floated closer so that his head bobbed nearer to Ashmedai's. "Aren't you going to congratulate me?"

"Oh? On what?"

"On how you and our sweet Stitches are soon to be godfathers." He gestured up at Klarent, and Ashmedai turned to gape in wonder, for the implication was clear.

Another babe.

While the news might have added to the weight that for so long had sat in the pit of Ashmedai's stomach, knowing now for certain that the curse would soon be behind them, all he felt was joy.

Then the performance began.

"CENTURIES PAST *when a different world reigned*," Klarent started in a loud bellow that caused everyone gathered to silence—the signal for Levi to begin as well, "*and denizens of Amethyst knew many mortal pains.*"

Levi fired images from his fingertips, purposely unfocused at first like palettes of color, until the rainbow swooped in front of where Klarent stood, hovered in the air for all onlookers to see, and formed into a miniature depiction of how the Dark Kingdom once looked.

The image of the city was exaggerated, like children's paintings from a storybook, but that this was Amethyst was still recognizable, even in the difference in the buildings, all normal angled and painted in an array of brighter pigments.

"*Lo, these lands did sparkle so bright,*" Klarent continued, the illusion of the old sunlit city leading the audience through its streets and down into the market, "*but Shadow was what saved us with the dawning of the night.*"

A lone figure appeared, simplistic in design per Klarent's direction, but still clearly Ashmedai, given the colors and long black hair.

"*Peace here, within, and for every mortal sin.*"

"*Rest we hope for our long-lost prince,*" Klarent went immediately into the next verse, and Levi added the figure of another walking beside Ashmedai, with violet clothes, half-elf ears, and brown hair, "*and woe to the demon who took him from us hence.*"

Where Ashmedai had been, a new figure pounced and pushed Ashmedai out of the frame, leaving behind a monstrous, hulking creature that towered over the Amethyst Prince, with the kingdom's gemstone distinct in the background.

"*Lo, the curse did spread from its source.*"

The demon snatched the prince up and dove with him inside the gemstone, turning it black, and darkness spread from it, the view changing again to show the whole city as the Amethyst Kingdom was turned into the Shadow Lands they knew.

"Our bright shining gemstone that sent us on this course.

"Peace here, within, and for all immortal sin."

The illusion zoomed back in on the gemstone as the demon leapt from it, returning it to brilliant violet, and off the demon zipped toward the market steps, where Ashmedai was seen again, getting back up to his feet, and he began to follow.

"Shadow, though foreign, did chase and defend, and run the demon out to prove our chaos could end."

Into the wood they went, with Ashmedai racing after the demon, accompanied now by a redheaded figure meant to be Braxton when his legs still worked, until the spread of darkness reached them. Braxton fell, and suddenly Ashmedai could go no farther, for a pulse of light indicated the barrier between him and where the demon had escaped.

"Lo, a wall was found to hold us here, but through this metamorphosis our story is clear.

"Peace here, within, and for everlasting sin."

Outward the illusion zoomed once more, showing the changed lands and populating person after person, all familiar, for Levi made one look like Daedlys, another Grillo, another Luccite, and so on, all staring in wonderment at how they had been changed.

"Diversity of people bless these lands, ruled ever-gently in the worthiest of hands."

Then came Ashmedai from the wood, carrying Braxton, and the people swarmed him, falling to their knees.

"Lo, tonight we celebrate our king, for peace and prosperity that no one else could bring.

"Peace here, within, and an end to every sin."

The images burst into prismatic distortions, the illusion fading and falling, leaving only Klarent behind it all, who took another deep bow.

The applause was wilder than any Levi had been privy to today, but as Klarent motioned him forward to take a bow beside him, Levi did so with his eyes seeking only one spectator.

Ash—who stared forward at nothing, looking unmistakably sad.

Levi realized in an awful rush of hindsight how foolish he'd been to go along with this performance, for of course this was a story Ashmedai would never want to relive. Yet he was forced to remember every Festival Day.

A pat on the back from Klarent made Levi startle, and he saw the same happen to Ashmedai as the citizens around the king crowded close to offer their praises. Ashmedai smiled in humble acknowledgment at all of them, but Levi knew it was a mask.

"Thank you, friend," Klarent said. "You don't know how much this meant to me."

Levi did. He understood. To everyone other than Ashmedai—and Braxton, he supposed—the curse was a source of eventual joy and fortune. They still feared the demon, the barrier, and wanted those threats gone, but no one considered what they had become a curse. Not really. Not anymore.

They didn't know how untrue that was for Ashmedai.

Klarent dragged Levi with him to descend the stage, a flurry of renewed pats on the back and accolades bombarding them as they made their way to Ashmedai's side.

"That was wonderful, Klarent," Ashmedai lied.

"The performance, I'll admit, was more a labor of love than anything," Klarent said, holding out the tome he had been saving, "but this book holds the true details, filled with the most accurate account to date. The poem merely kicks it off. For you, my king."

With hands struggling not to shake, Ashmedai accepted the book. As he touched it, the Source Crystal on the front glowed its signature violet. "Thank you. It's beautiful. And… congratulations, I hear." He mustered a more believable smile.

"Ah!" Klarent looked aside with a wriggle of nearly every tendril on his person. "You heard. Thank you, Ash. Now, I must attend to the following performer."

It seemed Grillo was next. Kenner must have been elsewhere, but Levi saw Yentriss in the crowd, clearly working to keep order, or at least a careful watch over the celebration, but upon seeing her husband take the stage, she came forward like many other gawkers, unable to hide her surprise.

"An ode to my beautiful wife," Grillo began.

Levi had been excited to hear the poem, but when he turned to Ashmedai, he found the king staring at the book with the same lost, melancholy expression.

"Ash?"

"Hm?" Ashmedai blinked away what were clearly tears.

"Shall we go for a walk?" Levi whispered, taking the book from him and linking their arms.

All Ashmedai answered with was a shaky nod.

Only the first few lilts of Grillo's poem reached them as they headed away.

"*Scales like a jeweled mosaic do shine.*

"*Upon one like no other womankind.*

"*Steel forged with grace who graced me that she's mine.*

"*My wife and muse who I am blessed to find.*"

Levi would have to ask Grillo later if Yentriss actually blushed.

Working swiftly through the crowd and doing his best to ensure they moved fast enough to not be easily stopped by passersby, Levi pulled Ashmedai toward the one place he knew would be quiet when all the Shadow Lands was reveling.

The wood.

"The performance really was lovely," Ashmedai said once the din of the festival was behind them. Levi had left the tome in a back nook of the very last stall, where he knew he could easily retrieve it later. "You have a true gift with your illusions."

"I'm so sorry, Ash. I should have known—"

"And told Klarent to cancel? You'd have crushed him."

"Still, forgive me. You told me you didn't like to talk about that night or the prince, and there I went helping Klarent spin the memories right before your eyes like a fool. Of course you wouldn't want to see that."

"It's all right," Ashmedai said, truthfully, Levi thought, and more clear-eyed with added distance between them and the stage. "It is good to remember sometimes."

They weren't using the path Levi had taken all those days with Grillo, but the main road the carriages used when traveling to and from Emerald.

"There is one thing I have wanted to ask," Levi broached cautiously.

"Go on," Ashmedai assured him.

"Did you love him?"

The king's pace didn't waver, like he had been expecting the question. "Yes. But he didn't love me."

"He didn't?" Levi was the one who came up short, blinking in surprise.

"No." Ashmedai turned to him. "To Cullen, we were friends, nothing more. If it has plagued you, Levi, I never knew with him what I have shared with you."

A surge of possessiveness filled Levi, like when he'd wished to be closer to Ashmedai than Braxton. He knew it was silly to have ever envied a dead man, but to know finally that only friendship existed between Ashmedai and the prince, even if Ashmedai had pined for Cullen, made what Levi had with Ashmedai even more special and solely his.

Tentatively, Levi reached for Ashmedai's face, which almost had a tinge of blue to its stark whiteness with the way the moon and stars reflected off the black trees. Levi kissed him, putting into it all his regret and love in equal measure. He never wanted Ashmedai to get that look of sorrow again.

Ashmedai's smile when they parted was a good start.

They kept walking, enjoying the quiet, with the sounds of the festival almost completely lost now. Then, up ahead, Levi spotted a mound of disturbed dirt.

"Like before," Levi said, rushing toward it. "Do you see? That's what I saw on the other side of the wood!"

"Levi, wait," Ashmedai called. "How far have we come?"

Levi kept onward, too entranced by the sight he feared he had imagined before. Though this was a different spot, surely, it was almost identical to the previous mound where something had been buried.

"Levi, wait!"

"But Ash, I'm certain—"

"*Stop!*"

The harshness—no, the *fear*—in Ashmedai's voice made Levi spin around. He had nearly reached the dirt pile, but Ashmedai hadn't moved with him, still several paces behind. Between them, parallel to each other on either side of the path, were trees with crystals at their bases glowing bright white. The line wasn't finished across the road, though Levi spotted a few dormant ones he had passed.

"You crossed the barrier," Ashmedai said in astonishment.

Levi stared at his hands, terrified for a moment that he would vanish, but he was still whole. Where he had crossed, there was a haze in the air, like the blending of colors on a painting, like the rainbow of Levi's own illusions before they formed, where the Shadow Lands and the rest of the world faded from one into the other.

He turned to look behind himself and saw… *snow* gently falling on normal winter trees.

"Did Brax… no, no…," Ashmedai muttered. "The crystals are still glowing, and I can *feel* the barrier. I know it's there."

Levi almost laughed, though he could tell Ashmedai was tense and frightened. He turned back, hoping to reassure Ashmedai but still curious. "How—?"

Levi's words were torn from him as something crashed into his side.

The next thing Levi felt was pain, not only from whatever had struck him, but because he was thrown to the ground, landing hard on his side, with one of his daggers digging into his hip. Arms surrounded Levi, and he registered a body plastered against him.

The demon.

Stunned and terrified, Levi couldn't think to fight right away as he was rolled onto his back, his body roughly pawed at, until his attacker found the buckle on his belt and began to unclasp it.

"Levi!" Ashmedai cried.

The *man* atop Levi wasn't from the Shadow Lands, but he was no demon. He was human, hair bedraggled and beard so bushy Levi could only just make out the glint of green in his eyes. He seemed so strange. So simple.

So ordinary.

The highwayman, for clearly that's what he was, was already fitting Levi's belt around his own waist, taking it for his own. Then he reached for the cuff on Levi's ear.

"No!" Levi swatted his hand away.

The man snarled, glaring at Levi for daring to defy him, only to seemingly just that moment take in how Levi looked and gaping at Levi's strangeness as Levi had gaped at him.

"What are you?" he asked hoarsely.

A roar sounded from inside the barrier like no beast Levi had ever heard, with both a reverberating depth and painful shrillness to its cry that rivaled Daedlys's scream. Levi and the man both turned, taking in the monster before them like something only a nightmare could create.

It wasn't only its shape that was frightening. It had wings and claws, a tail, jagged horns that spiraled upward from its head, and a mouth full of razor-sharp teeth. All those things Levi knew from people of the Shadow Lands—his neighbors and friends—but this creature was different. The feeling it evoked was a horror like no other, for it both seemed to have its shape and didn't. Its skin too was variable, like light and darkness warring for dominance, as if the beast was made of shadow.

The highwayman screamed, leapt off Levi, and took off in a frenzied run deeper into the snow-covered trees.

This was the demon, and though the highwayman had been able to run, all Levi could do was shiver and close his eyes in terror.

"Levi!"

Levi opened his eyes again, berating himself for forgetting that Ashmedai was there too. He was right there—where the monster had been a moment ago. Ashmedai looked sad again, maybe more so than Levi had ever seen.

Slowly, having lost his weapons belt but otherwise fine, Levi got to his feet. Ashmedai couldn't approach him, or else he would cross the barrier and not be as lucky as Levi had been. Yet, as Levi looked at the king, he had this odd sinking feeling overtake him that made it impossible to move forward himself.

"You... have illusion magic too?"

"It wasn't an illusion." Ashmedai's sorrow deepened further. "That is the real me."

"Then your secret, why the past haunts you so...." Levi swallowed low as he gathered his thoughts. "The prince didn't summon the demon, did he? *You* did and took it into yourself."

"No, Levi. I didn't summon the demon," Ashmedai said solemnly, and his eyes flashed in a way that made the whites of his irises turn black like the rest. "I am the demon."

CHAPTER 9

"COME ON, Ash, it's late," Cullen said, though he hardly portrayed any fatigue with the way he skipped onward, clearly enjoying being out in the square at night when most everyone else was preparing for bed or already asleep and the streets were empty. "What do you want to talk to me about that's so important?"

Ashmedai had been mustering the strength for weeks to finally confess. Cullen was just so beautiful to him. Not only his violet eyes and sweet face, or the way his brown curls tended to fall into his eyes and force him to flick them aside, but because of his heart, so big for his people, even though he doubted he could take on the role his father had left behind.

That was *part* of what Ashmedai wanted to confess.

"I know you've been debating passing the crown to someone else or calling for a vote."

Cullen spun around with a frown, still moving slowly backward, nearer to the towering Amethyst gemstone at the center of the square. His clothing always contained violet, and tonight he wore a violet and dark brown tunic with a deep indigo cloak. "I don't want to talk about that. Not now. I know I have to make a decision—"

"But you're basing that decision off the belief you're not good enough," Ashmedai cut in, causing Cullen to finally stop, his eyes even more brilliant violet with the gemstone's light shimmering behind him. "I simply want you to understand what you won't hear from anyone else. Maybe you won't believe it from me either, but I'm going to say it anyway. You would make an excellent king."

The usual indecision blighted Cullen's face.

"You *would.*"

Ashmedai had chosen to make himself look like an elf, because that was the form the first of his kind had taken upon returning to this world. He also thought elves beautiful. He thought dwarves and humans beautiful too. But the moment he met the half-elf prince, he knew he'd never known anyone quite as radiant.

"It's your doubt that proves how good a king you could be, because what you want more than anything is to see your people happy. You doubt you can do enough, that you can *be* enough, but that is how I know you will be. You are a remarkable man, Cullen. I have no doubts about that because…."

This was the second confession and much harder of the two.

"Because I love you," Ashmedai finished, closing his eyes with the admission.

The streets this late were usually quiet, but normally Ashmedai would at least be able to hear crickets, an owl, a cat prowling. While his eyes remained shut, everything around him was silent.

"Ash…," Cullen said at last, brokenly, and Ashmedai looked at him.

There was no indecision on Cullen's face now, only grief.

Only pity.

"I'm so sorry, I…. You know I care for you, but…." Cullen pursed his lips, like he hated that he had to say this, but his words were the truth.

"You don't feel the same," Ashmedai said, feeling an immediate sting of tears as he tried to look anywhere but at Cullen's remorse.

How had Ashmedai ever believed one of these beautiful creatures could love him?

Cullen gasped, and Ashmedai looked up again, blinking away his tears so he could focus on his friend—who was staring at him in fear.

Ashmedai gazed down at his hands. He hadn't been able to feel it amidst his heartache, but the pale color he had chosen for his skin was shifting, fluctuating through the monochrome spectrum from white to black and every shade in between.

"I'm sorry." Ashmedai lurched backward, trying to will his true form to not surface. He was upset. He didn't mean to lose the glamour. "Please, don't be afraid—"

"What are you?" Cullen snapped in accusation.

Ashmedai was failing to contain himself, seeming to lose more and more control the harder he tried to keep it. "Please," he said again, moving toward Cullen with a crunch of unexpected claws into the cobblestone. "I just wanted—"

"Stay away from me!" Cullen cried, backing toward the gemstone. His violet eyes were saucers of dread, and he reached blindly behind him, finding the Amethyst and pressing a palm to it. "You lied. You tricked us."

"No, I swear—"

"Stay away! I won't let you hurt my people." A pulse of magic surged from Cullen into the gemstone and back again, making it clear he was calling upon his birthright for the strength to fight the beast before him.

Ashmedai's clothing, his elvish facade, all of it had melted away, revealing him to be a thing of nightmares the people of this world had been happy to be rid of once.

Ashmedai never should have come back.

A spell started to spill beneath Cullen's breath, too quiet for Ashmedai to make out words other than "barrier" and "monster" and "forever." He felt a push from the crystal, as though it was trying to force him out of the square, out of the kingdom. Ashmedai should have let it banish him, but instead, he drove through the forces pressing against him, unthinking and desperate to at least say goodbye and rest his hand on the shoulder of a friend one last time.

The large Amethyst became a kaleidoscope, pulsing brighter against the shadowy abyss of Ashmedai's true self as he gave a final, foolish surge forward, one clawed hand landing on Cullen and the other on the gemstone's surface.

The flash was so blinding, the push so powerful, that Ashmedai flew backward through the air and landed hard on his outstretched wings. The light faded quickly, however, for the violet-colored crystal was turning black, and Cullen, eyes wide in panic, was being consumed by it as if swallowed by a ravenous fiend until he vanished into the void.

"*No!*"

"Ash…?"

Ashmedai jerked his gaze from where he was sprawled on the ground before the blackened gemstone. Braxton appeared from the other side, stunned and clearly wary, but not seeming as afraid as Cullen had been.

Braxton was a good man, a good friend. He was the first person Ashmedai had met when he arrived in the Amethyst Kingdom.

"*Brax*," Ashmedai lamented, his voice otherworldly in this form, making Braxton cringe. Like Ashmedai's physical appearance, his voice was variable, deeper and high-pitched, resonant and like a whisper. "*It's all my fault....*"

"It's okay." Braxton raised a hand as if to calm a spooked animal. "I knew you were one of them. I knew it. You were too extraordinary, too beautiful to just be an elf."

"*It's all my fault,*" Ashmedai said again, not really listening.

"No, Ash, I saw—"

"*It's all my fault!*" he shrieked and leapt back to his feet.

The gemstone was becoming brighter again, returning to violet, and in a sudden rush of hope, Ashmedai thought Cullen might be returned to him. He wasn't. Cullen didn't exist anymore. Whatever had become of him was seeping out of the gemstone at its base and spreading into the earth like a plague.

A scream, almost as shrill as Ashmedai's own, brought his and Braxton's attentions to a nearby shop. *Daedlys's* shop. In normal speech, Daedlys had a lovely tenor, but oh, how he could scream.

The white-haired elf was staring at Ashmedai like Cullen had.

"Wait!" Braxton cried when Ashmedai turned to flee.

Ashmedai was so distressed by what had happened, he could barely propel himself upward to take flight. All he could do was run, occasionally hovering in his scramble to escape, or leaping through shadows, headed into the wood to get as far as possible from the Amethyst and the kingdom he had ruined.

"WHAT ARE you...?" Levi gasped, stumbling backward, even though Ashmedai couldn't possibly come closer with the barrier between them. He hated that he was echoing what the highwayman had asked of him, but he didn't understand. "*You* caused the curse?"

"It wasn't on purpose," Ashmedai said, still and solemn, looking the way Levi was used to, with his white irises returning. But the memory of his true form, of a monster with shape and color and voice that made Levi's mind buzz from the dissonance, was impossible to forget. "A demon is as good an answer as any, I suppose, for what I am.

"My kind are from outside this world, connected but hidden. In ages past, we would cross over to explore. The people of this world called us... fairies. We were wild magic given form, but you—humans, elves, dwarves—you are what taught us to be individuals, to have wants and desires.

"We made ourselves look like you, acted like you. Over the centuries, we wanted more and more and more—just like you. We were already immortal, but in our growing greed, we wanted to be gods, to rule over all we had learned of this world. So we began to consume everything we could to achieve that end, and our ambition corrupted us.

"Some of us it destroyed. Some became such horrible villains that the people rose up to destroy them. And some of us... realized our folly and retreated home.

"More centuries passed, and a few of us wondered what had become of you, curious to venture back, though cautious of allowing ourselves to be corrupted again. The first who returned decided to stay, vowed to build something beautiful to make amends. Mavis, the Fairy Queen, they called her. Her certainty made me believe it was worth crossing over myself.

"I had new eyes after our years of solitude. At least... I thought I did. I believed I could control myself. But then I met Cullen, and I *wanted* again with all the madness of my kind."

A tear slipped free down Ashmedai's cheek, and he sniffled, almost angry in his rush to wipe it away.

"You... you were in love," Levi said, having stopped backpedaling while he listened, for the even tones of Ashmedai's voice made him feel less afraid.

"Yes. And look what that cost. I confessed, and he rejected me. He tried to be kind about it, but in my grief that he didn't love me back, I revealed what I truly was, and he was horrified. I was everything then that I had tried not to be—a demon unable to stop consuming what I wanted until nothing was left.

"He tried to cast me out, to banish the 'monster' from ever being able to enter his kingdom again. It was *me*, my magic that corrupted his intentions. I just wanted him to understand. If he didn't love me, so be it, but I wanted him to know me, to see me...."

Another tear fell, then another, too fast for Ashmedai to swipe at them all.

"He called upon the Amethyst for the power he needed. All the kingdoms have a gemstone somewhere, where magic congregates and the veil between worlds is thin. They're what my people used to amass more power once. I just wanted Cullen to understand, but when I tried to reach for him and touched the gemstone, I caused the curse.

"Cullen was eradicated into nothing. That would have been awful enough, but the darkness didn't stop. The barrier sprang up, and the curse spread to fill it, transforming everyone inside and imprisoning them forever.

"Like a coward, I fled. Everyone saw me, watching on, helpless, as the curse began to change them. Brax chased me into the wood, tried to get me to see reason. He'd seen everything and didn't reject me as Cullen had, but I was still so stricken by what I had allowed to happen, I didn't want to listen to him.

"Then the curse reached us. When I saw what started happening to Brax, I couldn't leave him. He was farthest from the Source Crystal, and maybe the most cursed because of it, because he changed so little but was never able to walk again.

"I tried to change back into my elven guise, but *this* was as far as I could get." Ashmedai lifted a hand to stare at his claws. His razor-teeth, his eyes, his ridges—it all made sense now, because they weren't from any legend or myth, other than stories of the demon itself.

"I carried Brax out of the wood," Ashmedai continued. "The people drew their own conclusions. I was going to tell them the truth, but Brax spun the tale—that it had been Cullen at fault.

"Cullen may have started the spell, but the fault was mine. Even so, seeing the distress on everyone's altered faces, these people who had become my friends, how could I not offer to lead in Cullen's absence? Someone had to. And, after all—" Ashmedai offered the solemnest smile Levi could imagine. "—I already knew what it was like to live as a monster."

A gasp left Levi before he realized how long it had been since he'd taken a breath. He watched the sorrow deepen on Ashmedai's face like fissures, and he knew the king believed history was repeating itself.

He was wrong. Levi had been afraid because he hadn't understood. Now the tale was told, the truth revealed at last, and as Levi took it all in and looked at Ashmedai, he had no doubts.

While Ashmedai's eyes were hooded and lowered to the ground, Levi strode forward, crossing back into the barrier and leaving the snow of the normal world behind. He took Ashmedai's face in his hands, and it was the king this time who gasped.

"The curse was an accident."

"It doesn't matter." Ashmedai shook his head, eyes squeezing shut as more tears fell. "It was all my fault… because he didn't love me."

"I love you," Levi said.

Ashmedai's eyes flashed open. "Levi…."

"I love you. And, if you need to hear it… I forgive you." He kissed Ashmedai, soft and gentle on tearstained lips.

Ashmedai's voice caught in a pitiable, choked sound as he fell forward. He sank against Levi with arms wrapping tight, face turning from Levi's hold and soft kiss to bury in Levi's shoulder, where he sobbed.

It was the least Levi could do to offer this mirrored support, but the least was hardly all he wanted to give. He held Ashmedai tightly, so the king would know there was no fear left in Levi's heart.

"I love you," Ashmedai wept. "Oh, how I love you… stronger than I ever thought I could love anyone."

Levi might have said such a comparison was unnecessary, but the selfish part of him enjoyed hearing that. It also made him wonder something he had dreaded before. "Forgive me that I must ask this, but… do you only love me because I remind you of him?"

Ashmedai's head snapped up from Levi's shoulder. "No. Your eyes and the faint resemblance in your face may have been what caught my attention, but I promise you, it wasn't what kept it."

The kiss this time was that familiar concurrent lean and press and tilt of their heads with mouths opening to claim something deeper than comfort. Knowing the truth didn't change the warmth Levi felt being in Ashmedai's arms, or how Ashmedai's lips and tongue made that warmth boil into a satisfying heat in the depths of Levi's belly.

More than anything, Levi still wanted tonight to end sharing Ashmedai's bed, where nothing and no one could touch them.

He was about to suggest Ashmedai whisk them away when he remembered the upturned dirt.

"Wait," Levi said, pulling from Ashmedai slowly before he turned to head back across the barrier. It was unnerving crossing intentionally, and Levi might have held his breath while he did so, but like before, nothing happened once he reached the other side.

He knelt in front of the dirt, casting a wary glance around him to look for anyone else like the highwayman, but once he was sure it was safe, he started to dig.

"What is it?" Ashmedai called. "What did that man bury?"

Levi's stomach churned and he jerked his hands back when he realized what he was uncovering. There were parts beneath the dirt.

Body parts.

Worse was when Levi looked around more closely and realized that although there wasn't disturbed dirt elsewhere, there were mounds like this one. Hundreds of them. Everywhere.

Levi leapt to his feet. "He's a murderer. There are bodies buried out here, countless bodies. Who knows how long that man has been burying victims where he thought no one would find them." With a shudder, Levi scooped the dirt back over the mound he'd uncovered and returned to Ashmedai. "I hope you terrified him so badly that he never returns."

"While normally I loathe instilling fear in anyone," Ashmedai said, "I agree. Now, I think it's time we left the wood, if you'd care to join me somewhere less daunting." He held out a hand, and Levi wasted no time in grasping it.

They started to head back down the path.

"I wish I knew why I can cross the barrier when no one else can," Levi commented.

"Braxton mentioned that creating you was part of his experiments toward weakening the barrier," Ashmedai said. "Clearly, he is succeeding if he found a way to let any of us cross it without disintegrating. Maybe he doesn't know or didn't want to risk having you test it. He told me tonight, though, that he is nearly complete."

"He was at the festival?"

"Briefly. I might get to walk with you in the sunshine yet." Ashmedai pulled Levi more tightly to his side as they walked.

Like many times before, Levi felt as though the shadows were watching him. After the highwayman and discovering all those bodies, it was no wonder, but Levi shrugged it off with a shiver. "What should we do about... all that back there?"

"Nothing tonight. I don't want to sour anyone's mood during the festival. He's gone. I'll tell Yentriss tomorrow to put up patrols and keep watch just in case. For now, I want to enjoy the rest of tonight. You've given me something I never thought anyone could."

They reached the end of the path, with sparkling lights calling to them once more beyond the wood's borders.

Levi turned to Ashmedai and took his hands. "Would you like to go back to the festival?"

"Would you?"

"I think I've seen enough."

There were shadows here too, maybe more so with the trees casting darker ones opposite the festival lights. Ashmedai gathered Levi close and leapt into the nearest patch of darkness just like Levi hoped he would.

HE LOVED him. Levi loved him, even after learning the truth.

Ashmedai had never felt so… full.

Aurora said hello when they first arrived back at the castle, but though Ashmedai and Levi both doted on her for a spell, she made scarce soon after, like she knew they wanted to be alone.

They had already been intimate once, yet the trek up to Ashmedai's bedchamber felt different. For the first time, someone other than Braxton knew who and what Ashmedai was and wasn't afraid. Better still, Levi wanted Ashmedai and sought his touch as boldly as he had before.

Their silk tunics were almost easier to lose than robes, the light, elegant fabric fluttering off their bodies like gossamer. They helped each other out of their undershirts and trousers, and Levi hardly seemed capable of keeping his hands from straying, if only to trail over Ashmedai's ridges.

Ashmedai's weapons belt had been set aside at the start, Levi's already gone, since it had been stolen, but the circlet and ear cuff they'd claimed at the festival remained. Ashmedai traced his fingers along the cuff and up to the tip of Levi's ear.

"The cuff can stay if it makes you look at me like that," Levi said, reaching to graze a thumb along the golden circlet with its scarlet gem resting upon Ashmedai's forehead. "I certainly wouldn't mind you keeping this on. The Amethyst King, who never wears amethyst himself." He chuckled.

"I suppose I've often given myself away with how I've never quite felt like I belong here, but red has always been more my color than violet. Let's save that hue for you, shall we?"

Naked now save their adornments, Ashmedai pulled Levi to him to feel their bodies flush and lazily kissed him. Even as their lengths grew, hot and leaking between them, they remained unhurried. And yet, within that lazy kiss everything seemed more acute, and Ashmedai felt Levi's stitches against his mouth.

It was never an unpleasant experience, or Ashmedai wouldn't have left those among the last, but it reminded him of Levi's true desire.

"Before we begin," he whispered, still standing at the foot of the bed, "shall I take the last of your stitches?"

"Yes," Levi said, like he had been thinking the very same thing. "I like becoming my own man beneath your touch."

Ashmedai knew there were many ways to interpret those words, and Levi meant them all. "I like helping you achieve it, just as you helped me see the truth in myself."

They were still embracing, pulses and breaths increasing to a matched fervor, with their cocks sliding past each other in promise, when Ashmedai forced a yelp from Levi by scooping him into his arms. Carrying Levi like a bridegroom, Ashmedai moved around the bed, sprawled Levi atop it, and crawled after him.

"I think, this time, I would like my mouth on *you*."

Ashmedai lifted Levi's knees and hooked them over his shoulders before the gasp had fully left Levi. He was almost entirely one perfect shade of blue now, with only the barest ombre at certain parts. The blue definitely faded to something darker between his legs, beneath his dark curls, and Ashmedai adored that beautiful indigo as much as he did when the blush was in Levi's cheeks.

He hollowed his own cheeks and sucked Levi into his mouth, careful of the sharpness of his teeth, though the faintest, featherlight graze of them when they did brush Levi's skin only made Levi moan louder.

There could be no greater gift than someone finally loving Ashmedai in return, and he would gladly spend lifetimes thanking Levi for that.

He coiled his tongue, allowing his natural malleable nature to let it spiral around Levi farther and tighter than any normal tongue was capable. With it, while still having his mouth all around Levi and salivating richly, Ashmedai stroked with his elongated tongue and sucked.

The sounds leaving Levi weren't mere moans, but plaintive whines, his hips arching upward to meet every one of Ashmedai's bobs and uncanny curls of his tongue. Ashmedai squeezed the soft mounds of Levi's backside and nuzzled into the sides of his thighs. Levi needed to know how special he was, how precious and incomparable.

Not having to hold back his true nature, the shadow magic seeped from Ashmedai's pores more liberally, seeking Levi almost hungrily. The shadows covered them both, so that when Ashmedai pulled up, knowing how close Levi had to be to spilling, Levi's entire body was glowing with black-purple light.

Ashmedai kissed him, stealing Levi's panted breath, and let both the salty taste he'd taken from Levi's length and the power of his shadows pass through the kiss—and smooth the stitches stretching Levi's smile.

Levi bucked into Ashmedai, as much as he could folded in half with his knees still over Ashmedai's shoulders. Ashmedai kept kissing him, letting the magic and his own mouth give Levi back the smile he'd once had and wanted to have again.

A shudder left Levi in the aftermath, like he might have spilled just then, but Ashmedai didn't feel heat or wetness. He knew Levi was close, and as he continued lightly kissing Levi even after the stitches were gone, he sent the barest tendril of his shadows to press against the budded entrance they had only begun to explore the first time.

"W-wait," Levi whimpered, and in an instant, Ashmedai stilled. Levi's vibrant eyes looked to him with heavy purpose. "Slower. Please. Or surely I'll make a mess of myself all too quickly again."

Ashmedai chuckled and summoned his shadows back, slowly lowering Levi's legs to rest on the bed. Whatever Levi wanted, Ashmedai would obey.

He wasn't quite ready, however, for what Levi asked of him next.

"Rest beside me and show me the real you again."

A cold ache twisted in Ashmedai's gut, despite having let some of his true self free already. "Levi, you don't have to be with that version of me to prove you love me. I know it's frightening. Once—" Ashmedai glanced longingly to the side. "—before our original corruption turned my magic to darkness, I looked more like something infused with light."

"Isn't that because you hadn't yet known desire or true emotion?" Levi's honest question brought Ashmedai's gaze back to him. "You said you weren't even individuals then."

"True. Our existence was different than life here."

"Would you change all that happened to bring you to this moment?"

Ashmedai wasn't certain at first when he began to answer, but the more the words left him, the more he knew the truth. "I wish I had caused less anguish, wish I had felt a little less of it myself, but if changing things meant I wouldn't be here with you now, then... no. I would have nothing different."

Even with his cheeks fully indigo from the lust burning within him, Levi's smile was sweet. "You are not darkness. You're shadow, and shadow cannot exist without light. I see both in you, in that form. Maybe that is exactly who you were always meant to become. Show me."

Ashmedai had rarely called upon that form since the night of the curse. Earlier, he'd only done so out of panic that Levi was in danger. Now, calling it out because he'd been asked felt freeing in a way he never expected.

LEVI WOULD be lying if he said there was no accompanying fear watching Ashmedai shed the visage he'd first known and fallen in love with. Ashmedai's true form was like some great gargoyle that almost seemed to not be solid, or one obvious color, or even truly real. It played tricks on Levi's mind that he was dreaming all this—or the highwayman had killed him.

Or crossing the barrier had.

But no, Levi was here with Ashmedai, and he had nothing to fear from the being in bed with him.

The more Levi looked, the more he could see Ashmedai's same face hidden within those varying colors and unpredictable textures. Ashmedai still had his long hair, but it too was in a constant flux of color and light versus dark. His horns were impressive upward coils from the top of his head, and as he lay beside Levi, his clawed hands and feet proved larger and more beast-like, but not reaching or rending with any vile intent.

The teeth were Ashmedai's teeth, and while his eyes seemed solid black, they also shifted, sometimes solid white, sometimes the white-on-black Levi knew.

Ashmedai was clearly a powerful being, deadly even, for Levi had seen him summon a part of this form when he devoured a gazellian during the hunt. The people merely saw it as shadow magic from the Shadow King, but Ashmedai *was* the shadows.

When Ashmedai's tail whipped upward like a cat's, slender and long, with a trowel-like tip, Levi laughed at how endearing that nervous flick seemed to him. Most extraordinary were Ashmedai's wings. Each half of them seemed nearly as large as the creature they sprouted from, yet one stretched upward behind Ashmedai, the other tucked beneath him with how he lay on his hip. Because of how he was made of shadow, the wing wasn't scrunched, but as though it had become a blanket for him to lie upon simply because Ashmedai needed it to. Only the circlet remained as it had been before, glittering gold with its red gem shining from within the shadows' shifting.

"You are like nothing I have ever seen," Levi said in wonder. Seeing Ashmedai fade to allover darker hues, Levi added, "You're *beautiful*," and reached at last to touch his king.

Daedlys and Aurora's forms had prepared Levi for the water-like give of touching something not quite there, but because Ashmedai wasn't truly translucent, there was a stronger solidness to him. Levi's mind couldn't fully comprehend it even as he felt it himself, but he knew the sensation under his fingers wasn't unpleasant.

"Oh!" Levi gasped when he felt up along Ashmedai's chest.

The ridges, almost impossible to see amidst the undulations of Ashmedai's form, were still there. Levi could feel them, almost deeper in each groove than normal but bringing a sense of the familiar through the contrast of this experience to everything he'd known of Ashmedai before.

"They're still one of my favorite things," Levi said, dragging his fingers down lower to feel the ridges along Ashmedai's hips, "like a secret I was the first to discover."

"*You were.*" Ashmedai's voice reverberated deep in Levi's chest. It still sounded like Ashmedai, just multiplied with variations in pitch overlapping.

"I think a few people saw your ridges today, wearing that tunic."

Ashmedai smiled. Levi saw it clearly, however different on this vessel. Ashmedai was something cosmic, hauntingly beautiful and all Levi's to explore.

He brought his hands up to Ashmedai's face and held it, looking into his eyes that were entrancing no matter the color. He kissed him, and the feeling was so instantly overwhelming that Levi forgot to breathe. Water and fire, hot and cold, the most intense pleasure and something not quite painful made his eyes water. The sensation was the same as what Levi felt when Ashmedai smoothed his stitches, but a thousand times more intense.

He pulled away with a gulp, heaving for the breath he'd forgotten.

"*I'm sorry*," Ashmedai said. "*I'll pull back.*"

"No! Then you won't be you. You shouldn't have to hold back. I can handle it. Besides—" Levi smiled as his pulse returned to manageable. "—it's my turn to pleasure you."

Ashmedai might be a demon—fairy—*god* creature that could devour Levi whole, but between his legs was still a thick ridged cock that Levi reached for brazenly.

A gasp from that multitoned voice was especially gratifying.

Ashmedai's ridges were more deeply grooved here as well. The dual sensations didn't stop either. Ashmedai felt both cool and searing hot, pliable and firm, but when Levi stroked the length in his grasp and found Ashmedai's tip, there was familiar wetness that proved Ashmedai was still something primal and virile and ripe with desire.

Levi aligned Ashmedai's cock with his own, still pumping with his hand but allowing their bodies to connect as he ground forward. He was calmed from how heightened he had been with Ashmedai's mouth on him, even after that shadow kiss took his stitches away, but feeling himself pressed up against Ashmedai in this extraordinary form was swiftly bringing Levi there again.

In the frenzy of their moving hips and Levi's stroking, Levi reached with his other hand to touch more of Ashmedai's body. His cheek, past the circlet into his hair, and up along one of his spiral horns. Then Levi drifted down again along the ridges of Ashmedai's chest, outward to trace one of his wings, and down his arm to find a much larger clawed hand, but that didn't mean Levi couldn't lace his fingers with it.

Levi stopped stroking Ashmedai's length, letting the collision of their hips and slide of their cocks be enough, because he wanted to keep hold of Ashmedai's hand while still touching him everywhere else.

The intensity from being in contact with Ashmedai, just like when Levi kissed him, was always just shy of too much, but it was also like finding release again and again despite not having reached completion yet.

It made Levi's hand tremble, moving around the ridges at Ashmedai's hip again, and then down his thigh. He wanted more but didn't know where else he might touch, so he took Ashmedai's other hand and brought the claws to his lips. He kissed the back of Ashmedai's fingers and squeezed the other hand in his grasp.

Levi could finish just like this, he thought, touching the one he loved and thrusting against him.

The world spun and Levi was on his back, staring up at an endless sky—but the sky was Ashmedai, celestial and luminous with his shadows pulsing.

Their bodies were still connected, only Ashmedai was atop Levi, and though his claws gently traced over Levi's body, making him shiver, it was the shadows that spread the farthest.

The shadows were what started to slip inside Levi.

"Ah—!" The cry caught in Levi's throat, his head dropping back as he arched into the feeling. He understood that even in Ashmedai's more elven form, the king wouldn't have been able to prepare Levi with his hands, not with those sharp nails. Levi knew what fingers with blunt nails felt like from his own tentative trials, but this was better.

The mere brush of shadows inside Levi the last time had brought him to a quick end. Feeling so many more of those shadows stretch him open, bringing fresh waves of hot/cold, pain/pleasure—*yes, yes, more!*— made him certain he would shatter like diamond dust against Ashmedai's heavenly backdrop.

Levi could barely feel anything else, his limbs limp as his hips were raised, and the shadows kept expanding, stroking inside him like licks of raw magic.

"I-I-I…."

"*Is it too much?*" Ashmedai rumbled.

Yes, Levi thought, but he wanted to crest the top of it, knew he could, and pursed his lips, shaking his head that he could take it. He should have released ten times over by now, but somehow his length bobbed against his stomach, ripe as ever.

The peak receded somewhat, as Levi believed it would, and he looked at Ashmedai above him. Levi was adjusting to the shadows, to their magic and the pressure of their stretch inside him. He nodded to say he was ready, and when he felt the hot, wet presence of Ashmedai's cock against his entrance, where the shadows still resided, Levi nodded more urgently.

He wanted this, to have the king all his own and be utterly one with him.

Ashmedai's cock was all the things the shadows had been as it pushed inside Levi, but even more intensely hot/cold and blinding with pleasure. The pain was somewhere far, far away now, and all Levi knew was ecstasy.

Words couldn't form, Levi's moans more like cries, weeping for how incredible it felt to have the one he cherished most fill him so completely. Ashmedai was holding Levi up, cradling him as he took Levi deeply, and in that safe embrace, Levi couldn't imagine a sight more breathtaking.

"Y-you're... so beautiful," Levi rasped, reaching for Ashmedai with an unsteady hand, but he managed to cup Ashmedai's cheek. "You're everything. You're *mine*."

Ashmedai swooped down to kiss Levi with such fierceness, he forced Levi's hand to drop and even more rivulets of pleasure coursed through him, so that Levi laughed in the aftermath.

"I love you," Levi said.

"*I love you*," Ashmedai echoed.

The intensity increased again, as did the speed and depth of Ashmedai's thrusts. The end was building for Levi as it seemed to be building in Ashmedai. Then Ashmedai's eyes, ever flickering from black to white and both, locked on Levi's neck.

As Ashmedai's large, clawed hand curled gently around Levi's throat, around the one line of stitches that remained, the extra pulse of magic that shot into Levi was the finale that made everything else burst.

Levi howled, his hips stuttering upward as he spilled. Moments later, a hotter pulse of that same magic shot inside Levi where Ashmedai was thrusting between Levi's thighs. All the mess was absorbed by the shadows, but the pleasure was tenfold what it had been. Levi thought he might sob from how good it felt, only to realize he already was.

Another pulse from Ashmedai's hand and a light back and forth with the pad of his thumb erased the last remnants of those final few stitches, with aftershocks flooding Levi and Ashmedai together, until Levi was truly, finally whole.

And he remembered *everything*.

Including how he'd been murdered.

CHAPTER 10

LEANDER COULDN'T run anymore. He'd run so far, for so long. It had been *days*. The prince had given him food and water to take with him in a rucksack, but the supplies were running low, and he had no idea how much farther it was to the Shadow Lands.

Anything is better than being sacrificed to the Ice King, he told himself as he stowed away what little provisions remained before beginning his third day of traveling.

The prince had saved him, the Emerald Prince himself. Leander had to survive. He had to reach the Shadow Lands and make something of the gift he'd been given to start over elsewhere.

He'd never done anything bad his entire life—other than be born a half-elf and show that he had magic, spotted accidentally one day, in his own backyard. Not even powerful magic, just illusions. That's all it had taken to condemn him. Retribution would have been just as swift if anyone had discovered Leander yearned for the company of men.

He didn't even know what had become of his brother, Leslie. He hoped their mother could continue keeping Leslie safe and hidden as a half-elf in a land that hated them.

Alone now and no longer needing to waste magic on glamouring his half-elf ears, Leander was exhausted. He knew little of where he was going. No one really knew what the Shadow Lands held. Their carriages would arrive without drivers, deliver goods for trade, and take back what Emerald gave them. The stories said that had been the way of things for centuries, stretching back even longer than tales of the Ice King. It was whispered to be a place of such powerful magic, no one dared question the carriages, stop trading with them, or ever send anyone into the wood to find the Dark Kingdom.

They called the lands that—Dark and Shadow—because the few people who'd ever ventured close enough spoke of how the wood turned to night even if it should have been morning.

That was how Leander knew he was finally getting close, because the sun had only just risen, and he'd walked for less than an hour when it seemed as though darkness might swallow him like he'd entered a cave.

Leander stopped. In front of him was a haze he might not have detected, where the wood opened into a wider path, and across that haze along the path was night—*night*, not merely dark, for he could see stars and a full moon ahead. The trees there no longer had leaves, their gnarled branches reaching for the sky. It was winter, but even the firs looked dead there, yet they were also beautiful somehow, sparkling as though covered in metallic shimmer. And, as Leander craned his ears, he would swear he could hear voices, happy, normal voices like townsfolk in a market.

Yes! There were lights in the distance! He was saved!

Terrifying as it was, and despite all the stories of dark magic and people being driven mad by this place, Leander had to press on, for he had nowhere else to go. Perhaps the Dark Kingdom welcomed those Emerald called corrupt, and all would be better for him there.

All would be well. It had to be. He was almost—

"At last. *You* are perfect."

Leander froze before he could take his first full step across the haze, hearing a strange voice coming from somewhere he couldn't see. "Who—"

Then everything stopped, the lights gone, the murmur of townsfolk stilled, and all curiosity wiped away, because a wicked fast slice had severed Leander's head from his body.

"Yes, you're perfect," the voice said again, the last thing Leander heard as his mind caught up to already being dead. "And not to worry. When you wake, you will be a brand-new man."

"LEVI!"

Levi sucked in a sharp breath as the memory faded. Everything leading up to this moment had been so blissful—achieving new heights of pleasure with Ashmedai in the king's true form. Now Ashmedai had returned to his white skin and less pronounced ridges, as if he feared he had somehow harmed Levi.

"Are you all right?"

"Braxton lied," Levi said, rolling onto his side to face Ashmedai.

"What? What are you talking about?"

"He lied. I remember everything now. You told me he said the people he killed to make me had started to transform and were panicked, beyond saving. He…." Levi clutched his throat at the sharp sting of memory. "I hadn't started to change yet. I hadn't even crossed the barrier. He said I was perfect… and then he took my head. He killed me. He murdered me and knew what he was doing. He murdered all of them—"

"*Levi*." Ashmedai gathered Levi close, hugging him tight, which helped still the terror that had risen in him. "I am so sorry. I'm sorry that happened. I'm sorry you have to remember it."

"The highwayman didn't kill those people and leave parts behind. Braxton did."

"But how? Brax can't cross the barrier."

"He was there. I know it was his voice."

"Are you certain? Maybe you're remembering wrong. This is *Brax*, your own creator and my closest friend. He would never—"

"He would never mutilate corpses and lie to you?"

The silence that followed was static and sharp, enough that Levi felt guilty for having to say it, but there were no doubts in his mind after reliving his death. That had been Braxton's voice.

Slowly, Ashmedai held Levi out in front of him, looking conflicted. "There must be an explanation."

"What if there isn't?" Levi asked.

"Then we will find out the truth. You're safe now. Even with that memory, I promise you are safe." He stroked Levi's cheek with a tender brush. "I will always keep you safe, Levi. Or…. *Leander*, I suppose I should call you now."

"No." Levi shook his head, pressing his face into Ashmedai's palm. "I remember everything, but I'm Levi. I'll always be Levi now. Leander simply needs justice. They all do."

"*Yes*," Ashmedai said with some of his true resonance slipping into his voice, "*they do*."

So as not to alert anyone at the festival that something was amiss, Ashmedai brought himself and Levi to the tower door using his shadows. The sounds of the festival were only faintly audible in the distance, like the most surreal of backdrops, since they were about to confront a friend for murder.

Ashmedai reached for the door, but Levi stopped him.

"Who was Braxton before the curse?"

The question startled Ashmedai, though the answer was simple. "Exactly who he is now—or so I thought. An alchemist, hungry for knowledge. If he is truly to blame for all this, I never would have guessed he'd be capable."

"The people of Emerald have become frightened of magic, outlawed it," Levi said, "yet they allow alchemy. There's still crime. There's still awfulness and death. But I've never heard of anything like what Braxton has done. I suppose even science can be frightening when wielded by the wrong person."

The sentiment was wise, but Ashmedai could tell Levi was haunted, because he too had never believed Braxton could be the *wrong person*.

"He owes us answers," Ashmedai said, reaching for the door once more, but also lifting his other hand to gently cup Levi's cheek like he had in the bedchamber. "If he did this, then all that matters is *why*."

Pulling the tower door open, Ashmedai went in first, with Levi following.

The tower was quiet, dark, with few crystals illuminating any part of the main living area.

"I don't see any pulsing, but he must be in his workshop," Levi whispered. "Unless he's still at the festival."

"Pulsing?"

"When he's working, lately there has been this purple light. It draws me in like I can't tear myself away."

Ashmedai frowned, continuing toward the closed workshop door, with one arm holding Levi behind him, though mostly to keep one hand laced with Levi's and know he was safe.

There was no noise from the workshop, no light either, but Braxton rarely kept it locked, and that was no different today. Everything looked as it had the last time Ashmedai was inside, except it was darker here, almost too dark for shadows, save a few at the base of the large black crystal in the center of the room.

At their approach, it pulsed with something almost the opposite of light, like Ashmedai's shadow magic—black with hints of purple, and only bright enough for them to see where they were going.

Ashmedai couldn't see in complete darkness, so even this lighting was difficult for him. His eyes were adjusting, but the clutter of the workshop, the shelving, the equipment, all of it could be hiding treachery where Ashmedai's eyes couldn't penetrate.

He opened his mouth to call out.

"Why, Levi, I believe you're missing stitches," Braxton called first.

Ashmedai looked around, but the voice had echoed, seemingly from everywhere, and he couldn't locate the source. "Brax? Show yourself! We deserve answers. Levi remembers his past life and believes you murdered him knowingly, on the other side of the barrier. Is that true? It that why you were keeping him from remembering who he was? Were you not forced to kill those people?"

"No, I wasn't," Braxton said. This time his voice seemed to come from behind them, but when Ashmedai pulled Levi closer and turned to look, nothing was there. "I needed them and their parts."

"Why?" Levi asked with a tremor in his voice. "Why did you need to make me?"

"It's the crystals. The black crystals are what will finally free everyone," Braxton said, not really answering Levi, with his voice coming from the walls this time, though Ashmedai couldn't tell which one. "That is all that matters."

"*Brax*," Ashmedai bit out sharply, hating that his voice tremored like Levi's. He'd never felt fear toward his friend before, but his instincts screamed at him to keep Levi close, so he gathered Levi in his arms and held him.

Braxton appeared finally from behind the large black crystal, wheeling forward like normal in his chair. "Do you remember when we met?"

Anger spiked through Ashmedai's chest. "You must answer for—"

"You found alchemy fascinating, so similar and yet different from magic. It didn't exist in your time, your world. Of course, I wasn't supposed to know what you were, but I saw when you arrived—late at night, when you thought no one was around.

"You blipped into existence out of thin air right in front of the Amethyst. There were stories of your kind. I knew what you were, what you had to be, much as I hadn't put much stock in myths before then. You were… ancient, with all the secrets of how magic could be harnessed within your grasp. You could have taught me endless truths of the universe, and all you cared about were the simple things—basic transmutation, farmers, children, walks by the lake."

At first Ashmedai thought Braxton meant to sneer at him, like Ashmedai had wasted his potential, but Braxton offered a rarely seen smile, tender even, as if he found it all truly endearing.

"Your kind once used the gemstones to heighten your already endless power and became gods, yet you were content to watch me tinker in my workshop."

"We didn't become gods," Ashmedai countered. "We corrupted ourselves."

"Perhaps. But you became more powerful, didn't you?"

"At a cost. Too great a cost. Brax—"

"Because you pushed for too much. You wanted the world. Someone's world can be as simple as their home or...." Braxton's smile turned tight as his eyes landed on Levi. "A gift from a lover."

Levi reached for the cuff on his ear, as if he could feel Braxton's gaze on it.

"Brax!" Ashmedai warned.

"You needn't worry. You know what matters to me is knowledge, not power or immortality. I already have enough of those."

"Then what—"

"I introduced you to Cullen, remember?" Braxton wheeled in front of the crystal, continuing a slow occasional spin of his wheels like a pantomime of pacing. "I hardly saw you after that, before everything changed."

"Enough!" Ashmedai snapped, tired of being interrupted. "You will answer me plainly!"

Braxton rotated his wheels to face Ashmedai. "Yes, I murdered those people."

Ashmedai didn't know what he'd expected, but part of him had hoped Braxton would have a different answer. "How? How did you cross the barrier, and why kill anyone?"

"I tried to do things humanely. Do you have any idea how many constructs I went through that you didn't even see? Do you think I did all that for a servant?" Braxton scoffed in a way that made Levi cower at Ashmedai's side. "I needed to learn what could and could not cross the barrier. I transmuted countless raw materials into copies of myself, but their life wasn't truly life. They didn't disintegrate when I sent them across the barrier, but they couldn't live anymore either and crumbled like useless dolls.

"I created the first black crystal to mimic the Amethyst while reversing its effects. If the Amethyst created the barrier to keep us in, the opposite should let us out. It didn't quite work that way initially, but I was able to use the black crystals to draw the lifeless constructs back inside the barrier so I could recycle them and start again. That process, however, had an unintended effect—it also sucked out the construct's residual life force and made the crystal pulse with power—like snuffing out one light to ignite another. That's what had been missing. I could mimic the Amethyst and alter its effects, but I couldn't harness enough power for anything living to cross the barrier safely. That's when I knew the answer to freeing us wasn't through life... but death."

He was mad. He was absolutely mad.

"I should have expected it. After all, the gemstones can harness the power of life and death, as you well know. They're how your people crossed over to our world and what you used to ascend. You exploited the magic of gemstones like the Amethyst to become what you are, and I used the Amethyst to create the black crystals and power my experiments— the very Source Crystal that cursed us.

"It still took hundreds of life forces from discarded constructs to allow me to cross over. I knew it would take too long to do the same for everyone else. Besides, one small crystal only let me leave our lands. It didn't make me human again or give me back the use of my legs.

"But oh, how lucky I was that day, exploring the outside world for the first time in so long. There was a highwayman in the wood who attacked me. I defended myself. Once he was dead, I pulled him back inside the barrier to see what would happen. He didn't transform. Being dead, he was unaffected by the curse. And souls don't immediately leave the body, you know. I had a hunch that if harvested quickly enough, a person's soul could power an entire crystal all on its own, and I was right. I tried once to use a soul from someone killed after they had crossed the barrier, but the curse rendered it useless. That's why the barrier destroys us. No, I needed uncursed souls.

"I continued experimenting with my constructs, but the real work was in securing a soul for every inhabitant of the Dark Kingdom. Don't you see? Any new spawn means a new sacrifice. With so many babes on the way, waiting any longer will only continue to postpone our freedom."

"That's why there were so many mounds," Levi said with a shudder, "so many more bodies than you would have needed to make me."

"There was the right amount to get what I needed." Braxton shrugged. "And maybe I enjoy killing people."

"You don't mean that," Ashmedai said, even if Braxton was mad.

"No? A thousand years is a long time to be alone, Ash."

"You weren't alone."

"And before that brief tea we had some time ago, how often did you visit?"

The truth cut Ashmedai deeply, but he shook his head. "I am sorry for that, but you can't blame my reclusiveness for you slaughtering innocents. Or your own choice to be reclusive. What you did is monstrous."

"Monstrous?" Braxton chuckled in such a dark, cruel way that Ashmedai didn't have to guess at the irony he was implying.

"I accept responsibility for my sins, but I never knowingly hurt anyone," Ashmedai defended. "And everything you did, everything you hoped to accomplish, none of it explains Levi."

Again, Braxton shrugged. "A single soul has its limitations. What good is crossing the barrier if we still retain our cursed selves? I knew there had to be an answer. I tested my hypothesis on animals first, simulating the frequency of the barrier here in my workshop."

"The pulsing," Levi deduced.

"Hypnotic, I'm sure, since it calls to the outside world. I wondered, if a true soul is more powerful than a construct's, how much more powerful would multiple true souls be if stitched together? You may only have one soul alive in you now, Levi, but you were made from many. Your unique soul can activate the others I've imprisoned in every black crystal in the kingdom, so that all at once, everyone will be capable of crossing the barrier and become who they once were, never at its mercy again. In that moment, with that level of power, the land itself will be cleansed and even animals can be saved. We can turn a monster back into a… mouse." He laughed.

Levi wasn't cowering anymore but gently pushed from Ashmedai's hold to step toward Braxton. "Then I truly meant nothing to you? I was just another experiment?"

Whatever else Ashmedai expected, it comforted him to see Levi's question cause a crack in Braxton's cold mask. "You are not nothing, Levi. You are everything. It took years to create you. Thankfully, highwaymen are plentiful. A few hired here and there ensured others were lured to the barrier for my use, and after I took what I needed, I'd simply bury the remains for the degenerates to loot later as payment.

"But you are not nothing. You were the first of my constructs to ever be truly alive, and you... surprised me, surpassing all my expectations. You will again when I use *this*." He reverently touched a hand to the large black crystal beside him, and it pulsed purple where his palm pressed. "My Onyx gemstone, the final step in not only freeing everyone but allowing us to become humans and elves and dwarves again.

"All that's missing is you." Braxton rotated his wheels again, pivoting to move behind the crystal, hiding him from view. "The right soul from the right body—one made from many."

"Levi!" Ashmedai cried, sensing the danger moments before Braxton struck.

Only *how* that was Braxton made Ashmedai freeze as he saw him, for a creature coiled around the crystal from the other side, not a man.

If Shevah was half spider, then Braxton was an amalgamation of spider and marionette. Extra limbs had sprouted from his body, stitched together from stolen parts. There were six of them, giving him eight when counting his original arms, which also extended unnaturally now, while his legs, honest at least in that they could not carry him, hung limp as his new limbs raised him up to a towering height.

Some of them lifted Braxton, others wrapped around the crystal for support, and more still lunged for Levi.

"No!" Ashmedai snapped to his senses, diving forward to intervene.

He had Levi by the shoulders, just as one of Braxton's limbs grabbed Levi's waist, while most of Braxton still touched the Onyx gemstone. It flashed with sudden power and light so strong that Ashmedai was flung backward.

"Noooo!" he cried louder, leaping back to his feet even while he couldn't see.

It was happening again.

It was all happening again!

"Levi!" Ashmedai screamed, seeking him blindly until the stars finally left his eyes.

The crystal was dimming back to black, and the monstrous version of Braxton was gone. The frailer, human Braxton lay on the floor in front of the crystal, unmoving, and Levi lay on the floor beside him.

"No, no, no." Ashmedai dove forward and laid a hand on each of them.

Braxton wasn't breathing. No pulse. Nothing.

And Levi....

A gasp came from Levi as his eyes sprang open and he sucked in a sharp breath.

Ashmedai focused on him, gathering him close and likely squeezing too hard as he fought for breath too. "Thank the skies and all the gemstones combined. Are you all right?"

Still gulping down air, Levi nodded but clung to Ashmedai weakly in return.

"You fool," Ashmedai said, looking at Braxton. "You were my friend. How could you do this?" He buried any remaining questions in the press of his face against Levi's hair.

It took some time for their panting and pattering pulses to quiet, but once they had, Ashmedai helped Levi sit up.

"A-Ash," Levi stuttered, swallowing and taking a breath to start over, as if still finding his voice. "W-what about the other crystals? The smaller black ones? Were they activated? They were everywhere, all throughout town...." He trailed off at the horror that might mean if Braxton was lying or if his intentions had been twisted, and Ashmedai understood.

He spared only a brief mourning glance at Braxton and then dove with Levi into the shadows at the base of the Onyx.

They arrived at the edge of the wood, between the tower and the town, but to their collective relief, nothing seemed to be amiss. They could see the jubilant people in the distance and hear the same faint music and celebration.

"Nothing's happened," Ashmedai said with a sigh.

"Something must have," Levi countered. "I can feel it. Can't you?"

Ashmedai didn't know what Levi meant, but then Levi had been created with a deeper connection to the crystals.

"The smaller crystals, powered by souls, were meant as conduits," Levi continued. "Even if no one noticed or felt anything, maybe that's all they did—spread the pulse throughout the land."

"To accomplish what?"

"What Braxton promised—to allow us to cross the barrier and become who we were."

They stared at each other, their eyes widening, before they turned toward the wood and began hurrying into the trees. They weren't near the carriage path this time, but Levi seemed to have a goal in mind, leading them swiftly.

He stumbled a few times in his haste, clearly still shaky from the blast, but each time Ashmedai helped him steady his feet, he pushed onward.

"Levi, wait!" Ashmedai called when Levi got too far ahead. "Even once we reach the barrier, how do we test this theory? If we're wrong, I can't cross it, and even if you could before, what if something different happened and you're no longer safe?"

The questions had the desired effect of slowing Levi's steps. They came to a stop side by side in the thick of trees, with Levi worrying his lip.

Rustling made Ashmedai grab Levi's arm and tug him closer. He wasn't letting anything happen to Levi again.

The rustling continued, and they both looked skyward. A glider monkey soared from branch to branch, heading deeper past them through the trees. They were close to where Grillo had his accident. Ashmedai could see the copse of felled trees a few yards from them, which meant the glider monkey was headed for the barrier's edge.

Ashmedai was going to call out, because usually the animals knew better, and the fresh crystals from the rebuilt perimeter still glowed, but Levi slapped a palm over Ashmedai's mouth and shook his head, pointing for Ashmedai to watch.

The glider monkey was leaping faster and faster, like it knew there was something to explore it hadn't seen before. After one final dive to reach a new branch, a ripple spread through the air, for the tree it had landed on was not shimmering black.

The glider monkey realized it too, but that wasn't the only new thing for the creature to discover. Its form was fading, but not like the horror of disintegration, just changing, becoming a simple gray squirrel.

The animal was certainly startled, but then it saw the snow at the base of the tree and scurried down the trunk to inspect the strange substance. A squirrel wasn't as dexterous as a glider monkey, but the creature was still able to dig into the snow, and then bundle up a bunch of it into a ball that it threw upward, clearly not thinking, since the snowball immediately came back down on top of its head.

Ashmedai and Levi laughed, drawing the squirrel's attention, which made it skitter back inside the barrier. It remained a squirrel—until it looked at itself and suddenly turned back into a glider monkey.

Levi started forward as the monkey, more skittish now with all the strangeness happening around it, leapt back up into the trees and hurried away.

"I think that was our test," Levi said and stepped across the barrier boldly.

The same ripple occurred, and Levi's skin faded to a pale peach, his eyes becoming blue instead of violet as he turned back with a smile and extended his hand, beckoning for Ashmedai to follow.

Levi was the strong one, of that Ashmedai had been certain for some time, but he knew he couldn't cower in his castle anymore when the chance for freedom was finally before him. Taking a breath, Ashmedai grasped Levi's hand and allowed himself to be pulled from the lands he had ruled over for a thousand years into the snow.

The whiteness of Ashmedai's skin also became peach-colored, his ears remaining long, though he felt his teeth lose their sharpness, and his claws became dull, blunt nails. He couldn't see his own eyes, but he imagined them now being a benign brown.

"You're not really an elf, though," Levi said with a sly grin.

"True, but I've always been able to bring out my real form. This was the version of me that was lost."

Levi shivered, and Ashmedai pulled him closer with a chuckle. It was colder on this side, where the winter season was more normal, and snow littered the ground around them. The temptation to explore was strong, but they agreed it would be safer and smarter to wait until more of the citizens had been informed and could join them, especially if more highwaymen lurked.

They returned to the Shadows Lands. Like with the glider monkey, they didn't immediately transform back. It seemed that had to be a conscious choice.

"To be honest," Ashmedai said, marveling at Levi's cream skin, "I think I might miss the blue."

"I think I'd miss your ridges." Levi alighted his fingers on Ashmedai's smooth clavicle, bared from the open collar of his red silk tunic. "And your claws. And your eyes. And your fangs."

Ashmedai laughed, and together, they returned themselves to the way they had been.

"I guess everyone can choose what they want," Levi said. "In a way, the barrier is still with us, but the people can be whoever they wish, even leave if they desire."

"I have a feeling most will want to stay exactly as they've been for a thousand years, or the way the newer ones were born. But now they have a choice. Imagine being able to travel again, to have visitors again. I just wish...." Ashmedai looked through the trees toward where he knew the tower resided. "I wish Brax...."

Levi hugged Ashmedai when no more words left him. "I know."

"He wasn't himself in the end. He wasn't. And I can't help blaming myself for that too. He was right about one thing. I wasn't there for him. I was so lonely for so long, but I was selfish, because I didn't see how lonely my friend was too."

Within their embrace, Levi lifted his hands to hold Ashmedai's face. "Everything can be better now, and we can make certain that every sacrifice was worth getting here."

He drew Ashmedai closer and kissed him.

This kiss was different than any before it, because Ashmedai was suddenly aware of how Levi's lips felt without stitches. As bittersweet as this victory was, he decided that nothing had ever felt so right.

BACK INSIDE the tower, in the abandoned workshop, while Braxton's body was still and empty and would remain so, the Onyx gemstone pulsed faintly at its core with one last hidden spark of light.

Of *life*.

And within that impenetrable prison, the real Levi screamed.

CHAPTER 11

"THIS CAN'T be real. I have to be dreaming," Levi said to an empty, terrifying echo.

There was nothing but blackness immediately around him, with the faint glow of violet light. He couldn't move. His voice, he supposed, was more something he wanted to hear, thoughts not words, because he had no mouth to speak.

Braxton had accomplished exactly what he wanted, and Ashmedai didn't know, because Braxton had taken Levi's body. He'd set them up, positioned everything perfectly, and now Levi was alone.

Levi could see outside the Onyx, but only the barren workshop it resided in, still dark. Braxton's body was sprawled on the floor, back to a normal humanlike figure, though Levi knew now how much that too had been a lie.

Unable to tell the passage of time, the wait for something, anything to happen, was maddening. What did Braxton want? What was he doing with Ashmedai? What did he plan to do with Levi? Would he force Levi to stay like this and slowly lose himself to the isolation?

As that thought crept in on Levi, he once again screamed.

"Urg, enough. No one else might be able to hear you, but to me, it's grating."

Levi stopped with a stutter, his scream fading as he tried to look around. It was surreal, because he couldn't actually look around or shift his line of sight, yet he could see in every direction around the Onyx without moving.

Through the workshop door strolled *Levi*.

Or rather, Braxton with Levi's face.

"Let me out!" Levi cried. "Please! Please don't leave me like this…."

"I have no intention of leaving you in there forever." Stranger still, perhaps, was hearing Levi's own voice with Braxton's cadence. He was dressed in the Emerald silk tunic, so it must still be the same night. "Your soul is strong, but soon the Onyx gemstone will drain you of your memories, and you won't fear anything anymore. Then you will get to start over. My gift to you."

"What...?"

Braxton came closer but didn't touch the Onyx. "You are my creation, Levi, my child. Of course I will remake you. You've accomplished everything I required of you. The spell is complete now, so it no longer needs your soul. I will give you a new life, a new body. But *this* one—" He pressed a hand to his chest. "—I made for me." He knelt then to pick up his own body—*his* body, because he was walking around in Levi's, and he planned to keep it.

"You can't! Please! Why do you even want my body? To walk again? You could—"

"Blind boy, it's not only that," Braxton spat, shifting the body in his arms to better balance the weight. "If all I'd wanted all this time was working legs, you've seen how capable I am at crafting from the bodies I've harvested. I needed the *right* body. Not only for the right soul to accomplish my plan, but a body he could love."

"But why...?" Levi trailed off even as the words formed, because the answer was obvious, but he *had* been blind. And so was Ashmedai. "You're in love with Ash. You've been in love with him from the beginning. But you never said anything. You couldn't have, or—"

"Or what? He would have had the chance to reject me outright? Before you, Ash only ever loved one man, a man who didn't deserve him and dared cast him aside, earning him his fate. I could have finished the spell years ago, but to make you right, I needed a face that would remind Ash of Cullen while still looking enough like me. I do have some vanity.

"I suppose my one regret is that you had the pleasure of touching him first. I waited so long to find a face as perfect as yours. I didn't even need to change your hair. Now Ash loves *me*, and we can both be happy and forget that prince ever existed."

"You can't do this!" Levi cried when Braxton began to walk away. "You can't erase me again! Please!"

"Don't worry. You took enough of the draught that the process should be easier this time. Eventually you won't even know what you've lost." Braxton paused at the workshop door and glanced back with a smile that Levi could only see as callous victory. "Just like Ash."

ASHMEDAI COULDN'T help feeling numb as they buried Braxton's body. He hadn't wanted to go back inside the tower to retrieve it, but Levi had volunteered, far stronger than Ashmedai felt. Levi carried Braxton's limp form with a solemn sense of duty that Ashmedai admired. He didn't even shed any tears, so Ashmedai did his best to not shed more either.

Whatever the crystal had done, Braxton's soul must have ended up powering it instead of Levi's. Part of Ashmedai wanted to think—good—but he doubted he'd ever fully see it that way. They buried Braxton behind the tower, amidst the flowers, and Ashmedai hoped that, someday, after they explained everything to the citizens, they could have a true ceremony to say goodbye.

They didn't return to the festival but retired to the castle. Explanations would come tomorrow. All Ashmedai wanted now was Levi in his arms and a bit of sweet oblivion.

"Prrp?"

Aurora's chirp was questioning as she appeared in the bedchamber while they were changing for sleep. She could always tell when Ashmedai was upset.

"I'm all right, my dear." Ashmedai petted her, and she pushed up into his hand like a rippling wave. "Sad perhaps, but also hopeful. She has a sense of things, you see," he said over his shoulder, as Levi moved toward them, "especially when I'm not myself."

Ashmedai wore a red silk nightshirt to bed, not unlike the tunic he'd been wearing most of the day, though longer and more flowing. He'd lent a second nightshirt to Levi, black, which billowed beautifully around his trim body as he moved.

With a smile, Levi reached to stroke Aurora's head, but she reared back and hissed at him before suddenly bounding through the bedchamber door, as if eager to escape.

"What on earth?" Ashmedai stared after her. She'd been so good around Levi so far.

"She must blame me for you being upset," Levi said, his smile quivering in displeasure.

"Or she doesn't want to share the bed," Ashmedai appeased. "I'm sure she'll warm back up to you in no time."

They headed for bed, and there was something so blissfully domestic about climbing under the covers with Levi that Ashmedai almost forgot to turn out the crystals lighting the room. He had a black dousing crystal like everyone else, and he almost hesitated using it to dim the lights all at once. Its true purpose had been revealed to be far more sinister, and an innocent soul had been sacrificed to power it.

Ashmedai tapped it and the lights went out. He sighed. All was as it should be.

"I'll admit I often wondered if you sleep," Levi said.

"I don't need to, but I enjoy it. Settling one's mind can be quite the relief."

"I couldn't agree more." Levi snuggled closer, the full line of his body pressing up against Ashmedai, which somehow felt more scandalous with thin silk between them than when they'd previously lain here naked. "We don't have to settle immediately, though... do we?"

"Did I not wear you out enough before?" Ashmedai laughed in surprise.

"A reminder wouldn't be remiss." With violet eyes darkening, Levi leaned in and kissed Ashmedai heatedly.

It was still strange getting used to the lack of stitches. Ashmedai almost missed them, but although kissing Levi felt different than it once had, he never wanted to kiss anyone else again.

He rolled and pulled Levi to him, giving in to the eager touches and deep probing of Levi's tongue. The silk contoured to them both and made the slide of their bodies softer. Ashmedai could already feel Levi hardening from the briefest thrusting of their hips.

Ashmedai was not, however. He didn't think it had anything to do with lack of desire for the young man clinging to him. It must have simply been too difficult a night.

Levi twisted the silk of Ashmedai's nightshirt, gathering it upward to reach between his legs, and Ashmedai hated that he had to stop him.

"I'm sorry. I can't. I think my mind is too occupied with all that's happened."

The disappointment was plain on Levi's face, but he nodded with a shuddery breath. "I understand. Being in your bed is prize enough. And after all, we have an eternity to be together."

"Indeed, we do, and despite everything else," Ashmedai said, still holding Levi close, as he shut his eyes for sleep, "that truly makes me glad."

"THE BARRIER'S gone?"

"Brax is dead?"

"How did this happen?"

The slew of questions from the citizens fed off one another until the grand hall was utter pandemonium with the overlapping of another question and then another. Ashmedai couldn't blame them. He still barely believed it had all happened either.

This council meeting was more packed than any before it, for attendance had not been optional. Ashmedai felt a bit bad waking everyone before dawn when several of the people were clearly hungover from the festivities, but it couldn't be helped. He didn't know what *day* would bring when so much had changed.

Since the hall was filled to bursting, the doors had been left open to keep the room from becoming too stifling. Ashmedai let the people's questions continue for a time, but then he stood to grab their attention and hushed them. All would be explained—and explain he did, with Levi standing where Braxton's chair would have been and filling in what Ashmedai couldn't answer as if part of Braxton lived on.

Because the change was minimal within the barrier, the curse having been altered rather than eradicated, the belief was that adult citizens would continue to be unaging, but beyond that, much could be different if they wished it. There was confusion, skepticism, and awe, but eventually the truth hit home for everyone, and talk turned to what to do next.

Yentriss demanded patrols, especially after learning of the highwaymen. They couldn't simply venture outside their borders without taking precautions. Levi had spoken of distrust among the other kingdoms of magic and elves, so Ashmedai agreed patrols and vigilance were necessary, since there was no way to know how outsiders might react to them, even if they would look "normal" upon leaving their lands.

"From our tests, it seems anyone can take on their former self if they choose, even now, here, while still within the barrier. Levi and I did so and were able to change back, so the choice is yours."

That brought a fresh hush upon the crowd, many looking around as if wondering who might try it first.

No one did.

"Can I have wings?" a small voice asked.

Kenner waved from where he sat in his father's lap.

"I don't think it works that way, Kenner," Ashmedai said. "You can look as you would have should your parents have had you when they were, um…." He looked to Yentriss beside him because he didn't remember anymore what she and Grillo were.

"An elf," Yentriss said, with a fondness rarely heard from her.

"Human," Grillo called in kind.

"Then you might look a bit like Levi," Ashmedai said to Kenner, "just not blue."

Kenner had seemed intrigued when Ashmedai first said Levi's name, but those final words made him grimace, like not being blue made the whole thing far less appealing.

Ashmedai was going to recommend they test things slowly, only if people wanted to, and with careful consideration, sharing all findings to be certain there were no unforeseen side effects—when another hush struck the crowd as light began to filter in through the open doorway.

Bright light.

"The sun is rising!" someone cried, and an immediate dash began for the door.

"Everyone, please!" Dreya tried to retain order, but the excitement was too great for anyone to listen, and Ashmedai reached over to rest a hand on Dreya's arm.

"I think such a sight happening for the first time in a thousand years is something everyone deserves to see." Ashmedai smiled and watched the excitement fill Dreya's face too before she spun around and yanked a surprised Luccite from her chair to lead them both out the back door.

"Go," Ashmedai told Yentriss, who bowed in thanks before hurrying to join her family.

Levi waited for him, and they walked hand in hand down the center aisle to exit out the front doors after everyone else had gone. All the details they still needed to settle paled in comparison to seeing the sun brighten the once Dark Kingdom.

It *was* bright, something none of them were used to, and some, like Dreya, had never seen the sun before, yet somehow it didn't seem to bother anyone or cause them pain. It merely took them a moment to adjust. The city looked so different in daylight, since everything was otherwise as it had been all these years, from the angled buildings to the distant trees shimmering black.

"What does this mean when everything else still looks the same?" Luccite asked, farther out since she had come from around the back with Dreya, still holding her hand.

Ashmedai picked a flower from a bush blooming in front of the grand hall's front windows and willed it with a thought to become how it had once been. Instead of blue luminescence and a winding black stem, the flower became a long-stemmed red rose.

Mindful of the thorns, Ashmedai handed it to Levi, who smiled.

"We get to choose," Ashmedai said, "so let us do so wisely."

Everything became more of a celebration after that, different but just as glorious as Festival Day. There were some things people wanted to remember of their old lives, and so they would change objects to that other form, sometimes to stay that way, sometimes to change back. But few who changed their bodies left themselves as human, elf, dwarf, or half.

Like Daedlys, who had once been a slender white-haired elf, or Klarent, a brown-haired human with a handsome beard. Grillo, who'd also been human, had still been broad and tall, but with dark skin and tightly coiled black hair, whereas Yentriss was an elf with paler skin, long golden braids, and green eyes. Kenner tried very hard to follow their example, a half-elf with medium skin between their two shades and brown hair with golden highlights, though he didn't seem capable of willing his horns away—or didn't want to.

Dreya was especially fascinated with Luccite's red curls when she took on her dwarven form, her button nose still looking quite catlike. Dreya herself, like Kenner, couldn't fully form a "normal" persona, and only managed to rid herself of bark and hooves.

Almost everyone eventually returned to their cursed selves, however, as Ashmedai had suspected. Titles like "monster" were in the eye of the beholder, and a thousand years was a long time to learn that.

There would be order, more tests, and exploration—eventually— but for now, people were content to have a day in the sunshine.

Ashmedai thought Levi looked especially radiant in brighter light, his red hair proving to have even more variations in shade than Ashmedai had ever noticed. His blue skin too.

"What next, my darling?" Ashmedai asked. They hadn't chosen a destination, though their impromptu stroll had ended with them at the top of the market steps.

Rather than head down, Levi motioned farther along the path. "While a walk by the lake would be lovely, I should clean up the tower."

"Oh? I was hoping you might continue staying with me at the castle."

"I was hoping the same." Levi took Ashmedai's hands. "But I'd like to keep the tower as well, maybe even continue some of Braxton's experiments. *Humanely*. There are great things that can be done with alchemy."

"True. You know, there's one thing I don't understand about what happened last night. Brax made it sound as if it had to be you, your soul to accomplish all this, but in the end, it didn't matter."

Levi's smile turned thin, as though the reminder pained him. "I guess not." He kissed Ashmedai, and once more Ashmedai was struck by how different it felt to kiss Levi without stitches. He hadn't noticed as much when he first took the stitches away, but then they had been quite a bit more amorously involved at the time. Still, it was definitely different now, more starkly different every time, in fact, almost like Ashmedai was kissing someone else.

That thought stirred unease in Ashmedai's stomach.

"I'll come with you to assist—" he tried when Levi turned away.

"*No.*" Levi whirled around. "No thank you. I'd like some time alone if that's all right."

"Of course," Ashmedai said. Levi needed to mourn too, and it was an understandable request. There was no reason for Ashmedai to feel like anything was off, and yet there was… *something* he couldn't identify, sitting in his stomach where the unease had swirled.

The last thing Ashmedai wanted was to be distrustful of Levi, but that feeling in his gut didn't fade. He decided, at least for a few paces, he'd follow Levi by shadow to ensure everything was okay.

There were more shadows than ever with the sun shining above, so finding several along the road was easy, and Ashmedai leapt from one to the next, keeping his distance and always staying out of sight. He was being protective, not suspicious, he told himself.

Then, when Levi got to the portion of the road that would either continue toward the tower or curve into the wood, he went into the trees.

Ashmedai slipped back out of the shadows and stared. Why would Levi not mention he planned to enter the wood? That gnawing, unsettled feeling might have prompted Ashmedai to continue following Levi, but there was also something about the tower being "cleaned up" that gave him pause, and in one swift pivot, he turned for that destination instead.

Before anything was changed, Ashmedai wanted to see it again for himself.

LEVI WAS already starting to forget things. He couldn't remember his brother's name anymore, and he had only just recalled it the day before. His old life seemed to be fading first, but Levi didn't want to lose any of it again. He'd already been robbed of himself once.

Not knowing the passage of time was worse. There were no windows in the workshop. He knew it had only been hours, but how many? And how many more did he have before he would forget everything?

Footsteps drew his attention to his surroundings. Braxton's presence wouldn't be welcome, because it meant he'd be working toward giving Levi a new body, a new life, and Levi didn't want to give up this one.

The sight of Ashmedai walking through the workshop door made him lose all other thought.

"Ash!" Levi shouted. "I'm here! Ash, I'm here!"

Ashmedai didn't appear to hear Levi, for his pace was slow, moving around the workshop with a scrutinizing eye, as though looking for something.

"I'm here…," Levi said, weak and defeated, because Ashmedai wasn't looking for *him*. He had no reason to believe he didn't already have Levi with him.

It was good to see Ashmedai, though, beautiful as ever, walking with his fluid grace as if the shadows themselves carried him forward. Maybe he simply sought a book or some token to remember Braxton by. His expression was pensive, however, as he trailed his claws along the shelving and pored over notes scrawled on scraps of parchment on various tables. None of it seemed to satisfy what he was searching for.

"You must know something's wrong," Levi said. "That's why you're here, isn't it? You must be able to tell he's not me. He's not me, Ash. *I'm* me!" he finished with another shout.

Ashmedai's head whipped toward the Onyx.

"Can you hear me? Ash!"

Ashmedai didn't answer, but his brow scrunched as he began to approach.

"Yes! I'm here! I'm here! Please hear me!"

Ashmedai's frown deepened, and he eyed the Onyx gemstone from its base to the ceiling. He couldn't hear Levi, but he must be able to sense something.

"I don't care if you can't hear me. I'm still going to speak. I don't want to forget you. I don't want to be someone else. I think I've forgotten my old name again, but that's not the name I need. I'm Levi. I'm *yours*. Please sense that I'm here, Ash. Please...."

If Levi still had his body, he would have gasped when Ashmedai's eyes stopped their searching inspection and landed square on the center of the Onyx, as if looking right at him. Levi couldn't see himself, but he must be nothing but a spark inside a void of blackness. Still, he willed with all the conviction in him that Ashmedai somehow know that spark was him.

Ashmedai reached forward—

"What are you doing?"

Braxton stood in the doorway when Ashmedai spun around.

"No!" Levi screamed, as loud as he could. "That's not me! That's not me!"

Braxton cringed as he came forward, since he *could* hear Levi, though he tried to hide it.

"Your hands," Ashmedai said, noticing smudges on Braxton's hands and dirt beneath his fingernails.

Braxton stared at them, cringing again, but allowed the expression to transform into something sorrowful. "I... started thinking about the mounds, all those... parts." He shuddered, as believably as if the real Levi had done so. "I wanted to be sure the first one I saw was covered in case anyone ventured to the barrier. I know everyone agreed not to, but I didn't want anyone to have to see that."

"So that's what you were doing," Ashmedai said, sighing in audible relief. "I thought...."

"What?"

"I don't know what I thought. It's been a trying few days. I'm sorry. I'll leave you be."

"No!" Levi cried again. He'd been so close to having Ashmedai notice him. He was certain of it. "Ash! You can't leave me, please! I'm here! I'm right here!"

Braxton flashed Levi a cold look before turning with a smile to follow Ashmedai's retreat.

"Ash!" Levi bellowed.

Ashmedai stopped. "The first mound?" He turned around slowly. "That one was already covered. That's why we couldn't find it again after Grillo's accident."

"Right. I know," Braxton said. "I just wanted to be certain to ease my mind."

"He's lying!" Levi cried, watching Braxton flinch once more, noticeably enough to tighten his shoulders. "You know he's lying! Ash!"

"Something isn't right." Ashmedai headed back into the room. "I don't know what, but I know something isn't right. *You're* not right."

"What are you talking about?" Braxton straightened, pivoting to position himself squarely between Ashmedai and the Onyx.

"You've seemed strange ever since Brax died. I didn't notice right away, but I know you've been acting different."

"How should I act? Everything changed last night. I'm simply adjusting like everyone else."

"What were you doing in the wood?"

"I told you—"

"You're lying. You've never lied to me. What were you doing there?"

Braxton's tension increased. He didn't have an answer.

Ashmedai moved past him toward the Onyx.

"No! Don't touch it." Braxton grabbed his arm. "You'll disrupt its power and seal us in again."

Ashmedai looked at him and then at the hand tight on his arm.

Braxton let him go with a start.

"Why would you think that?" Ashmedai asked. "You weren't aware of what Brax was doing."

"I... was looking over his notes—"

"You weren't here. You went into the wood. You haven't been back here to read over any notes."

"It doesn't matter. Don't you understand? Everything is fine. Everything is perfect. Just leave it be."

Ashmedai backed toward the Onyx and then turned to face it again. "What if I destroyed this thing completely?"

"No!" Braxton lurched forward. "You'll condemn everyone!"

"Will I?" Ashmedai glanced back. "Or just you.... *Brax*?"

Ashmedai filled his hand with sudden shadows, faster and more concentrated than any he'd used to smooth Levi's stitches. Before Braxton could stop him, or Levi could do more than stare in wonder and hope—Ashmedai slammed his hands against the Onyx gemstone's sides and the shadows burst.

"No!"

ANOTHER BLINDING flash and explosion threw Ashmedai across the room. He didn't know if some of what Braxton was saying might be true, but he didn't care. What he did know was that the real Levi was somewhere else, and the Onyx had to go.

Unlike last night, Ashmedai didn't hurry to his feet. He was too afraid of what he might find, or worse, that he might have been wrong. When he finally did get up and blinked the spots from his eyes, his fears were realized, because the Onyx was in pieces—and Levi's body lay limp on the floor.

"No...." Ashmedai dropped to his knees beside Levi and reached for him with a hesitant hand, fearing he would find an empty body like Braxton's.

His worry worsened when Levi didn't gasp awake or sit up with a start, but then, finally, when Ashmedai's hand landed atop Levi's heart to search for a beat, violet eyes fluttered open.

"Levi?"

"I-I... was Leander," Levi croaked as if he hadn't spoken in days. "My brother's name is Leslie."

"What?" Ashmedai asked with a frantic laugh, scooping Levi into his arms.

"The gemstone was making me forget again," Levi said with a weary smile, despite the horror of those words, "but I remember now."

A sob caught in his throat and tears started to form to quickly stream down his cheeks. He tried to blink through them, but upon failing, he let himself cry and pressed his face to Ashmedai's chest.

"It's really you this time," Ashmedai said, not asking, as he hugged Levi tightly. He felt Levi nod, and in the depths of his soul, he knew it to be true. "I'm so sorry it took me so long to realize."

"But you did," Levi said, looking up with wonder and love in his gaze. "You—"

An eruption and inhuman shriek thundered in the distance from somewhere outside the tower. They both sat up, looking to the workshop door.

"If I'm back in my body...." Levi began.

"Then Brax is back in his," Ashmedai finished.

He helped Levi up, and they rushed for the back door, with Ashmedai not losing contact with Levi for a single moment. He would not lose Levi again, but they had to confront Braxton once and for all.

Once outside, the source of the noise was clear—the garden, where they'd buried Braxton. Dirt shot upward and rained down again as Braxton fought himself free, his added limbs returning from however they stayed hidden within his body. He looked even more monstrous than before with the way dirt and mud covered him, and his eyes were wild with fury.

A sack lay on the ground near him with body parts spilling out of it. At least Ashmedai knew why he'd gone into the wood.

"I was going to remake you!" Braxton bellowed at Levi, striking out with one of his elongated limbs to spill the bag of parts over the ground. "But no, you had to be selfish! You had to draw him to you, like some demandable siren! I waited a thousand years, and you ruined everything!"

The way he rose up and charged toward them—toward Levi—with impossible speed, made it clear he had no intention of sparing Levi this time.

Ashmedai tucked Levi close and jumped into a pool of nearby shadows. They reappeared again halfway down the road toward town. Ashmedai turned to Levi to begin working on a plan, but Levi was gazing upward, staring at the sunlit sky. Ashmedai had nearly forgotten that the real Levi had yet to experience it.

"I remember the sun from my old life, but... it's beautiful." He smiled in wonder.

"I know." Ashmedai allowed the quiet moment, but like their limited time with a once friend turned enemy in pursuit, the sun's rays appeared to be out of time too. Clouds were forming to block it. The sky was growing dark, and Ashmedai couldn't be certain if it was natural or magic and alchemy at work. "We may have undone everything...."

"Maybe," Levi said, with the shadow of guilt erasing his smile. "Braxton said he didn't need my soul anymore, but I don't know the consequences of destroying the Onyx."

"I don't care." Ashmedai looked at him squarely. "If I never get to leave these lands or see the sun again, it'll be a worthy sacrifice to have you."

As a new smile brightened Levi's face, another rumble sounded in the distance, and they looked to see what appeared like a monstrous spider clinging to the side of the tower. When Braxton spotted them, he leapt from the tower with ease and again began to charge, moving faster than a rollhound with the way his many limbs carried him forward.

"Run!" Ashmedai urged Levi down the path, and they sprinted together, just as the clouds that had started to appear blotted out the sun entirely.

"What are we doing?" Levi asked. "What can we do?"

"I don't want to raise my hand or sword against a friend, but I won't let him touch you," Ashmedai said. "We can't let him reach town either. The wood! We must lead him into the wood. We must get him to cross the barrier."

With the Onyx destroyed, Ashmedai wasn't certain if crossing the barrier would make Braxton human or kill him, but it was the only way to give Braxton a chance while keeping Levi and the citizens safe.

They were already past the path into the wood closest to the tower. Running in blindly without a path could be as dangerous as what pursued them. They had to make it to the main road. Which meant everyone would be able to see them—and Braxton.

"Ash? Levi?" Grillo called from the edge of town, where he'd just come up the market steps with Yentriss and Kenner.

Someone screamed, and since literally everyone had already been outside enjoying the sun, they all heard the disruption and turned to look.

"Is that... Brax?" Kenner gaped.

"Stay back!" Ashmedai shouted. "We'll handle this!"

He owed his people that. He only wished he could pass Levi to Grillo and Yentriss and keep him from having to be part of this too, but Levi was who Braxton was after.

"Hurry!" Ashmedai grabbed Levi, leaping through nearby shadows to ones at the edge of the wood, putting them farther ahead of Braxton, but still ensuring he saw them and would follow.

Follow he did, so Ashmedai started running again, keeping Levi close.

Braxton only had eyes for them, uncaring of the townsfolk, and barreled after them like a force of nature.

"He's too fast," Ashmedai lamented, "but if I shadow jump too many times, he might realize what we're planning."

"Then we'll have to give him extra targets," Levi said, his tears long dried, with a determination settling on his face that belied all fear before it, "because I am not letting him touch you either."

With a brief squeeze of his eyes shut and a spread of his arms outward, suddenly there were a dozen more of Levi and Ashmedai all branching away and falling behind them to dart off into the trees.

Ashmedai stared in awe—only to spot a swarm of jackalopes headed toward them. He grabbed Levi by the shoulders and held him back so the jackalopes could dart past, thankful they were clearly more interested in escaping Braxton than ramming into passersby with their antlers.

Behind them, Braxton was distracted enough by the copies that he was swatting at any of them he could reach and punching through trees. Upon impact, the copies would disappear, and Braxton would howl and swipe at another. It wouldn't be long before he spotted the real thing.

Renewing their run, Ashmedai urged Levi on beside him, sparing only an occasional glance back to track Braxton's progress. The copies were many, but Braxton was no fool. He realized his prize had remained on the road, and he and Ashmedai locked eyes.

A rustle in the trees above made Ashmedai look skyward before he could look forward again. Glider monkeys were also fleeing. With another glance back, Ashmedai even saw a family of gazellians running across the path, and they never ventured this close to town. But then, even on the hunt, no one ever made as much noise as Braxton was now.

Braxton swung outward with two of his formidable gangling limbs, and the gazellians flew like rag dolls into trees before scampering back up and limping in a frenzy to get away.

"There!" Levi called, just as Ashmedai and Braxton locked eyes once more, and Braxton hurtled himself forward that much faster.

Ashmedai looked forward to gauge the distance to the barrier, waited until just the right moment, and then grabbed Levi about the waist and spun them, setting Levi directly behind him as he came to a stop.

"Enough!" Ashmedai held both hands outward with a surge of shadows like he'd used to destroy the Onyx. He stared Braxton down, daring him to continue coming. "Do you hate me so much for what I did that *this* is how you're punishing me?"

Braxton's anger flared visibly in his expression, but he brought himself to a stop, his spider limbs planting into the dirt to hold him up as tall as possible. "What *you* did? You fool. You didn't curse this land. Don't you understand that yet? Don't you remember where I was when it happened? *I* altered the spell Cullen tried to cast, not you."

"What?"

The townspeople had followed despite Ashmedai's warning. They came running down the road after Braxton, wielding magic and weapons, like an army come to Ashmedai and Levi's aid, but at those words they stopped and stared, just as Ashmedai was.

"My research into the gemstones back then was far from complete," Braxton went on, "but I was able to manipulate what Cullen tried to do, so that instead of keeping a monster out after he discovered you were a demon...."

Ashmedai would have flinched at his secret being revealed for all to hear, but he couldn't focus on the stunned faces of his people enough to care. "The Amethyst turned everyone *into* monsters and kept them in," he finished breathlessly.

"Exactly. I was trying to protect you, to keep you here instead of letting Cullen banish you like some beast. Sacrificing him to complete the spell was a bonus."

All this time, Ashmedai had been so certain it was his fault, certain Cullen being taken by the void was because he couldn't control himself in his grief over being rejected. "But why? Why all this? Why murder and lie and try to take over Levi's body?"

"Because he's in love with you," Levi said softly from behind him.

"What…?" Ashmedai sputtered again.

"Even now it is a surprise to you," Braxton huffed, stomping with his stolen feet. "I have always been the one who loved you. *Me*. But you never saw it. You only saw Cullen, which was why I knew you would see him." He sneered over Ashmedai's shoulder at Levi. "I needed to manipulate enough parts to look like Cullen but still like me so you would forget whatever parts of me weren't enough. Then I simply needed to make Levi fall in love with you."

Now it was Levi who sputtered, "Make me? What do you mean?"

"Your draught wasn't only to keep your memories at bay, silly boy. It made you susceptible to suggestion. I knew you'd catch Ash's attention—I'd made you for that purpose—but I had to be sure he would catch yours. The first time you ever took that draught was when I told you about him. Afterward, you just needed to see him. To know him. I even knew he would be compelled to smooth your stitches. You were bound to love him after that, as I do."

Love. All the pain and suffering these many years hadn't been suffered by Ashmedai alone, but the cause was the same.

With them at a standstill, Ashmedai couldn't help feeling sorry for his friend, and he owed him the truth.

"I do love you, Brax."

A smile slipped into Braxton's cold expression.

"But not the way you want, and this isn't the way to change that."

Braxton stomped again with several of his feet, his smile crumbling, as he readied to charge. "That is *my* body."

"No, it isn't." Ashmedai kept Levi behind him.

"You would take this from me? You would reject me as you were rejected? His love for you isn't even real! Mine is. My whole life was dedicated to becoming what you wanted."

"I never asked that of you. Brax, please—"

"No." Braxton shook his head. "I have waited too long. I am through being patient! I will find another way. I will show you."

"Brax, don't!"

He lunged, but Ashmedai was ready for it, waiting for a shadow to appear, cast by Braxton's towering height, and then he dove with Levi out of harm's way.

Braxton surged forward from the momentum, not stopping until he crossed the barrier, and as Ashmedai and Levi reappeared just inside the line of trees, where one of the taller trunks cast another shadow, they could only watch with bated breath to see what would happen next.

To Ashmedai's honest relief, Braxton didn't disintegrate. Whatever finishing the spell last night had accomplished, destroying the Onyx hadn't undone its effects. Braxton's added limbs faded and he fell, landing with a gasp on sturdy legs that held his weight for the first time in centuries.

He shifted on his feet in shocked silence. As he stared at himself with those first few tentative steps, he almost looked close to tears.

"There you are, old friend," Ashmedai said, stepping onto the road with Levi beside him. "Please, still be my friend. You have done terrible things, but this doesn't have to end with more loss. You cursed these lands, but you also freed them. Be free with us."

Ashmedai took another step forward and outstretched his hand. All that stood between him and Braxton was the barrier, a nearly invisible wall separating man from monster.

Braxton turned to face him. He didn't look all that different, other than not needing his chair, for he had always maintained most of his human appearance. The tears in his eyes didn't fall, however, but held steady.

"A thousand years ago, that might have been enough. But I have waited too long." He walked determinedly through the barrier, and the fierceness on his face made Ashmedai stutter backward, dropping his hand, for he knew it would not be taken.

As Braxton crossed over, his spider limbs regrew in the same breath that his real legs failed him, and he was raised back up to that menacing height.

"Brax, you can't force me to love you," Ashmedai tried once more. "Who knows better than I that you can't force anyone to love you? But you can choose how you react when they don't."

Braxton winced at being told once more that Ashmedai would never love him the way he wanted. "No. Nothing matters without you. You're mine. You were supposed to be mine! Not his." His eyes fell to Levi, who had stepped parallel with Ashmedai. Whatever love Braxton once had for his creation, there was no sign of it now.

He lunged for Levi like before, and Ashmedai knew in the scant seconds he had to act that he had been left with only one choice.

Moving with matching swiftness, he stepped between lover and friend and met Braxton in a clash that was far from equal, for Ashmedai became a deadly, shadowlike wave that flooded over Braxton to consume him. Nothing would be left behind, because Ashmedai couldn't bear seeing remains when he had already buried Braxton once.

One moment Ashmedai was shadows in ravenous motion, and the next he stood where Braxton had been. The usual satiation and instant desire for more flooded through Ashmedai, but as much as he hated this part of himself, he knew he could control it.

He didn't reform himself completely to his usual guise, however. He owed it to the audience he hadn't forgotten the chance to see what he truly was. Surely they already guessed, given what they'd overheard, but still, slowly, Ashmedai turned to face Levi and his people farther behind, for the first time not hiding any part of himself.

All weapons and magic had long since dropped. Not everyone had a clear view of what was happening, but the truth was clearly being whispered and passed down the line. No one screamed. No one ran. But no one moved toward the terrifying shadow demon in their midst.

Not until Levi, tears in his eyes, with a mixture of heartache and affection on his face, leapt upon Ashmedai and threw his arms around him. He gasped, for the feel of Ashmedai in that form was still intense, but he didn't loosen his hold.

Ashmedai held him back tightly, and finally faded into the version of himself he preferred, pressing his pale white face against the softness of Levi's hair. He closed his eyes, expecting to be driven out, condemned, shunned, but at least he knew Levi would be with him.

A force suddenly collided with their legs, nearly toppling them. Ashmedai and Levi jolted apart to untangle from each other and look, but they couldn't untangle completely.

Kenner was wrapped around their legs, joining the embrace.

Levi laughed, but Ashmedai could only stare—at Kenner and at the crowd of townspeople moving forward. No one looked as though they wished they held a pitchfork.

"You're not so scary for a demon," Kenner said. "Brax was the scary one."

Ashmedai hugged the boy back, overwhelmed by his response.

The others swarmed closer, and though Kenner eventually ran back to his parents, the overall look of acceptance on everyone's faces didn't change.

"It was my fault," Ashmedai said, the mantra he'd told himself for a thousand years.

"Really? Didn't sound that way to me." Daedlys floated out of the crowd with a smirk on his translucent face. "Kenner said it right. You only looked frightening all those years ago because we didn't yet know what a real monster looked like. Even if Brax hadn't interfered, sounds like the curse started as a misunderstanding and poor choices all around. You think we'd blame you for that after all this time?"

Another laugh left Levi, drawing Ashmedai to look at him, still close at his side. Levi's smile was somber, but he spoke plainly as he faced Ashmedai. "You loved someone, that's all. You loved this place and its people. All these years, you've taken responsibility for something that wasn't within your control, but knowing the truth doesn't change who you are or how we feel about you."

"You are our king," Yentriss affirmed, standing beside Grillo. She rustled her son's hair, and then stepped forward to drop to one knee with her head bowed.

Grillo and Kenner followed, and like a ripple starting from the front of the crowd and spreading backward, everyone began to kneel, revealing just how many people filled the length of the road, all willing to believe in Ashmedai still.

Something similar had happened once, all those years ago, when Ashmedai carried Braxton from the wood. It hadn't felt earned then. Ashmedai didn't know if he'd ever feel like he'd earned it, but he bowed back in acceptance of the heartwarming gesture.

"Thank you. All of you."

As the people began to rise, Klarent, up front by his husband, suddenly said, "Oh dear, my gift was in terribly poor taste, wasn't it?"

Daedlys laughed, and Ashmedai finally had to laugh too.

"My friend," Ashmedai called to Klarent, "I think I can forgive you."

Before anything more could be said, the clouds that had blocked out the sun proved to be only clouds, just as the barrier had proven to still be crossable.

Snow began to fall, at first only a few lazily drifting flakes, and then more, bringing everyone's attention toward the sky, and turning what easily could have been renewed mourning back to celebration.

The people started heading down the path toward home, enjoying the new snowfall as much as they had the sun.

"Ash." Levi stopped him from following and held Ashmedai's hands between them. "There's one more thing I need to say. Please don't think my love for you isn't real. I stopped taking the draught days ago, and my love only grew stronger. I love you because of our time together, because of everything I learned of you, because of *you*. I refuse to second-guess that just because of what Braxton said.

"Please tell me you won't either. You found my soul and knew my heart even when I was nothing but a dying light. And I reached out to you…." He raised one hand to hold Ashmedai's face. "Because I love you."

"I know," Ashmedai said without an ounce of doubt. Everything Levi had spoken was how Ashmedai felt too. His only regret was that the lessons he'd learned from loving and losing Cullen, and then loving and being loved by Levi, hadn't been something Braxton could learn too. "Never doubt, my darling, that I also love you," he asserted and kissed Levi soundly.

CHAPTER 12

LEVI HAD no need to hide his face with a hood as he headed toward the market. After all, he didn't think himself ugly, even if, compared to everyone else in the Shadow Lands, he was almost... ordinary.

Especially without his stitches.

Although he was very fond of the permanent ink he'd had etched around his neck, mimicking the way the stitches there had once looked. It honored his past life, because he wasn't Leander anymore, though the memories remained. He was Levi, and he felt more fulfilled and complete in the Shadow Lands than he had ever been allowed to be in Emerald.

Of course, it helped that Levi was walking through town with the Shadow King's hand clasped in his own, having left from the castle instead of his once-home in the tower.

One consequence of the Onyx gemstone's destruction was that the rest of Braxton's black crystals no longer worked. Levi could only hope that meant all the souls captured over the years had been freed, even if they didn't have living bodies to return to like he had.

When the time was right, Levi did plan to visit his mother and inquire after his brother, Leslie. Maybe he would even visit the Diamond Kingdom to find out what had become of his father. At the very least, he wanted to give Leslie the music box, but the life he would live from now on would still be this one—with Ashmedai.

The usual crowd had gathered in the area before the market steps, waiting at the end of the long road that led out of their lands. Today was delivery day, when the carriages from Emerald would arrive.

The festival stalls had all been taken down, their lumber added to other structures or put away to be used again next year. Some remnants of the festival remained, like a string or two of crystal lights, but for the most part, the festivities were complete.

Everyone had already agreed that the tradition would continue, however. They knew the full story now, but the impact that night had had on all their lives was the same.

"Strange, isn't it?" Ashmedai said as the caravan appeared, cresting the exit from the wood and heading toward them. "This is the last time those carriages will return without passengers. I'm still unsure about sending a delegation, but I know we can't stay hidden any longer with the barrier open."

"Remember what I told you of the Emerald Prince," Levi assured him. "He is a good man. He saved me. He means to change things back home. And his father is a good king, if misguided. The first delegation is only meant to test the waters anyway. They won't even know our true faces at first."

"And after all!" Dreya bounded through the crowd, dragging a somewhat stumbling Luccite after her. "You're sending us! Of course all will be well. Who better than the voice of the people, and our most powerful healer to make sure I stay safe?"

The assumption was, since being within the barrier required them to will themselves to look human or elven or what have you, anyone new entering the Shadow Lands wouldn't be affected unless they chose to be. People from other lands could finally visit or move here without fear—if only they could be made to understand and accept the nature of this place.

Dreya had indeed been chosen as voice of the people, though Luccite was selected mostly because she'd insisted, and because she was an alchemist by trade, which the Emerald Kingdom allowed.

Standing before Levi and Ashmedai, Dreya didn't immediately release Luccite but kept hold of her arm. They had been seen like that quite a bit lately and, given how much Luccite used to drape herself near Dreya in obvious if unspoken affection, the healer didn't look all that bothered by the manhandling.

"I've been practicing," Dreya announced, and with a wiggle of her nose, her more chimeric characteristics faded, leaving her looking quite human—except for her hair. "What do you think?"

"You might want to lose a few leaves." Luccite snickered.

Dreya moved her head as if trying to get a better look, and Luccite rolled her eyes in dramatic fashion. With a shrug, Dreya returned to her normal self.

"Good thing crossing the barrier should do the hard work for you," Luccite said.

After a giggle and pressing a loving kiss to Luccite's cheek, Dreya headed up front to help Yentriss with the delivery, but since the crowd was continuing to grow, Levi and Ashmedai were soon met by another set of friends.

"Hello, Ash. Dear Stitches," Daedlys greeted as he and Klarent came over to wait next to them. "And may I say, I appreciate you left me with a way to continue calling you that." He nodded at Levi's finely inked design.

Levi smiled and then noticed how Klarent's robes looked slightly more distended than usual. "Why, Klarent, are you starting to show already?"

"Indeed, I am." Klarent stroked a hand down the slight bump of his belly. "Luccite said the gestation might be shorter than anticipated. They've even been kicking already. Oh!" His hand jumped where he had it rested. "And they're doing it again. Would the godfathers like to feel?"

He didn't wait for Levi or Ashmedai to respond but grabbed both their hands and rested them where his had been. After a moment, Levi distinctly felt a kick.

"Incredible!" he exclaimed. "We are so happy for you."

"What are you hoping for?" Ashmedai asked, his own grin quite wide after feeling the baby. "Wisps or tentacles?"

Daedlys and Klarent both laughed.

"I just hope they don't come into this world screaming like their father," Klarent said with a nudge at Daedlys's floating form. "That might make poor Luccite's ears ring for days."

"If that happens," she deadpanned, since she was still nearby, "I'm letting you two finish the birthing on your own."

They laughed again.

She was definitely joking, Levi thought.

Maybe.

It had taken until the festival structures were coming down before Levi and Ashmedai remembered the gift from Klarent had been left behind one of the stalls. They'd reclaimed it then, and for all the sadness the memories of the night of the curse once stirred in Ashmedai, he'd found a place of honor for the tome on the mantel of the hearth in his bedchamber.

"Levi! Ash!" It was Kenner, sitting on Grillo's shoulder, held up by his lizard arm, which he was more than used to by now. "Do you think anything exciting will be in the carriages?"

"Isn't there always?" Ashmedai answered. "Is Grillo going to let you claim something, Kenner?"

"Within reason," Grillo said.

"You know," Levi mentioned to Grillo, "I never got the chance to ask you something. I didn't hear the end of your poem to Yentriss. Did you get her to blush?"

"Spectacularly." Grillo beamed. "Even better, if anyone asks her about it, she blushes again, such a lovely shade of forest green. You'll have to try it sometime." He winked.

At long last the carriages came to a stop at the end of the road, and the usual bustle broke out, with people vying for items after those already spoken for had been claimed. Several spools of soft-looking yarn were heatedly sought after, Levi assumed with the intent of knitting a baby blanket, since the combatants were all those with child, the winners eventually being Amuro and Pentelyn, whose pregnant belly was also noticeably larger.

Nothing called to Levi to have as his own the way the music box had, though he thought he might get a few more tunics made in Emerald silk—for him *and* Ashmedai.

All too quickly, the spectacle was wrapping up, but before Dreya could announce the last carriage was empty, Gordoc let out a cry from inside where he'd been inspecting corners for anything forgotten.

"Ash!" He appeared in a flurry, waving something above his head. "There's a note!"

Levi and Ashmedai turned to each other in surprise and then swiftly began to push through the crowd, which parted for them once the initial shock wore off. In Gordoc's hand was indeed an envelope—with the Emerald Kingdom's royal seal holding it closed.

Ashmedai took it, and a hush fell over the crowd. Then, as soon as he had it open, Daedlys yelled, "Well, read it!"

Ashmedai chuckled but raised his voice for everyone to hear. "Dearest people beyond the wood. We call you Dark Kingdom and Shadow Lands, though I have learned of late that such titles are not always true of the places we fear. I write to you first in hopes that the young man I switched places with as sacrifice to the Ice King reached you safely."

Not exactly, Levi thought, though all had turned out well in the end.

"He was wrongly condemned for having magic, and I have since encountered much magic myself. I swear to you and to him that no one will ever be called corrupt again for having magic or being of elven lineage in my kingdom. We have reunited with the Frozen Kingdom, ended their curse, and all is well."

Ashmedai met Levi's eyes, pausing in his recitation, since Levi had explained to everyone about the current Emerald Kingdom and the Frozen Kingdom they feared.

"The prince saved the Ice King?" Levi asked in wonder.

"So it would seem," Ashmedai said. He continued reading. "What I experienced is too long a tale to write here, but its happy end means that soon, in the once again Sapphire Kingdom, I am to be wed, uniting Sapphire and Emerald for myself and the Sapphire King to rule over both together."

Now Levi was truly shocked, for he had heard rumors whispered about the Emerald Prince, but he'd never expected a royal wedding between kings.

"I would like to formally invite your own royal family and whoever else may wish to attend to join us on the date in the enclosed invitation and reunite your kingdom with ours as well. I do not know why we lost touch. I do not know if the stories my people say of your lands are true. I was told to expect monsters in the Frozen Kingdom, and while in some ways, that is what I found, I also learned that monsters are not always who they appear to be.

"So, I say to you now—you are welcome, and if you be monsters, we only hope you are kind ones. Signed Prince Reardon, House of Thom, of the Emerald Kingdom. Well." Ashmedai's sharp-toothed smile widened as beautifully as ever as he looked out at his people and lifted the note into the air. "It would seem more than Dreya and Luccite need to prepare for a trip. We've been invited to a wedding!"

The crowd cheered.

In all Levi's wildest dreams, both as Levi and Leander, he'd never once believed any of this could be possible. Now, as he looked at his king, his love, and the beautiful golden circlet with its red gem that Ashmedai wore often now, glittering in the sun, just like Levi's ear cuff, he saw something so much better than what could be offered by a mere dream or illusion.

He saw possibility and a future all his own—one he would share.

"I will have to give this Emerald Prince my eternal thanks," Ashmedai said softly, for Levi's ears alone.

Levi leaned toward him and lightly kissed Ashmedai's lips. "As will I."

SEVERAL WEEKS LATER

NEMIRAC KEPT a keen eye on his surroundings as he exited the wood's path and continued into the Amethyst Kingdom. It was late, the land cloaked in darkness like it had been for a thousand years, with stars and a bright full moon above. Come dawn, however, the sun would shine on the strangely angled black buildings and gnarled black trees.

No longer was this the Shadow Lands or the Dark Kingdom, as it had once been called, but even so, already Nemirac could tell how different Amethyst was from the Mystic Valley. Also known as the Diamond Kingdom, the Mystic Valley was Nemirac's home, where he had lived his entire life, secluded with the rest of his people until *their* curse had been broken, almost overlapping with the curse broken here.

Nemirac hadn't initially planned to travel, but after word spread of Amethyst's curse also coming to an end—more or less—Nemirac's mother received a letter from the Shadow King. Finally, upon reading the letter, she told Nemirac the truth. He wasn't simply the Diamond Prince. All his life he had been the Fairy Prince anyway, after his mother, the Fairy Queen. But they were no fairies, and they were certainly not elves.

They were demons.

Nemirac reached a set of steps at the edge of where homes began to line the streets, leading to the spire-topped castle in the distance. What appeared to be a recently crafted sign was planted into the ground beside the steps, mentioning a market below and an inn "Newly Added" that wouldn't have had any use until recently.

The inn would be Nemirac's first stop, though he had no intention of spending the night.

"Hail!" someone shouted the moment Nemirac entered. "Another new face, eh? Have a seat, anywhere you like. We welcome all kinds here."

The construction of the building was nice enough. Every plank of wood was black, the inn made from the same black trees as almost everything else. Nemirac had seen a few people on the streets, but here he could truly appreciate the myriad of beings that inhabited this place.

He couldn't say he had ever seen the likes of such… monsters, other than in storybooks. There were creatures like centaurs, nagas, harpies, and some seemed to be a combination of several. There were also humans, elves, and dwarves, some visiting, like him, no doubt, and some who may have once been creatures themselves but had chosen to change their forms with the breaking of the curse.

The bartender, who had called to Nemirac, was something like a fish-man, with puckering lips and finlike fingers. Nemirac tried not to let how strange this all was to him show, for though he had seen many wonders in his homeland, filled as it was with magic, he knew very little of the outside world, and Amethyst was hardly an ordinary example.

"Are you also the innkeeper?" Nemirac asked the fish-man, approaching the bar where a few patrons were seated, enjoying drinks.

"Not one for pleasantries, are you? I'm Gordoc," the man said. "And yes, sir, this is my establishment. Just opened. You're one of the snazzier elves we've had come through. You some sort of noble?"

"I'm looking for other travelers, not conversation," Nemirac said shortly.

He'd also thought he'd chosen a more neutral outfit when he set out from home all those days ago, but looking around at everyone here, he supposed his trousers and black and silver tunic would have been better on their own, with a more basic cloak, instead of what he had selected. He just felt incomplete without his red wizard's mantle that buttoned into the tunic like a high collar and covered his shoulders, along with the accompanying half robe that attached at his hips and billowed low nearly to his ankles.

He was a prince, after all, but at least he had foregone his coronet for simpler adornments like his yellow leather belt. His staff was ostentatious as well, he supposed, with its large diamond at the top. The staff was crucial for channeling his magic, however. He was only half-elf—half-*demon*—so his innate magic was not nearly as powerful as his mother's.

For now.

"Excuuuuse me," Gordoc said with an exaggerated raise of his finned hands. "If you're only interested in other travelers, everyone tonight who doesn't look like a local isn't one. Take that as you will. Now, are you in need of a room and drink—"

"That's all, thank you." Nemirac turned from him without further comment and ignored the irritated huff the man released at Nemirac's turned back.

There were many in attendance who were not monsters, but after a longer scan of the room, no one looked like someone who had seen battle or even a bar fight. There was a young human couple laughing at a table, an older dwarf drowning in ale who could have been a grandfather, and several half-elves playing a game of cards, none of whom wore weapons belts. Everyone else was just as unexceptional.

Since there were half-elves and at least one full elf in attendance, some of whom might be from the Mystic Valley, just to be certain no one might recognize him, Nemirac drew up the hood from the back of his mantle, forced to pull his long braid forward to drape over one shoulder. Even while intricately plaited, his hair was long enough to nearly reach his waist, silver-colored, practically white, as if it were made from diamond dust itself—or so his mother used to lie.

The last of the people Nemirac noticed was a cluster of young women of various races in the corner, none of whom looked formidable enough to protect Nemirac should his plans go awry.

Safe within his hood, but having come up empty, Nemirac started to turn back to the bar, though he doubted it would be fruitful to ask Gordoc if there were other inns or places travelers frequented.

A boisterous laugh from the corner drew Nemirac's attention—a male laugh, deep and resonant, amidst the gaggle of women. Nemirac headed that direction, finally seeing that the women, five in total, weren't clustered for their own sakes but clustered *around* a man, who seemed quite pleased by the attention.

As Nemirac continued to approach, he saw more of the man revealed—human, with tanned skin, brown hair to his shoulders, a neatly trimmed but full beard, and lively green eyes. He looked large, thick with muscle beneath his teal and purple surcoat. He also wore an overcoat with fur along the collar, and a floppy cap that tilted to one side in the same teal and purple colors, but with a green feather.

His laugh was infectious, though Nemirac assumed his admirers were there more for the strikingly handsome figure he cut—and because he appeared to be the one supplying the booze.

"Another round, eh? Don't you lovelies go anywhere now," he said, sliding around several of the women to get out from behind the table.

One of them must be a local, judging by her blue amphibian-like skin, and two of them, Nemirac realized, were actually slight and very pretty young men.

Nemirac changed direction to head the man off at the bar. He was indeed large, well over six feet tall, whereas Nemirac was barely five foot ten and willowy, with minimal muscle. Nemirac wasn't built for combat outside throwing spells, but this man clearly was. He had an axe on one side of his weapons belt and a short sword on the other. He wore bracers, leather armor hidden beneath his overcoat, and the well-worn boots of a wanderer.

Perfect.

"Another round for my table, Gordy!" The man pounded a rowdy fist on the bar top and dropped a small pouch of gems upon it, spilling out a few that he passed to Gordoc, whose eyes sparkled at the sight almost as brightly as the stones themselves.

"Right away!" Gordoc gathered the gems greedily.

At Nemirac's approach, the man turned with a grin and raised a questioning eyebrow, one with a scar clean through it that added to his rugged attractiveness.

Not that Nemirac *cared*. What he was after was a bodyguard.

"Are you for hire?" Nemirac asked.

"Forward, aren't you?" The man's deep, boisterous voice made Nemirac's stomach grow hot. "That's far too fair a face to be hiding in a hood. I wouldn't be opposed to being *sold*, pretty thing, but I'd take you to bed for free."

"I-I meant as a sellsword!" Nemirac barked, feeling his cheeks grow as hot as his gut.

He was often called pretty back home, but he'd only recently come of age at twenty-two and often avoided anyone trying to court him. Books and magical study were easier to lose himself in than people.

Nemirac recognized his own attractiveness, however, combining the beauty of his dark-skinned elf-looking mother and his fair human father. He'd always wondered why his hair was silver instead of blond, however, just as he'd questioned the gold color of his eyes, when his mother's were dark and his father's blue.

At least he'd wondered before discovering his true lineage.

"I'm interested in hiring a combatant, not... *dallying*," Nemirac spat.

"Pity," the man said, eyeing Nemirac openly from head to toe.

"Are you for hire or not?" Nemirac wanted this man because he looked the strongest and was honestly the only option right now. It had nothing to do with the appeal of his broad shoulders, the twinkle in his eyes, or the single dimple on his cheek beneath the scruff of his beard.

Gordoc began placing flagons upon the bar, and the man claimed one, taking a long drink before he answered, "I can be. What are you offering in exchange?"

The man's gems were impressive, but Nemirac had something better.

He dropped his own pouch on the bar and opened it to reveal diamonds, causing Gordoc's eyes to saucer. "I need you to do as you're told and not ask questions. This will be a long-term arrangement, likely lasting several weeks, and I won't be staying in Amethyst, so if you intended to remain here tonight, that will change. Do we understand one another?"

The man opened the bag of diamonds farther, that same scarred eyebrow rising, though he otherwise remained impressively neutral. "The world has suddenly opened, offering many new lands for adventure. Frankly, I'm up for anything."

"*Do we* understand each other?" Nemirac asked again.

"Yes. I can follow orders just fine." He winked.

Nemirac ignored the gesture. "Where do you hail from?"

"Originally? Ruby."

"Ruby? You're not a dwarf."

"Not only dwarves live in the Ruby Kingdom, pretty, but I suppose people from other lands have forgotten that. Where do you hail from?"

"Not your concern." Nemirac lowered his voice, since Gordoc had finished with the flagons but was hovering a little too closely. "Meet me in the square in three hours, after all is still and everyone has cleared out,not amoment later. We will be making a hasty retreat, and I need to know you'll be timely." He sneered over the man's shoulder at the group of admirers watching with obvious annoyance that someone new had the man's attention.

"I'm always timely—even when dallying," the man added in a mock-whisper. "You have a deal, pretty. I'm intrigued."

"My name is Nemirac." This man hadn't come from the Mystic Valley, and since those lands had been cordoned off for two hundred years and Nemirac was still young, no one outside his home should know his name.

"Pleasure to meet you, *pretty*. I'm Janskoller," he said with a tip of his hat. "Janskoller Thah."

"Janskoller the what?"

He chuckled, more like giggled, which should have seemed disjointed coming from such a masculine specimen, yet it suited him perfectly. "T-H-A-H. But if you're asking—Janskoller the mighty? The handsome? The virile? Take your pick. Most people know me as Janskoller the bard." He bowed deeply.

"Bard?" Nemirac hadn't noticed before, but leaning against the wall beside the table Janskoller had come from was a lute. "I need you to fight, not serenade me."

"Why not both? I can fight, don't you worry about that. The serenading I'll throw in for free." He winked again. "Would you like a demonstration—"

"Three hours," Nemirac interrupted, even if the lute had him curious. He had a feeling he had just made a terrible mistake, but at least the view would be pleasant.

Nemirac turned before Janskoller could say more. There was planning to be done before they met again and made their escape. It was time for Nemirac to claim his birthright—starting with the Amethyst gemstone.

But that is another story.

Keep reading for an excerpt from

Coming Up for Air

by Amanda Meuwissen!

CHAPTER 1

IF HIS life had gone differently, maybe Leigh Hurley would have been an engineer working toward his master's in thermodynamics by now instead of sinking to the bottom of the river.

At least he couldn't tell how filthy the water was since it was midnight and he was plummeting fast into the dark depths, the glimmer of moonlight above him quickly disappearing. He was a good swimmer, not that it mattered with twenty-pound weights attached to his ankles. He had about two minutes before he passed out, and then it would be curtains.

Fighting against the panic clawing at his chest the same way his lungs begged for air, he forced his body to curl downward in a frantic attempt to reach the weights. They were cinder blocks attached with actual shackles. Under normal circumstances, he might have been able to remove them using one of his lockpicks, but he couldn't see. A bitter mantra of "if only" followed his path downward like the bubbles of air escaping as he tried to think of some other way, any way to get out of this.

If only he wasn't a criminal. If only he hadn't been so damn opportunistic. If only he hadn't gotten caught.

It had been a smart plan. The streets by the docks where Leigh lived were split in half between the Moretti brothers and Arthur Sweeney, who might have been Irish to their Italian, but that wasn't the root of their animosity. Everything revolved around power in Cove City. At the end of the night, what mattered was which family had the most territory, like some old-fashioned trade of land equaling wealth, which was always true, and Leigh owned nothing, not even the apartment he could barely pay the rent on.

Since his best friend was *Alvin* Sweeney, Arthur's son, Leigh played for their side, hoping to rise in the ranks on more than nepotism. Looking good to Sweeney Senior meant making a splash on the scene, so Leigh had been working overtime for months on small thefts that caused an increasing decline in how much the Morettis brought in from their protection racket.

Leigh gave most of what he stole to Sweeney, but some he returned to the neighboring mom-and-pop stores as a good Samaritan, and a little he kept for himself. This made the Morettis look weak, like they couldn't protect their own. It was all about the long game and how it would make things easier for Sweeney to claim those streets in the months and years to come.

It would have worked, too, if they hadn't been waiting for Leigh tonight.

"Nobody crosses the Morettis," Leo, younger brother to Vincent and in charge of their muscle, had said before his goons dropped Leigh over the side of the docks.

Now he was going to drown with no one to remember him other than Alvin and maybe the handful of people in his building who relied on his technical talents and didn't care if he was a runner for a mobster as long as their TVs and dishwashers worked.

It was such a waste, pushing him to struggle harder to swim upward after he gave up on the shackles, vainly trying to beat back fate, even though he knew he wasn't strong enough and barely made an inch of headway before he continued to sink.

Soon he'd disappear, another good riddance that he doubted even his parole officer would miss for how often she sighed and told him to make something of himself instead of falling back into bad habits. But what was there to make of a life without privilege? Leigh had no prospects, no family, no education, only honed skills of survival. He'd been a thief since he could fit his hand inside a passing pocket. With his record, even at only twenty-five, there was no hope for him in this city that didn't lean on Arthur Sweeney, and now he'd lost that opportunity too.

The water was cold even in spring since this part of the river was wider. The docks wouldn't see any activity until morning, and not much then either at this location, though with a few shortcuts, it wasn't far to Leigh's apartment. He'd die close to home, if that meant anything. He just wished he'd been smarter, faster, and had another chance to do things better.

Those two minutes had to be up, because it was getting harder to fight, his mind sluggish and unable to think of a solution to save him. He was even starting to hallucinate, maybe dreaming, maybe already dead and fading away. A light shone in the blackness as he hit bottom.

More like a glimmer of bare skin, because he'd swear he saw a face approaching as his mind grew hazier and his vision dimmed.

Somehow the face became clearer, though, beautiful too, like something ethereal—flawless features, concerned eyes, dark hair swaying in the water. If he was real, he would have been the exact sort of man who would have made Leigh take notice. Maybe the man was an angel, and Leigh's passing wouldn't be as painful or as terrifying as he'd feared, despite his lungs burning with the struggle to breathe.

But he didn't deserve an angel. He wasn't good in any sense of the word or worthy of heaven. He didn't believe in love, not even in saying the words, because that was more damaging and hollower than being hated if it came from somewhere fake or turned into rubbish along the way. His father had taught him that early, and life only reaffirmed the dangers of love and trust over the years.

Scared as Leigh was, part of him believed he had this coming, but the angel in the water didn't snarl or fade away. He came close enough that Leigh could make out every detail of his face, including occasional freckles and a wide smile. Then the beautiful man floated closer, looking back at Leigh in wonder, and captured his lips in a cold kiss.

A song filled his mind like when one got stuck in his head, playing distantly and sweet like he imagined this man's voice might be—lovely but understated, just a tune without words.

Leigh was dying. He should have been filled with terror, but in his last moments, he felt calm to have had such a pleasant final dream.

The next moment, he was gasping for breath, somehow on shore, on the riverbank far enough from where he'd been dropped that Leo and his goons couldn't see him, but still close enough to walk home. It didn't make sense. The man in the water couldn't be real. Cove City didn't produce unknown saviors, yet when Leigh looked down at his ankles, the cinder blocks were gone.

Coughing into the sand and dirt, unsure how he'd been saved or if he'd been touched by some miracle, all Leigh knew was that he had to get home, and after he rested, he'd have precious little time to prevent this same fate from befalling him again tomorrow night.

With a mighty push, he thrust up onto his knees, staggered to his feet, and began the slow trek back to his apartment, trying to banish the vision of that lovely face from overriding what he knew could only have been a trick of the mind.

LEIGH DIDN'T mean to fall asleep when he reached home and shed his soaked clothing. He only planned to rest his eyes for a moment, but he'd underestimated how exhausted he was, and when he roused it was to a loud knock at his door, with the clock on his nightstand blinking 7:00 a.m.

He didn't have time to be tired. That could already be Moretti goons or Sweeney himself, furious at Leigh for failing. It didn't help that he didn't feel as though he'd slept. His dreams had been filled with the face he imagined in the water. He didn't think he'd ever seen a man like that before, but his mind had conjured such a perfect specimen for his final moments.

The kiss had been nice too.

Leigh couldn't get distracted by phantoms, though. While he had no idea how the weights had come loose from his ankles or how he'd ended up on shore, it couldn't have been some mystery man.

"I'm coming!" Leigh called when the knocking refused to cease. It wasn't the Morettis or Sweeney or they would have kicked down the door by now. It had to be Miss Maggie. Only she ever got this uppity before 9:00 a.m.

Yanking the door open, Leigh stood in his sweats and long-sleeved T-shirt, barefoot and still chilled from his time in the river, but clean after a shower when he'd arrived home. He rubbed the sleep from his eyes and scrubbed at the closely shorn length of his hair.

"What?"

Miss Maggie was indeed the person on the other side of his door, but she looked particularly surly this morning. "William," she said sharply, using his given name, which he despised. "About time. I might be an old woman, but that does not mean I want to see some young man walking buck naked through my halls at all hours just because you had a wild night."

"Excuse me?" Leigh took a moment to process what she was complaining about. He hadn't started to undress while still in the hall last night, had he? He was out of it when he returned home, but not that disoriented.

"You know I support your lifestyle, whatever it may be, just so long as you keep the volume down after 11:00 p.m. and act respectfully, but this was just vulgar. Are you playing some game with the boy?"

"Game? Miss Maggie, I have no idea what you're—"

But before he could finish, she yanked someone else into view, who was wearing what appeared to be one of her housecoats and nothing else, not even shoes, though that wasn't what stopped Leigh short.

It was the man from the river. Same hair, same eyes, same everything.

Leigh really had died last night.

"*William.*"

Which meant he was in hell if he was still dealing with Maggie's temper.

"Keep your evening activities confined to your apartment. Now, mind yourself, young man," she said to the flesh and blood figure who'd saved Leigh's life, "because I expect that nightgown returned at some point, preferably washed."

She shoved the man into Leigh's arms, and he had barely a second to register the full form of him, slim and tall, maybe half an inch taller than Leigh, and just as beautiful as he remembered, before Maggie hurried down the hall in a huff.

Leigh stumbled backward, causing the man to stumble with him, and pushed the door closed more on reflex than conscious choice. The man was real. Leigh hadn't imagined him. But if he'd saved Leigh's life, why was he only showing himself now?

And why the hell wasn't he wearing any clothes?

"I found you," he said in a breathless voice, as if in awe of Leigh, immediately evoking the memory of that same voice *singing*. "I knew I would, but still, I found you."

Carefully Leigh pushed at the man to hold him in front of him so they could get their bearings. He didn't seem very stable on his feet. Had he been drunk last night? Was that why he was swimming in the river at midnight naked and wandered all the way here in the same state? His eyes, large and almond-shaped, didn't look intoxicated. With olive skin, a reddish tint to his black hair, and freckles, he looked as likely to be of South Pacific descent as Greek or Jewish, maybe all three.

"You are even more handsome than when I saw you in the water," he said, with an intensity to how he stared that made Leigh shiver. The peek of long legs out of the housecoat was not helping his straying thoughts.

Leigh's generally fair looks with blond hair and blue eyes had gotten him out of sticky situations before. He knew what he had and how to use it, but he didn't think he compared with this lithe elfish beauty before him with a smile that lit up the whole apartment.

"It's you," he said, unable to articulate anything more than that. He pulled his hands from the man's shoulders, thinking it too intimate considering he was wearing nothing more than a nightgown.

"Yes." The man stepped into his space as if beckoned by a magnetic pull.

"You saved me. You found me."

"My apologies it took so long. I hesitated to follow, and once I decided to, I had trouble finding my feet, as they say. I knew the Breath of Life would lead me to you, though. Our souls are intertwined now, William. Ah, but you prefer Leigh, don't you?"

How…? "How do you know that?" And what was he talking about?

"You know my name as well."

"No, I…. Tolomeo. Tolly," he said before he could finish denying it. Had they met on the shore after all and Leigh simply didn't remember?

"Yes," Tolly said, smiling wider still.

This was too strange. Leigh's head was pounding, he was exhausted, and he still had to worry about Sweeney and the Morettis. He could not get caught up with some weird nudist—flower child—whatever this man was—when his life was in shambles.

"Look, I don't remember everything from last night, so if you explained this before, who you are, I'm sorry. I appreciate what you did. You saved my life, but it won't stay saved for long—"

"Those people who tried to drown you will continue to wish you harm," Tolly said.

"Yes. So if you came here expecting something more than my thanks, I hate to disappoint you, but I don't have much to offer."

"Oh, I am not like my brethren, I swear to you. I wish for no boon or life debt."

Okay. Was this guy a method actor or something? Maybe he was just crazy. "What do you want from me, then?"

"I wish to stay with you," Tolly said as matter-of-factly as asking for cab fare. "Forever."

Definitely crazy.

Holding up his hands to ward off whatever reaction might come next, Leigh chose his words very carefully. "Tolly, I will give you something to wear and then maybe there's someone we can call, okay? Or a hospital you came from?"

"I came from the sea," Tolly said, unfazed by Leigh's line of questioning. "Well, the river in this case, but all water is connected in my world. We can transport between depths through magic. I like bodies of water close to cities. The rest of my kin stay away, which I prefer, and I get to experience more of the human world."

"Human world? Your… kin?"

"Merfolk."

Leigh curtailed his reactions as best he could. "Tolly, is there anyone I can call to come get you?"

At last, a bit of that sunshine disposition flickered. "I have no one. No family or friends to speak of. That is why I chose to follow you. I was drawn to you, Leigh"—he stepped forward, making Leigh step back—"in the water, in your last moments, like I have never been drawn to anything. Others of my kin would have let you die, drowned you themselves, or forced a more self-serving pact, but I knew I had finally found the one who could give me legs."

If this guy snapped, Leigh was fairly certain he could take him, but he hoped it wouldn't come to that. "You are not a mermaid. You're a man. You're on legs right now. You did not have a tail last night."

"You only saw my face."

"You didn't have a tail because mermaids don't exist!"

"I shall prove it to you. I need only to submerge in water to call out my tail. Then will you believe me? Your bathroom should have what I need." Without waiting for an answer, he glanced around the apartment and pushed past Leigh, deeper inside.

Leigh needed to get this guy out of his home, even if he had saved him last night.

Merfolk? Seriously?

Tolly found the bathroom quick enough and proceeded to turn on the taps to the tub before Leigh could organize his thoughts for a proper protest.

He tried anyway. "Listen, I don't have time for this."

"I am used to cold water, but perhaps I shall try something warmer," Tolly said as he held his hand under the water and adjusted the taps accordingly. "Is warm water nice?"

"I… yeah, usually. Can we please just talk about this—"

Tolly disrobed without shame, right there in front of Leigh, just shed the housecoat and stood there nude. He was even more beautiful bare, entirely hairless below the neck, thin like a swimmer but well-muscled, without a single scar or imperfection other than the sunspots that Leigh thought only enhanced how beautiful he was.

Being gorgeous and naked in Leigh's bathroom did not change that he was clearly insane, however.

"Tolly, you can't just…. We need to talk about this." Leigh turned to stare at the wall. He was a hardened criminal. Sort of. *Sometimes*. It should not be this difficult to throw someone out of his home!

"Not until you believe me. Our conversation will go nowhere if you think me mad."

He was a smart crazy person at least, but that didn't help the situation. Leigh had to focus on the Morettis, on what to say when he saw Sweeney, on how to get himself out of this mess so he didn't end up dead some other way tonight, without having to flee the city. He'd break parole if he did that, and the money he'd saved so far wouldn't last him long on the run.

Maybe the Morettis didn't know where he lived. If they did, surely they would have sent someone to rummage through his things, looking for that extra cash. Maybe they did know and someone was on their way now. No point in rushing over when they thought him dead.

"Tolly, just put the housecoat back on or grab a towel. I'll get you some clothes—"

"Do you not find my form pleasing?"

Out of the corner of Leigh's eye, he could tell Tolly stood facing him, hands running down his hips and thighs like he really was unused to legs. "It is very pleasing, but it's not…. I hardly know you."

"Ah yes, human decorum. I might fail at that on occasion, but I will try my best. I know so much of your world, but I have not experienced it firsthand. Still, you know me better than you think through our connection. The Breath of Life is a powerful bond. I am yours now. You are welcome to look at me."

Leigh was certain some of the porn he'd watched over the years had lines like that. "Tolly…."

"I do not wish to make you uncomfortable. I will get into the tub to conceal myself until the water is high enough. Hopefully you will not find my tail displeasing."

Tolly lowered himself into the tub, and Leigh allowed a glance in his direction. Even mostly hidden, he was enchanting to look at. Despite having come from the water last night, his hair had perfect body and poof to it. Why did someone so gorgeous and who had saved Leigh's life have to be nuts?

"I have to figure out how to handle those men who tried to kill me. Do you understand?"

"Of course. I will help you."

"No offense, but you're a little skinny to be a bodyguard. This is going to take strategic planning."

"I am an excellent planner. I often have to dodge others of my kin. I am not popular, as I do not conform to the merfolk ways. Kill or be killed—it loses all the magic of life, even when magic surrounds me in the water. How can one live like that?"

Leigh almost took the words as an attack, though he knew Tolly didn't mean it that way. He'd never killed anyone before, but his plans to rise in the ranks with Sweeney meant one day he would. Kill or be killed was the only way he could survive in this city.

"You were right, warm water is nice, though the cold can be pleasant too." Tolly tilted his head back and sank lower into the tub.

Scrubbing a hand down his face, Leigh was thinking of how to get this naked delusional poet out of his apartment without drawing the attention of his neighbors when he heard a strange wet slap and a contented sigh.

"There, you see? I am merfolk, but you gave me legs, and now, I am yours."

The red glimmer in Leigh's periphery before he looked up had to be an illusion because of how tired he was. There was no way it could be anything else.

But when his gaze focused on Tolly in the tub once more, it wasn't a pair of feet propped on the edge but the unfurling of the most beautiful deep red tailfin he had ever laid eyes on, trimmed in gold-tipped scales.

"Holy shit."

AMANDA MEUWISSEN is a bisexual author with a primary focus on M/M romance. She has a Bachelor of Arts in a personally designed Creative Writing major from St. Olaf College and is an avid consumer of fiction through film, prose, and video games. As the author of LGBT Fantasy #1 Best Seller, *Coming Up for Air*, paranormal romance trilogy, The Incubus Saga, and several other titles through various publishers, Amanda regularly attends local comic conventions for fun and to meet with fans, where she will often be seen in costume as one of her favorite fictional characters. She lives in Minneapolis, Minnesota, with her husband, John, and their cat, Helga, and can be found at www.amandameuwissen.com.

THE PRINCE
AND THE
ICE KING

A Tale from the Gemstone Kingdoms

AMANDA MEUWISSEN

A Tale from the Gemstone Kingdoms

Every Winter Solstice, the Emerald Kingdom sends the dreaded Ice King a sacrifice—a corrupt soul, a criminal, a deviant, or someone touched by magic. Prince Reardon has always loathed this tradition, partly because he dreams of love with another man instead of a future queen.

Then Reardon's best friend is discovered as a witch and sent to the Frozen Kingdom as tribute.

Reardon sets out to rescue him, willing to battle and kill the Ice King if that's what it takes. But nothing could prepare him for what he finds in the Frozen Kingdom—a cursed land filled with magic… and a camaraderie Reardon has never known. Over this strange, warm community presides the enigmatic Ice King himself, a man his subjects call Jack. A man with skin made of ice, whose very touch can stop a beating heart.

A man Reardon finds himself inexplicably drawn to.

Jack doesn't trust Reardon. But when Reardon begins spending long days with him, vowing to prove himself and break the curse, Jack begins to hope. Can love and forgiveness melt the ice around Jack's heart?

www.ingramcontent.com/pod-product-compliance
Lightning Source LLC
Chambersburg PA
CBHW051643260626
47170CB00004B/1300